Cougar's Mate

TERRY SPEAR

Also by Terry Spear:

Romantic Suspense: Deadly Fortunes, In the Dead of the Night, Relative Danger, Bound by Danger

The Highlanders Series: Winning the Highlander's Heart, The Accidental Highland Hero, Highland Rake, Taming the Wild Highlander, The Viking's Highland Lass

Other historical romances: Lady Caroline & the Egotistical Earl, A Ghost of a Chance at Love

Heart of the Wolf Series: Heart of the Wolf, Destiny of the Wolf, To Tempt the Wolf, Legend of the White Wolf, Seduced by the Wolf, Wolf Fever, Heart of the Highland Wolf, Dreaming of the Wolf, A SEAL in Wolf's Clothing, A Howl for a Highlander, A Highland Werewolf Wedding, A SEAL Wolf Christmas, Silence of the Wolf, 2014, Hero of a Highland Wolf, 2014, A Highland Wolf Christmas, 2014; A SEAL Wolf for Sale, 2015; A Silver Wolf Christmas, 2015

SEAL Wolves: To Tempt the Wolf, A SEAL in Wolf's Clothing, A SEAL Wolf Christmas; A SEAL Wolf for Sale

Silver Bros Wolves: Destiny of the Wolf, Wolf Fever, Dreaming of the Wolf, Silence of the Wolf; A Silver Wolf Christmas, 2015

Highland Wolves: Heart of the Highland Wolf, A Howl for a Highlander, A Highland Werewolf Wedding, Hero of a Highland Wolf, A Highland Wolf Christmas

Heart of the Jaguar Series: Savage Hunger, Jaguar Fever, Jaguar Hunt, 2014, Jaguar Pride, 2015

Vampire romances: Killing the Bloodlust, Deadly Liaisons, Huntress for Hire, Forbidden Love

Heart of the Cougar Series: Cougar's Mate, Call of the Cougar, 2014

PROLOGUE

Shannon Rafferty woke to the sound of her boyfriend arguing with one of his triplet brothers in the kitchen of their rural two-bedroom house. She hadn't expected Ted to be home for another week. He was supposed to be at some specialized police training program. And now Hennessey was here? Fighting with him?

What... what was going on?

She'd already packed up her car and had planned to move out first thing in the morning. She wasn't sure where she was going exactly, thinking she might drive to Oklahoma. Three different times, she'd run off while she'd lived with foster families until she was finally old enough to support herself, using false IDs to get jobs.

Her brother and his friends, including two of her prior boyfriends, had all been on the wrong side of the law for years, until her twin brother and each of her subsequent boyfriends had been killed in violent crimes in Florida. She'd run off, moved far away to a little town in Texas, and turned over a fresh leaf. No more associating with guys who were in trouble with the law in her new life while she waitressed in a local diner. She'd run as a wild cougar at night in the Palo Duro Canyon, which is where she'd met Ted Kelly, a cop in his cougar coat. He'd chased her down, but only after she finally let him.

And then she began dating him.

Except Ted hadn't been right for her, either. Keeping secrets. Insisting she didn't work. That he'd provide everything for her that her heart desired.

She thought he was seeing another woman, but something else was going on, and she suspected it had to do with the illegal sale of drugs and that was the end of it for her.

The sound of the escalating, angry voices in the kitchen made her skin prickle with concern. She was certain Ted would attempt to stop her if she tried to leave him. If she'd known he would return home so soon, she would have left already. Why did it seem she was always on the run?

She hurried to slip on some clothes. She'd have to sneak out the bedroom window, get into her car, and leave now. Forget about waiting for morning.

He'd been so controlling, not allowing her to have a job, and she had liked that he had wanted to support her, but something wasn't right. Something she hadn't been able to put her finger on. Not since they'd met a month ago when she'd tried to erase her prior life. He hadn't seemed to care about where she'd come from or anything else about her past. That had suited her fine. And he'd provided her with what little she'd wanted or needed. But the secretive calls at strange hours of the night, and his trips to who knew where didn't seem right either, making her believe something else was wrong. And the time had come for her to go.

A crash sounded in the kitchen. Her heart jumped. She threw her handbag strap over her shoulder.

"I told you what I'd do if I caught you cheating us out of the money again," Hennessey growled.

"I swear I gave you and the rest a fair cut of the profits. I had expenses, man."

"You lying bastard. I knew you couldn't be trusted."

A drawer jerked open. Something banged into a cabinet.

"No!" Ted shouted. "God, man, no! I swear I'm telling the truth."

Her heart thumped hard as she tried to open the bedroom window. No, no, no! It was stuck.

Her fingers cramping around the metal, she tried again and again, shoving at it, but it wouldn't budge. She had to chance slipping out of the house through the front door and pray they didn't notice her. She opened the bedroom door as quietly as she could and crept down the hall. A short wall blocked her view of the kitchen and their view of her. But as soon as she had to make a dash through the living room for the front door, one or both of the men could catch sight of her.

Barely breathing, she couldn't do anything else. She had to run, now.

Ted gasped for air, and she figured Hennessey had hit him hard and knocked the breath out of him. She glanced in the direction of the kitchen. Ted was sitting on the floor, holding his stomach, blood all over his hands.

Oh...my...God. Her breath hitched.

"Where is the damn money?" Hennessey growled.

Ted glanced at her, his breathing labored, his face turning gray. "Shannon," he gasped, and in that instant she thought she saw regret—that now she would be murdered next. And he hadn't wanted her to know... or to be a witness to this. Or to die.

Hennessey's broad back was to her, but he turned, bloodied knife in hand, and stared at her—for just a moment. His blue eyes cold with fury, his black hair trimmed short—cop style—he made a dash for her. Everything happened in fractions of heartbeats. Everything blurred as tears filled her eyes.

Breathe! Move!

She bolted for the front door before she'd consciously thought of doing so. She hadn't even considered that the door would be locked. She just twisted the handle and it opened. Thank God.

She threw the door open and ran outside into the still warm October night—the unsettled weather in the Texas Panhandle doing its usual highs and lows and everything in between.

She dashed for her car and saw a couple taking their small son and dog for a stroll down the sidewalk. The perfect family, she thought in that instant, and they could all be murdered if she let on what had happened inside the house. With a forced smile, she said hello, and hit the unlock button on her keypad.

They couldn't know it, but they had saved her life. She jumped into the driver's seat and saw Hennessey shrink back from the doorway, unable to come after her while wearing his brother's blood on his hands, the knife, and his clothes.

The family had moved far enough away now that as soon as she started the engine, she threw the car into reverse, drove onto the street, gunned the gas, and then headed anywhere away from here.

She was on the run again. Only this time for her life.

CHAPTER 1

The police were supposed to be the good guys, Shannon thought bitterly as she spent the fourteenth night, she thought it was, in the Colorado Rocky Mountains after four weeks of running as a puma. She was more used to rural life than living in a skyscraper city. Rural—as in having a small town nearby to shop at, restaurants, movie theaters, the usual. Living like this was something she'd never bargained for. Not in her worst nightmares.

As soon as she had to struggle to survive, her puma instincts had come to bear, but this wasn't the real her—a pure mountain woman—living as a puma—who survived off the land and craved that way of life. Shannon had ditched her car, clothes, and ID, and had been on the run ever since as a wild cat, casting aside the raven-haired human part of the equation to meet the challenges of the rugged wilderness.

Had she run far enough? Hidden her tracks well enough?

She doubted it. Suspecting she had killed the cop, the whole world would be looking for her. But not everyone would be out to arrest her. At the very least, one of her kind wanted to kill her. To silence her. To make her the patsy for his crime. Others, who would believe her accusers' tales, would feel the same way—and want to end her puny existence to ensure no one knew what she truly was because if she went to prison and turned into a puma—well... the notion was unthinkable.

She was a fighter, her brother having taught her some killing moves because of the crowd he ran with, until even he had to deal with badder ass men than him and had gotten himself murdered.

She sniffled, hating that she'd lost him, her only family. The one who had taught her how to endure in nearly any kind of conditions or she would never have survived even for this long.

She had no one to turn to. And no idea where to go to next.

Her tail swished back and forth as she leapt from one rocky ledge to another until she reached the cave she planned to sleep in for the night. She peered into the dark abyss high up in a rocky area, a waterfall cascading down one side into a deep pool of water below. Forest covered much of the area, giving her good cover when she was moving around below, but it also hid anyone from her view who might approach the rocky formation when she was up high above the treetops. The sound of a river rushing over rocks a couple of miles in the distance and the whoosh of the wind as it tossed about the kaleidoscope of colored leaves stole her attention. She breathed in the pine fragrance and smell of granite, of the fresh water spilling over the rocks. That was the part she loved about nature. If she hadn't been running for her life and fearing what else she might chance to meet out here: bears, wolf packs, hunters, even another cat that didn't appreciate her coming into the puma's territory, she would have enjoyed a trip to the wilderness. Just a trip, not a new way of life.

She didn't know exactly where she was and wouldn't have even known this was Colorado if she hadn't crossed a road where a sign marked the border between Oklahoma and Colorado a couple of weeks back. At least she thought it had been a couple of weeks ago. Lately, she'd been losing track of time. She had no idea if this was a Monday or a Sunday, or any day in between. She was certain it had to be November by now though.

Did they hunt cougars in this area? *Crap.* What if they did? What if the hunting season had already started? That meant she could be one of the ones hunted—not just by the police and the puma shifters, but by hunters looking to take down the big cats for trophies or the thrill of the hunt. Many areas *did* have legalized hunting seasons for cougars.

She studied the cave further, her ears perked, listening intently, her whiskers testing the cold night breeze, her nose twitching as she smelled for any sign of an inhabitant. Nothing. The cave was empty, thank God.

She still couldn't believe it had come to this.

She had the propensity for dating the wrong guys. That's how this had happened. She liked the cads. The bad boys. All because of her brother's influence. And from associating with his wild friends. When her brother and two of her boyfriends had died on her—due to one fatal mistake or another—she'd changed her whole way of life.

So what did she do? Dated a cop! And now she was on the run.

How long before her luck would run out? They wouldn't let her go. They'd keep tracking her. They needed her. *Dead.* If someone else didn't shoot her first.

Unfortunately, pumas or mountain lions or cougars or catamounts, whatever people wanted to call them, had a bad reputation. The more people there were, the more they encroached on the cougars' territory, the more incidents there would be. What did people expect?

She feared she couldn't win. She couldn't shift without clothes and she had no ID. If anyone learned who she was, the police would be all over her. Running as a cougar for the rest of her life wasn't an option, either. She needed her humanity, just as much as she needed her wild cat side.

And she needed food, her rumbling stomach reminded her. That was one of the problems she'd had to deal with on this journey, the inability to take down four-footed prey. The instinct existed, but the human part of her saw Bambi, not a meal on hoofs. Or Thumper, not a bunny that would ease the ache in her belly. She'd been living off fish, a rattlesnake, and a few prairie chickens when she could catch them.

Satisfied the cave would provide her a safe resting spot for the night, she jumped down to the next rock ledge to check out the pool of water down below to see if she could catch dinner. She leapt onto another outcropping further down when a child's terrified scream and then a loud splash below the waterfall sent chills up her spine.

The only way she could reach the child quickly enough from this height was to run to him in her puma form—but if anyone with a rifle saw her...

Listening, she waited a heartbeat to hear if anyone was coming to the child's aid. Shannon couldn't wait any longer. The child's terror overrode her fear for her own safety.

The child screamed again and Shannon leapt onto a ledge below the one she'd been on and then another and another. When she reached more of a slope, she raced down toward the waterfalls where she'd heard the screams, her heart beating hard, her temple pounding furiously.

The whole time all she could think of was rescuing the child and how difficult that would be. If anyone saw her, they'd think she had every intention of eating him instead. And the child itself would most likely think the same.

She dove through underbrush and a grove of trees, her paws sliding on the fallen leaves and loose rocks, and reached a rocky ledge.

The child was a boy of maybe six or seven—his forehead bloodied as he clung to a rock in the frothing, icy cold water. She wanted to shout to him that she was coming, but her shout would be a mountain lion's snarl, terrifying, when she wanted to reassure him in the worst way.

When he saw her, his eyes widened. He shook so violently, she was afraid he'd lose his grip on the rocks and drown if she didn't reach him quickly enough. As it was, he could still die of hypothermia. Cougars didn't care for the water like jaguars and tigers did, but they did swim well in the water. She quickly looked around and saw and heard no sign of any help coming for him.

She jumped up and into the air and down into the water, hoping she wouldn't break a leg on the rocks. That would be the end of her running from the law. And the end of her life. She sank deep into the water, no impact with rocks, but it was too deep to stand up in, even if she'd been in her human form. As far as she'd gone under when she jumped in and had to swim to the surface, she guessed it was around ten feet.

The water was cold, but it didn't bother her while she wore her cougar's coat. She dogpaddled toward the boy, who looked like he wanted to let go of the rock and get away from her, but he was too scared to release his hold either.

The boy's eyes couldn't have grown any bigger. She wished she could shift and tell him she intended to save him. She imagined that would likely cause him to go into a worse shock.

She finally reached him and licked his cheek with her sandpapery, warm, wet tongue, trying to show him she was not going to bite him. That probably didn't help, either. He might think she just wanted a taste before she bit him. There wasn't any other way to do this. She reached down and bit into his jacket. He screamed and flailed his arms and legs.

So not good. But she had no alternative. She pulled him from the rock and paddled with him to the base of the opposite cliffs and the small rocky beach, her teeth holding on for dear life as she didn't want him to wriggle free. Halfway there, he stopped fighting her, for which she was extremely grateful.

When they reached the beach, he shook violently from the cold, his lips blue, and he didn't move away from her or try to get free. She pulled him up to the rock wall and under the overhang for a bit of shelter. No one seemed to be coming to his aid. She assumed a family was camping nearby, but in her puma form, she had no way to let them know the boy was in trouble.

Again, she did the only thing she could, knowing that if the family saw her, they'd think for certain she'd claimed the boy for her meal but wasn't hungry enough to eat him yet. She began to lick the water off his face in an effort to dry him a little and to help the circulation in his skin. He was so cold, terrified, looking up at her with huge, haunted brown eyes and didn't utter another sound. Then she cuddled against him, trying to share the heat of her body, as if he was her overgrown cub.

When he fell asleep, she moved more of her body over his, trying to warm him. The temperatures dropped as the night progressed and he continued to shiver, but not as violently with her helping to warm him some. She remembered reading about an autistic boy who had wandered off in the middle of the night from his tent, and the family dog had found him, curled up with him, and kept him warm during the drop in temperature that night. When they'd located him, the dog was praised for saving the boy's life.

With her? They'd shoot her.

By morning's first ribbon of pink light, she heard people shouting in panic. "Mikey! Mikey, where are you!"

Shannon licked the boy's face, trying to wake him so he could call out to his family. She couldn't leave him until she was certain they'd find him and carry him to safety.

She licked him again and purred. His eyes opened, and he looked even more terrified in the early dawn light.

"Mikey!" a man hollered in the woods still too far away.

She was afraid Mikey thought she would bite him if he tried to warn his family he was here. Despite not wanting to leave him until his family located him, she leapt into the water and swam away from the rocky beach.

As soon as she did, he began to yell, "I'm here! Over here! By the waterfall!" But his words were weak, and she wasn't sure his family would hear him.

She leapt onto a rock, then looked back at him. The voices grew closer.

Men yelled again.

"Here!" the boy said and started to cry. "Here!"

She swallowed a lump in her throat.

Three men broke out of the woods and spied her across the water, standing on the rock ledge. One of the men was armed with a rifle.

"Here," the boy cried and they looked over the overhang to see him.

Two of the men scrambled down the rocky cliff to

reach him, the one remaining behind pulling the rifle to his shoulder.

She leapt onto the next ledge and disappeared into the brush and prayed the boy would recover from his injuries.

She knew she couldn't stay here now.

***

Glad the last of the campers staying at his rustic cabins in the Rockies had packed up and left, Chase Buchanan liked it just like this—no humans talking and shouting and laughing. Just the breeze fluttering through the leaves, the birds singing, and the water lapping at the lake's beach nearby.

After cutting up vegetables and adding water, stew meat, and spices in the crockpot, Chase started cooking the Irish stew on low. He had his day planned out for him. He was about to begin work on one of the cabin roofs when he got a call from his US Army Special Forces buddy and now sheriff of Yuma Town, Colorado. Trouble, Chase imagined. So much for his plans.

He lifted the phone to his ear. "Yeah, Dan?"

"If you can put on your deputy's badge, I need some help."

"What's up?"

"We have a big cat near Carver's Falls that dragged a six-year-old boy from the pool after he'd left his tent in the middle of the night and wandered off. He must have fallen off the cliff. His mom said he regularly sleepwalks when he's overly tired. Now we've got to hunt down the cougar."

"Did the cat hurt the boy?" Chase was certain Dan would have told him right off if the cougar had killed the child.

"No. Just licked him and dragged him to shore, then stayed with him."

Which meant the cat must have fed recently. "Are we

using tranquilizer darts?"

"Yeah, we'll turn it over to the local big cat reserve or to a zoo if we can take him in all right. But I don't want anyone hunting for cougars in the area this early. Our people are doing their last minute runs in the wilderness before cougar hunting season begins in two weeks. A couple of other men—strictly non-shifters—are still at the campsite at Lake Buchanan. They helped track down the boy and witnessed the cougar. The family has packed up and gone home."

Sheriff Dan Steinacker and Chase had seen a lot of missions together while they served in the army, and Dan knew he could count on Chase for anything.

"I hear you." Chase had planned to run tonight himself after dusk, just like most of his shifter kind did once many of the tourists went home after summer break and before cougar hunting season began. "Where do you want me to head?"

"Southside. I'll take the north. That's the way the cat went, according to the family."

"Not one of ours, is he?"

"I had my dispatcher call the alert roster, but everyone is accounted for."

Chase sighed. "All right. I'm on my way there now." His cabins were about a mile from the location and the town, seven. He'd make it to Carver's Falls before Dan arrived to check out the area. "Call you with an update later," Chase promised, grabbed his rifle and darts, and headed outside to his vehicle.

So much for reroofing a couple of the cabins he owned in the next couple of days. This time of year when the tourists were gone, he repaired the two-hundred-year-old log cabins before winter arrived. He was thinking seriously about what his grandmother had said concerning the

Buchanan of old. How they'd been castle builders in Scotland, replacing the wooden Roman fortresses with stone keeps and curtain walls that could keep out the invaders.

Not that he needed stone fortifications for the security. All he wanted was something that wouldn't need constant repairs.

When Chase finally reached Lake Buchanan, he saw just three tents in one of the camping areas. Wearing parkas, three men were fishing at the edge of the lake, the chilly breeze whipping about them.

"Howdy, folks," Chase said, stalking through the woods to reach the rocky beach.

A black-bearded man nodded in greeting. A younger redheaded man, looked to be his son, maybe in his early thirties, stood next to him. Another man, blond, same approximate age as the black-bearded man, watched Chase approach, looking a little wary.

"I'm Chase Buchanan with the sheriff's department," Chase said, having been deputized by Dan when he first arrived in town four years ago, but he wasn't on the regular payroll and didn't want to be. He liked managing his cabin resort just fine. Because of that, he wasn't dressed like the sheriff and his full-time deputy—instead wearing his western boots, blue jeans, western shirt, sweater, and parka coat—not at all the look of someone serving on a police force, though he flashed a badge. "Were you with the family whose boy was injured on the cliffs?"

"Not exactly with them, but camping nearby. My son and I went with the boy's dad to search for him when they discovered the boy was missing. I have to say I've never heard of anything like it. The cat pulling the kid out of the water and then sleeping with him. He said he woke a couple of times and the cat was covering him with his body. We

21

figure it had recently eaten and was saving him for later."

"Yeah," the son said. "We had a housecat that brought a mouse in from outside. A live mouse and put it in her dish. She planned to eat it later. Of course, as soon as she let go of it, it ran off."

"Right, gentlemen. Thanks," Chase said. He didn't like having to take down cougars, but he didn't have much of a choice in a case like this. Word would spread, and gun-toting hunters were sure to take down the kid-eating cougar. That meant any cougar they spotted would be a target. Forget licensing or limits.

"Are you going to kill it?" the first man said.

"Tranquilize it if we can locate it. He might have moved on." But Chase doubted it. Cougars were territorial and if he found this to be a good hunting ground, he'd stay nearby. Wanting the men to be safe, Chase said, "You know the rules at these campsites."

"Yeah. Don't leave any food out that'll attract wild animals," the younger man said, the other men nodding.

"If you've got guns, no shooting the cat," Chase said. "We'll take care of it."

"Unless he attacks us without provocation," the younger man said.

"Right." Chase had to agree that if they were attacked, they had every right to protect themselves.

He said goodbye to the men, then headed for his vehicle. He drove around the lake to the south side and parked, then grabbed his rifle filled with tranquilizer darts, a canteen of water, and binoculars. He could see well with his cat's vision, especially when something moved. But he wanted to catch sight of the cat well before the cougar caught sight of him.

Cougars were solitary animals, normally yielding to other large predators like bear and wolves in a pack. So he really didn't believe he'd have much trouble with it. But if he tracked it down too far away, he would have a time carrying him back to his vehicle so he could take him to a cat reserve that was nearby until they could find the cat a more permanent home. Most zoos raised their own cats from cubs and didn't take in wild ones. But sometimes they did. He even knew of a wild male cougar that had mated with a cougar raised by the zoo, which brought some much needed new genes into the gene pool and she had three healthy cubs as a result. So it could happen.

He trudged through the woods, the stands of golden aspens' quaking leaves turning, some already a blazing yellow, others still a summer green, and others turning golden orange, shimmering in the fading sunlight. Cottonwoods along Cougar Creek were fading into gold, and scrub oak sported its fall finery from rusty to pinkish red, oranges, and yellows, the evergreen pines mixed among them. At the highest elevations, a fresh blanket of snow covered the upper peaks of the mountains.

He sniffed the brisk, cool air. And then he caught the big cat's scent. The cougar had come this way. Only *he* was a *she*.

Chase just hoped he could capture her and that someone would want to take her in without causing her too much trauma. If she was young, even better. Sometimes an older cat that was used to hunting might have to be dropped off in the wilderness somewhere else to fend for herself, or be put down.

Hating this part of the job, Chase continued to track the she-cat up into the rocks.

CHAPTER 2

Shannon Rafferty's schedule was all screwed up. She hadn't eaten for two days now, when she'd had every intention of finding a cave to sleep in, and then hunting for some dinner. Instead, she'd had to rescue the boy. She hoped Mikey's head injury wasn't too bad and that he hadn't suffered too gravely from the effects of hypothermia. Or that her rescuing him hadn't given him nightmares. But she was afraid it would.

She had slept most of the day in another cave farther away from the first and then when it was dusk, she would have to risk hunting.

The sky grew darker as Shannon stared out the entrance of the cave, watching for any sign of danger. She hadn't seen any hikers or hunters. Yes, she'd noticed the tents at the campsite near the lake. She'd even considered that after the men retired to their tents and their sleeping bags tonight, she could go there and catch a fish in the lake. The campers wouldn't be able to see her at night. Then she'd have it made. But once she'd rescued the boy, she nixed that idea. If they somehow did catch sight of her, they would know she was a dangerous predator, looking for a new source of meat. Maybe even them.

It didn't matter. She couldn't have let the boy drown. Several times she'd woken during the day, thinking she'd heard a child screaming. Forget *his* having nightmares about last night. *She* was having them!

The moonlight softly illuminated the golden aspen, the leaves fluttering in the chilly breeze. She closed her eyes briefly.

She had enough nightmares to deal with without piling up any more on top of those. She had intended to stay here in the area because she hadn't located any sign of wolves or black bears. If she ran into a black bear or wolf pack? Both predators would push a cougar out of their territory or kill him.

She hadn't smelled either in the vicinity. Only cougars. And a lot of them. Cougars didn't run in packs. Which was why a cougar would be at risk when encountering a wolf pack. A lone wolf was no match for a cougar's claws and teeth. But with a lot of cougars congregating together? It had to mean they were shifters. And they kept the other big predators away. So she thought she had half a chance at surviving here. Bears and wolves would find some other place to hunt.

She'd never smelled so many cougars in one area before though and it did worry her that they'd locate her and then what? Interrogate her. Why would a female shifter run in the wilderness by herself with no camping equipment anywhere?

Even if they didn't learn who she was, she couldn't go to any of them and ask for help. Not in her cougar form. Without clothes, she couldn't just walk into town naked, either. Besides, she was a wanted woman, and she was certain no one would believe her word over the rest of her boyfriend's family. Not when Hennessey Kelly was a cop, which meant she was on her own.

The crimson sky turned to blackness and all that was left was the moon and a sprinkling of stars. Shannon rose, listened, her ears perked, trying to hear anything other than the sound of the breeze rustling the leaves down below. She heard no sign of humans and leapt down to the next ledge. Thankfully, her kind could leap eighteen feet in one bound, up or down. And horizontally? As much as forty to forty-five feet. At a sprint, she could run full out for short distances at forty to fifty miles per hour, which was what she had planned—to race back to the lake, despite discounting the idea earlier, and then take however long it took to catch her meal.

She'd made it to the second rock ledge when she saw something move in her peripheral vision. A man standing on a lower ledge off to her right, his hands reaching for his rifle, slung over his shoulder. How could he see her at dusk?

He moved quickly as if he was a military man and not just a hunter. Before she could leap at him, he fired a shot, the sound ringing in her ears, echoing across the rocks. The last thought she had as she collapsed on the rock ledge above him was that she had lived a month longer than she thought she would have ever managed.

***

As soon as the she-cat landed on the stone, asleep, hopefully, Chase struggled to reach the ledge she was lying on. If he'd been in his cougar form, no problem. But to reach her as a human, he could have used climbing gear.

He hated having to shoot her as much as it felt as if he were shooting one of his own people. But he wasn't. He had just knocked out a wild cat protecting herself that might have killed him, based on survival instinct alone.

He grasped the top of the ledge, got a couple of toe

26

holds with his boots, and pulled himself halfway up the rock face when he saw a naked woman lying on the granite, her back to him, and his tranquilizer dart in her shoulder. Shocking him to the core, he gaped at her. *Holy shit.*

Silky, dark brown, nearly black hair draped around her neck, the rest of her tan skin covered in chill bumps from the cold. Before he could climb on top of the ledge to reach her, and while he was still processing that the cougar was a shifter, and not a full she-cat, his cell phone rang.

His nerves, normally made of steel, shattered into a million fragments. He climbed up onto the ledge and hurried to pull the dart out of the woman's shoulder, then jerked off his parka. After rushing to lay it on the ledge and then lifting her onto it, he pulled her arms into the sleeves and then buttoned it up to her throat. The parka only came to high thigh, but he couldn't do anything about that for now. He glanced up at the cave above them, assuming she must have been staying there.

His breath coming out in a misty fog and his heart pounding hard, he made the rest of the arduous climb to reach the cave to grab her clothes and ID. He stalked inside, used his cell phone to provide some extra light as pitch black as it was in there, and found—nothing. Not a backpack, not a stitch of clothes. Certainly no ID. And she wasn't anyone he remembered ever having seen before.

He hadn't thought he could be shocked any further.

"God, what a nightmare." He had to get the nearly naked, sleeping woman down the cliffs somehow. And he had to keep her warm until then.

He called Dan to give him an update. "Dan."

"Yeah, I tried calling you to let you know the cougar headed in this direction at some point, but I haven't found any sign of him. Have you discovered anything your way?"

"Yeah. I sure as hell did. I'm in one hell of a mess. I

need your help... pronto."

***

Dan immediately headed back south. In all the years he'd known Chase, he'd only heard him sound this frantic about anything twice in his life. The first time was when three of their team members had died in a mine blast during a combat mission and neither could save any of them. The second time was when Chase's family had been murdered.

"Okay, slow down and say everything after: you have a naked woman in your custody."

The last Dan had recalled, he'd sent Chase to track a cougar and... *Ah, hell.*

Sounding startled, Chase said, "Just a minute."

But Dan couldn't wait to hear what was going on. "Don't tell me she's the cougar we were trying to track down. The one who saved the boy."

No answer.

"Chase?"

No answer.

"Chase!" He had to get coordinates from him if nothing else. And he damn well wanted to know what he was up against, so he knew how to get Chase out of the mess he was in, whatever it was.

"Yeah, yeah, yeah," Chase said, sounding totally rattled. He quickly spouted off coordinates. "I'm in a cave above where the woman is. No ID, no clothes, nothing, but she's been sleeping here. I need to get back down to her."

"She's sleeping, naked, in this cold weather on a rock ledge below a cave," Dan said, still not believing it as he strode through the woods, figuring it would take him an hour to reach the location.

"I tranquilized her before she leapt at me. I didn't know she was a shifter."

"One of our kind." Dan didn't say anything for a moment. He couldn't imagine shooting one of their own people like that. But at least some of it made sense now. "No one we know, I take it."

"No. We've got to get her down from here. I'm afraid if we allow her to come to, she'll shift and run off. We're going to have a hell of a time getting her down from here safely."

"Run off... because she wouldn't come into town initially."

"I didn't find any sign of hiking gear or anything else. So it looks like she arrived here as a cougar from somewhere else. She might have a tent somewhere and just went for a run as a cougar. This is one hell of a mess."

"All right. All right. We're fine. We'll take care of her and then we'll find her stuff and marry them up. If you've knocked her out, it might be awhile before we can locate anything for her."

"True. Are you on your way?"

"An hour to your location. What are you going to do for now?"

"Get back down to the woman, pronto. She's wearing my parka for now, but it's not near long enough. I don't know how we're going to get her down these steep rocks. I barely made it coming up here myself. Without climbing gear, I'm not sure how we're going to carry her down."

"Okay, I'll have to detour and get climbing gear and a blanket out of my vehicle. Be there closer to an hour and a half. Sooner, if I can."

"You didn't know anything about this, did you?" Chase asked, frazzled.

Dan laughed. "No, but I can't think of a better man to handle the job." He paused. "What does she look like?"

"In her cat form, narrowed golden honey-colored eyes,

reddish-gold fur. In her human form, dark brown hair, in good shape, but a little thin, maybe twenty-five or so? Not sure."

"No sign of a male, or any other cougars in the area?" Dan was moving as fast as he could over the uneven terrain as he headed for his vehicle.

"No male scents up here. Just hers. None of our people around here. No other predators scented."

"So you're good for the time being," Dan said, relieved.

"Hell, no... we're not good. We're in a hell of a fix," Chase growled.

Dan smiled a little. "All right, but you don't have anything trying to eat you or chase you off or—"

"Ah, hell," Chase said.

"What now?" Dan asked, his heart pounding, the adrenaline rushing through his blood. He hadn't even reached the lake where his vehicle was parked and from there, he'd have to hike through the woods to the mountain like Chase had done. Except at least he had the coordinates to their location, whereas Chase had been combing the area, searching for the cougar, so he hadn't known exactly where she was.

No answer. Damn. "Chase? What's going on?"

The line clicked dead.

***

As soon as the woman moaned down below, Chase feared she'd be so disoriented, she might roll off the ledge and kill herself. Or attempt to shift and kill him. But he thought he'd knocked her out well enough that *that* wouldn't be an issue.

Yeah, he was grasping at worst-case scenarios, but he couldn't help being worried about what she might do. The chance of her rolling and falling off the ledge was his greatest concern. He ended the call to Dan and concentrated on the woman.

He couldn't see her the way the ledge to the cave jutted out. He called out to her just in case she stirred even more from her drugged state. "Miss, I'm a deputy with the local sheriff's department—situated in Yuma Town, Colorado." She most likely knew she was in Colorado, but just in case… "My name is Chase Buchanan. I've called the sheriff, and we're going to help get you down to the town and look after you. I've given the sheriff the coordinates, and he should be here within the hour." Hopefully.

"Miss, can you hear me? I'm coming down."

She didn't answer, and he suspected she'd gone back to sleep. He hoped she had. The only way he could ensure she was still in the same place was if he stretched out over the edge to see the ledge directly below.

He moved to the edge so he could peer over it before he began the climb down. All that was there now was his parka coat lying on the rock slab. The woman had vanished.

The blood pulsing in his ears, his heart thundered. She couldn't have fallen, could she have? He felt sick to his stomach and scrambled to his feet.

Then something moved up above him. He turned and looked up just as the cat leapt from the rock ledge, slammed into him, and knocked him down. The back of his head hit the granite hard. A sprinkling of stars appeared against an ebony night. Before he could clear his vision and move, the cat turned into two cougars and stood watching him.

He sat up, grew dizzy, couldn't tell if two cats stood there, or he was just seeing double. Then the cat leapt off the ledge.

"No!" he shouted. *Damn it to hell*. She couldn't run half-drugged and if hunters had received word a cougar had dragged the boy out of the waterfall pool, they could be out to get her.

His head throbbing with pain and his vision still fuzzy, he fumbled to get his cell out of his pouch. "Dan, *damn it to hell.*"

"What's going on?" Dan asked, sounding relieved to hear from Chase, but apprehensive that he wasn't going to hear any good news.

"She about cracked my skull in two and took off."

"The woman? When she was drugged?"

"Hell, yeah. Well, she shifted first. But she's in no condition to be on the run."

"Okay, I'll be there in thirty-five minutes."

"I'm tracking her."

Dan didn't say anything.

Chase was untying his boots. "I've got to watch her back. Talk to you later." He hung up on his buddy, needing to get out of his clothes ASAP, and shift. He couldn't track her half as fast as a human.

But it was a lot harder than he thought it would be. His head was splitting in two, he was still seeing double, and he had a devil of a time untying his boots and unbuttoning his shirt. If he felt this bad, how did the half-groggy she-cat feel?

Somehow, he managed to strip off the rest of his clothes, then at least had the presence of mind to shift and the ability to do so. He studied where the next ledge was that he could jump down to. The whole thing was wavering. He took a chance and leapt as close to the cliff face as he could. He did the same on the next two ledges, but overshot the last one and ended up landing on his feet on the grass below, thankful that he hadn't injured or killed himself in the process.

Then he chased after the she-cat's scent trail, determined to stop her in her flight.

***

How come some deputy sheriff had come after her? Hennessey Kelly had to have learned Shannon was here and notified the local authorities. They'd take her back to town, thinking everything was as he said it was and turn her over to him. And then? She was a dead woman.

She should have known she hadn't run far enough. Not knowing the area that well, she had no idea how far Yuma Town was from Canyon, Texas. But not far enough. Apparently.

She'd been running for a month, was exhausted, worn out, and barely able to keep going as a cougar. Except for doing so on a jaunt in the wilderness sometimes, she'd never had to live as a cougar 24-7 like this and couldn't believe how tough it was.

Now she was running again. Only this time, half-doped up. She'd stumbled so many times, her mind drifting, that she wanted to sink down into a bed of flowers. Except there were no flowers and the night air was getting colder as she felt her step growing ever slower.

She hoped she hadn't hurt the deputy sheriff too badly, or he would think everything Hennessey told him was the absolute truth. She was a deranged killer.

When she finally reached a river, she wanted desperately to swim across it to disguise where she was going. Not that she had any idea where she was headed. But she couldn't do it. Not with as groggy as she felt. She would surely drown. She growled, not believing the deputy had gotten the upper hand and drugged her so easily.

She stumbled again and felt as though she was the lion in *The Wizard of Oz*, ready to lie down in that field of magical flowers and sleep the rest of her life away.

***

Frantic to reach the she-cat, Chase felt like his head would crack open from the pain any minute. He kept searching the ground and the air, smelling the panicked cougar, trying to catch up to her. His legs were longer, his stride lengthier, but his vision was damned blurry. He'd run into three different trees, thinking that they were farther over than they were, scraping one shoulder one time, the other another, and then his right, a second time.

He felt like he'd been binge drinking, when he'd only gotten plastered on special occasions—like when his team members had died, and when his wife and child were murdered.

He wondered what had spooked the woman so. She had to have smelled his scent on his coat, indicating he was both a human and cougar. So she had to know he knew she was one, too, and had only her best interests at heart. That drugging her had been an honest mistake on his part.

Worse, she was in no condition to run. Just like *he* was in no condition to run.

He shook his head, trying to clear it, then saw her, or double of her. He wasn't sure what he was going to do now. She stood next to the river, contemplating crossing it. She couldn't. Not as deep and swiftly flowing as it was here. He didn't bother to try and sneak up on her. Though their cougar kind were normally ambush predators and didn't stalk their prey, he had no choice. He raced after her in a sprint, attempting to reach her before she could bolt and particularly before she could dash into the water, if she thought to.

He leapt, a perfect leap that would have brought her down, only, he leapt at the double vision and missed her completely. Not to be thwarted, he tried again. She'd been so shocked to see him come out of nowhere that she hadn't escaped yet. This time, he leapt on her and pinned her down against the ground.

He'd never tangled with a she-cat before like this. She immediately rolled over on her back, kicking with both feet and bared her teeth at him. She was as feral as a wild cougar and he couldn't understand why she was so afraid of him. She hissed, growled, and screamed at him. Humans rarely realized the screams they heard out in the wild were a cougar's vocalization, but hers were wild and angry enough to make his cougar hair stand up on end.

Her lips curled back, she bared her pearly whites at him, her nose wrinkled, eyes narrowed, and her ears were back. She was spitting mad.

And scared. He wanted to tell her he wasn't going to hurt her, but he knew there was no convincing her of it.

He wanted to earn her trust in the worst way. He wanted to talk to her, persuade her he didn't mean to hurt her in any way.

The only way he could do that was to shift. Damn it. His head throbbed as he got off her, then stood his ground. She jumped to her feet, crouched, and was steeled to leap, to kill him. Hating to do it with the chilly breeze whipping around them, afraid that she would run off again, he called on the urge to shift into his human form to show he wasn't going to harm her.

His head splintered with pain and the next thing he knew, he was lying on the ground, face planted in the tall grasses, the sound of the river rushing by.

CHAPTER 3

Barely able to stay awake, Shannon stared at Deputy Sheriff Chase Buchanan lying on the ground in a dead faint. Why in the world did the deputy sheriff shift? And then, pass out?

Shannon thought at first that he was just faking it. But she'd gotten close enough to his face to lick his ear and he didn't stir.

Now what? Shannon couldn't just leave him here like this. As cold as it was, he'd end up with hypothermia. She nudged at him to wake him up. Was she crazy? She was liable to pass out right next to him. She should just leave. Now, before she fell asleep. She was fighting the drug slipping through her blood stream, but barely.

She had to get away. She couldn't stay. What if the sheriff wasn't the only one coming after her? Up until now, she'd only worried about this cougar trying to chase her down. She hadn't thought she'd have a whole slew of trackers on her back. She suspected the sheriff and others were shifters, just like she'd smelled in the area—lots of cougars. Cougars that were not shifters would probably be thoroughly confused if they came into the territory.

Maybe other trackers would stay with Chase Buchanan, take care of him, and she'd be long gone by then.

She looked back the way they'd come and saw no one. Heard no one.

What if a predator came upon him and thought he was... wounded prey?

She glanced back at the river. She should run. She had the opportunity. What if she never had the chance again?

Annoyed with the deputy—first for shooting her with a tranquilizer dart, and then for passing out on her and forcing her to protect him, Shannon lay down nearby to watch over him. She was starving and she had to get out of the area. She would leave just as soon as she heard someone who was human who could take care of the deputy—hopefully another shifter and not a plain human who would think the deputy had been mugged or something. Well, and worse, that she was watching over him because she'd claimed him for her next meal. She would really be gaining a reputation then. First, the boy, now, a grown man.

Shannon watched for any sign of anyone coming, listened hard, intent on bolting as soon as she knew the deputy would be taken care of. She glanced again at the naked man, handsome, light brown hair, a five-o'clock shadow, and when they'd been staring up at her right before he shot her, the prettiest green eyes. He had well-toned muscles, was in great shape, tanned, and hot. Not that she should think of him in that way, not when he would see her as the enemy, and certainly not after he had shot her.

She let out her breath in exasperation. She should run. What was she waiting for? She had to be crazy!

***

Chase didn't remember passing out, and when he had come to, he had wanted to jump up and hunt the cougar down again, until he heard the she-cat approach. He'd smelled her concern and played dead. With a real cougar, that was not a good idea. Running either, or they would chase and pounce. Playing dead meant a perfectly docile meal. But she wasn't a full cougar, and she was concerned about him, as evidenced by the way she had licked him, and then he heard her settle down on the grass nearby. To watch over him?

Or had she fallen asleep from the tranquilizer slipping through her system. He couldn't believe she'd fought it this long.

With his enhanced cat hearing, Chase heard the she-cat's stomach grumbling. If she'd stayed with the boy all night to keep him warm, as he suspected now, she probably never had a chance to hunt for a meal. He risked opening his eyes to see what she was doing, hoping that she wouldn't realize he'd come to, become alarmed, and take off again. She was watching for Dan or anyone else who might be headed their way, her head resting on her paws, but her eyes were half open and her ears twitched back and forth. She was vigilant and wary, albeit fighting sleep. He realized the she-cat looked hungry, thin, and malnourished, like she'd been on the run and living in the wilderness for some time. Not like she'd been camping nearby and was just taking a run on the wild side.

He took a deep breath and slowly let it out, not wanting her to know he was awake. It was times like this that made him miss his wife and baby all over again. Though for the past four years, he only dated a couple of times and that was enough to make him realize he wasn't ready for it. Yet with this woman, his protective instincts came into play. She was scared of something. No way should she be out here trying to take care of herself as a cougar on her own. Not alone as a shifter. Cougar shifters could manage when they had no other avenue available to them, but they were too human to be completely wild.

He wanted to take her home and feed her some of his beef stew, the recipe passed down for generations on his Irish side of the family. He was definitely a meat and potatoes man. But he knew someone else in town would take her in. Someone more suitable to watch over her. Unless they were afraid she'd run off, or that someone was after her. And then, she'd need someone's protection. Like the sheriff's.

He smiled at the thought that Dan might get that role. Wouldn't he be surprised?

When Chase smiled, the she-cat lifted her head and stared at him. She had caught him in the act. He was freezing and shivering, his body trying to warm him. He had to shift soon. Still, he didn't want to if it alarmed her.

Silently suffering from the cold, he stayed where he was instead and said, "Miss, no one is going to hurt you." Though he had no intention of telling her anything about himself or his past, he thought it might help to ease her worry. "I lost my wife and baby five years ago and that's one of the hardest things I've ever had to live with. I swear to you, no one wants to hurt you. You need food and shelter. If you'll permit me, I'll escort you back to where I left my clothes. I'll dress and try to make it down the rocks without killing myself..."

He paused when she appeared to smile a little. At least her teeth showed a little.

"Then I'll take you back to my vehicle. It's parked at the lake. I'll drive you to my rental cottages if you like, and warm up a batch of to-die-for Irish stew, homemade, and already made up. You can stay in one of the cabins I own and manage. Can you nod your head in agreement, and then I can shift so I'm wearing my cougar coat? I'm freezing."

She just watched him.

He sighed and shivered. "You're malnourished. You can't run forever. Cougar hunting season begins in two weeks. We'll talk. You tell me what's wrong. We'll figure out a way to help you no matter what the trouble is."

She looked back toward the forest.

"The sheriff's on his way. Since he's on foot, human style, it'll take him a while." He didn't want her to think they were going to gang up on her if Dan suddenly made an appearance.

She swung her head around to look at Chase again, panic in her expression.

"We're buddies from the war. Special Forces. We've known each other forever."

She again looked warily at the forest.

"He's a good guy. He's the reason I returned here after my family died. The whole place is cougar shifter run. We all do our own things, but we all watch out for each other also. You're safe here. We might have to take it a little slow on the return trip, though."

She stared at him now.

"After you knocked me down, I think I suffered a bit of a concussion. When I shifted so I could talk to you, the pain in my head was so great, I guess I passed out. I kept seeing two of you. I ran into trees, and before that, I missed the last ledge I meant to jump down to get off the mountain. Luckily, the drop was only about fifteen feet or I could have killed myself."

He really hadn't meant to mention that part, either. It didn't sound macho enough. On the other hand, he really wanted to impress upon her that he wasn't in any shape to chase after her, she wasn't in any shape to run, and they'd all be better off sticking to his plan—going with him to his home.

So when had he forgotten the part about how Dan was supposed to take her home with *him*?

Maybe because Chase thought the she-cat might be beginning to trust him a little and hadn't run off, and because he did have a separate place for her to stay so she didn't have to feel closed in or smothered. Or that she was a prisoner of sorts, her every move being watched.

"The places I rent are all empty now with the tourists gone. So it's quiet. The grocery store is already closed for the night, but I can run into town and get you some food for tomorrow. You'll have everything you need, free of charge. Kitchenette, hot showers, and a comfortable bed. What do you say?"

She heard movement in the trees, and he prayed it was Dan and not someone else who might think the cougar had injured him. Even though she had.

Then he saw Dan stalking out of the trees. He was carrying Chase's rifle, a backpack, and Chase's coat was tucked over that so that it appeared he'd retrieved all of his things. Chase hadn't relished climbing back up the mountain and back down again, in the event his head was still not quite right.

"Thank God, you're here." Chase turned to tell the woman he was shifting back into his cougar form, but she'd bolted. "Hell and damnation." He was so cold and stiff that he welcomed the change in his skin and muscles and bones, the warming effect and the fur protecting him from the chilling night breeze. At least he didn't pass out this time. His head still throbbed, but he was seeing clearer now.

He swayed a little on his feet, but then he went after her.

"No!" Dan said. "I've got all your stuff. Here, change, I'll run her down."

Chase was on it. He didn't want to run as a human,

41

though he realized he wasn't quite moving at his usual cat-in-a-rush speed. He heard Dan dump everything and run after him, and even as a human, he caught up to him.

Then he saw her up ahead, lying on her side, panting, her eyes closed. Was she faking being knocked out? He never would have imagined she could have lasted this long though. Still, as he approached her, he used caution.

Dan's footfalls were heavy behind him as he ran to catch up.

"Is she out for good?" Dan asked, drawing up close to Chase, but waiting for his say so.

Chase growled a little. He moved up close to her, meant only to nudge her, but licked her cheek instead. She didn't growl, snap, or react in any other way. She was completely wiped out.

"Okay, I'll carry her back. You grab your stuff and we'll take her into town," Dan said.

Chased waited while Dan lifted her into his arms. Then he turned around and loped toward his gear, still feeling a little under the weather, his head pounding, and he hoped he was running in a straight line or else Dan wouldn't go along with his plan—to let the woman stay at one of his cabins.

When he reached his gear, Chase hesitated to shift. It was bad enough he had passed out the first time in front of the she-cat. He really didn't want to do it in front of Dan. Then he realized he probably shouldn't drive his vehicle, either.

He shifted, felt his head splitting in two, and sank to his knees. Damn it.

Dan was at his side in a second, crouching with the sound asleep cat in his arms. "What the hell's the matter?"

Chase realized then despite Dan carrying the cat, he had still moved nearly as fast as Chase had in his cougar form.

"I'll be all right," he grumbled. "Go ahead. I'll catch up."

"Like hell you will," Dan said, now sounding just as annoyed. "Hey, buddy, we go a long way back. I know when you're not all right. Are you gonna be okay?"

Chase let out his breath in a rush. "Yeah, yeah. Hell."

"What's wrong?"

"Nothing. I just got a little dizzy."

Chase took forever to dress, having nearly the same difficulty in buttoning his shirt, getting his feet into the right pants leg, and tying his boots.

"Talk to me," Dan said.

"I fell. All right?" He didn't want Dan to think badly of the she-cat. She had only been protecting herself. She hadn't bitten him.

"All right." But Dan looked him over, trying to see where he'd been injured, and Chase knew he'd insist on sending him to see the doc.

"I'm fine," Chase said again, and stood. So far so good, but when he bent over to grab his backpack, the blanket, rifle, and the climbing equipment, he felt the earth tilt on end.

And he woke to find himself planted face down in the grass again.

CHAPTER 4

Dr. Kate Parker raised her brows at Chase as he found himself lying in a clinic bed, railings up. Her red hair was pulled up in a bun as usual when she was on the job, her green eyes studying him closely, her peach-colored lips turning up a tad.

"You sure had the sheriff all shook up. He called his dispatcher and then had everyone on the emergency roster notified of the situation. I swear he thought he was in the Special Forces again, ordering everyone about as if he were on the battlefield and ready to lose a couple of men. Or in this case, you and a she-cat. How are you feeling?"

"Better." He tried to sit up, but a jolt of pain crashed through his skull. He collapsed back on his pillow.

"Just lie back. Take it nice and easy. You've suffered a concussion. No brain damage that I can see." She shook her head. "I can't imagine how the cat got the best of you."

"Where's the woman?" he asked, not wanting to admit the trouble the cat had caused him and everyone else on the alert roster who had been called to assist. Everyone in town probably knew about it by now.

The doc motioned to the curtain shielding the other bed. "She's sound asleep. I put the two of you in here together because I was certain you wouldn't stay in bed unless you knew she was close by and you could watch her for me." The doc smiled again, but then she grew serious. "That doesn't mean you're to leave that bed for anything. Just ring me or Helen. We'll come and get anything that you need."

That was the nice thing about a clinic for cougars. The doc saw to minor emergencies, but everything else was shipped off to the hospital two hours away. She was mostly here just for their shifter kind. So they had two nurses and one doctor on staff at the six-bed clinic.

"You'll be better before you know it. I just want to keep you overnight for observation. Do you want me to pull the curtain aside and let you get a look at her?"

"Yeah, thanks."

The doc pulled the curtain aside. He expected to see the woman still in cougar form. Instead, she was in her human form, her dark brown hair spilling in curls against the white pillow, her eyes closed in sleep, her breathing light.

"She shifted some time ago. She woke to find herself in a hospital bed, and I think she got scared that someone might see her as a cougar, shifted into her human form, and fell asleep. I don't think she realizes she's in a cougar-run town. I've got her on an IV as she was dehydrated and malnourished. When she wakes, I want her to eat well."

"Hell, my stew," Chase said, trying to get up, worried that it had burned up, but Kate grabbed his shoulder and eased him back into bed.

"Dan ran by your place to drop off your rifle and lock it in your rifle cabinet, then found your stew simmering in the crock pot. He said he had to sample a little to ensure it was still all right." Doc smiled.

Frowning, Chase didn't mind if Dan ate some, but he had hoped to "sample" some himself.

"He said he left most of it in there for you. And he put

the rest in the fridge for you. The stew will be there when you're ready to return home. So, did you learn anything about the woman? Who she is? Where she's from?"

"No. She was in her cougar form the whole time, except right after I shot her."

The doc smiled a little and shook her head. "Not a great way to start a relationship."

He snorted.

She chuckled. "See you later." The doc left the room, closing the door behind her.

He wasn't certain if the doc's closing the door alerted the she-cat that she was gone, or if it had just awakened her, but she turned her head in Chase's direction, looked at him for a moment, then groaned and closed her eyes at the same time.

"You," she said under her breath. "What are *you* doing here?"

He smiled. "You pounced on me and gave me one hell of a headache."

Her eyes remained shut, but she smiled a little. Then she frowned. "Why did you shoot me?" She looked at him then, her golden eyes narrowed.

"Sorry about that. I thought you were a wild cougar," he said.

"I... *am*."

He laughed. "Yeah, I kinda learned that a little too late."

"Where are we, exactly?"

"Yuma Clinic. It specializes in our kind. I'm Chase—"

"Buchanan," she said, running her hand over her forehead.

"Are you okay?"

"Yeah, considering that you drugged me." She sat up in bed and groaned, then lay right back down. "Dizzy. I guess I need to eat something. I couldn't convince you to take me to your place and get a bite of that Irish stew, could I?"

"They'll be serving us something to eat soon here, Doc said."

"I'm fine. I'll get something on my own." She sat back up and started to get out of bed, then realizing she was hooked up to an IV, she removed it.

"Whoa, where do you think you're going?" He sat up quickly and wished he hadn't as a wave of dizziness rushed through his brain.

"Didn't I already say that I was fine? Oh, wait, you want me to pay for a stay here that I didn't authorize or need? Isn't that against the law? Forcing someone to be a patient against their will? If that person had been awake enough to object?"

"Town's taking care of the bill. Let me give the nurse a call and see if she'll get the doctor to release us."

"Just *me*. You probably need to stay here a while longer."

"I'll take you home." He tossed the cover off him and realized the gown had bunched up to his lap.

She studied his legs and smiled.

He got out of bed. "You can't go anywhere until you have some clothes."

"Then give me yours. You can get some others."

He chuckled and shook his head, which was a mistake. The pounding had renewed as soon as he sat up in bed, then worsened as he stood.

"I can use your coat again." Then she shook her head. "Won't work. You didn't drive yourself here, did you?"

She was bright. He'd give her that. "I'll call the sheriff."

Her expression changed from playfully teasing to worried. She *had* to be on the run.

"Listen, I don't know what's wrong, but I swear to you

that you'll be safe with me, with..." He motioned to the town. "With us. Trust me, all right?"

Her expression said she didn't trust him. He feared the worst. She had killed someone and the police were looking to arrest her.

"No matter what you've done, I swear we'll figure it out."

"I've got to use the bathroom," she said, then moved slowly, as if she was still groggy. She finally reached the bathroom, the back of her hospital gown open as her cute little ass was on full display.

He told himself to look away, that as out of it as she was, she hadn't held her gown closed. But he also told himself that he was watching her in case she crumpled before she reached the bathroom, in which case he had every intention of rescuing her.

When she made it into the bathroom all right and shut the door, he quickly called the nurse. He wasn't leaving without letting everyone know what he intended to do. Besides, he needed to secure a ride.

Hell, he didn't even know what to call the woman. "My roommate and I are checking out," Chase told the nurse at the nurse's station.

"Let me get the doc."

"All right." He called the sheriff. "Dan, can you spare a minute to take me back to my place?"

"One of the men left your hatchback in front of the clinic. I left your keys in your jeans pocket. I figured you might want to leave sooner than the doc suggested if you were feeling well enough. How's the woman? Is she awake yet?"

"Yeah, she wants to go to my place."

Dan didn't say anything and Chase didn't want him to get the wrong idea.

"I had offered to feed her some of my famous Irish beef stew. She's hungry. What can I say?"

A long pause ensued as if his friend was considering the ramifications of him doing such a thing. Then Dan finally said, "She has no clothes."

Chase smiled a little, forgetting that scenario. Then he sobered. "Yeah, well, I can get her a pair of scrubs, and she can wear my coat over them."

"Okay. We can fix her up with some other clothes later. No word as to what's going on with her? Who she is? Where she's from?"

"No, but I'm hoping to learn something soon."

"She could be real trouble, Chase."

As if reminding him just the trouble she had already been, he felt another stab of pain in his skull. "Tell me something I already don't know."

"When you learn something, call me."

"Will do. Talk later." He ended the call just as the woman left the bathroom.

"It's free if you need to use it. Did you get permission for us to leave yet?"

"It's coming. And I've got a vehicle to drive. So we're all set. I'll get you a pair of scrubs you can wear, and you can use my parka to stay warm."

He headed for the bathroom and closed the door.

A few minutes later, he heard one of the nurses say, "Chase? Are you in there?"

"Yeah, be out in sec."

"Where's the woman?"

***

As soon as Chase Buchanan entered the bathroom, Shannon seized his parka and tugged it on, and fumbled in his jeans pockets to locate his car keys, if he'd had them on him. Her hands shook as she pulled them out, trying not to let them jingle before she clamped her fingers around them, and then rushed out of the room.

She felt disembodied—she suspected partly from the drug and partly from not having eaten for so long. She hated to have to do this, but it was all his fault she was here. She noted no nurses were manning the station, thank God.

Shannon hurried down a hallway past several hospital rooms, their doors closed, to what looked like a back door, a lighted exit sign displayed overhead. She pushed open the door, thankful it didn't set off any alarms, and stalked outside. The chilling wind swept across her bare feet and legs. Shivering, she poked at the keypad, desperately trying to find the right vehicle. No car headlights came on. *Damn it.*

Then she realized this was probably the staff parking lot and Chase's vehicle would be out front. She hurried around the side of the building.

At least the parka kept some of her warm, but her legs and feet were freezing. Unfortunately, the "cute" penguin gown she wore looked too much like a hospital gown, and she had to hide it pronto. She hated to take Chase's car also. Then again, she wouldn't have it for long. Only as long as it took her to reach a wilderness area where she could park it, then ditch the clothes, shift, and get the hell out of Dodge, or technically, Yuma.

Shannon had to admit she admired the deputy for chasing after her when she must have hurt him worse than either of them had suspected. She really did feel bad about that now, since it appeared he'd only wanted to help her. But after all that had happened to her in the last few weeks, she couldn't really trust anyone that easily. Before that, she was way too trustworthy.

She knew she didn't have much time to do this. That

every second that went by meant Chase would learn she was gone, that his parka was gone, that his keys were gone, and he could guess all the rest. Then he'd call his sheriff buddy who would put an APB out on Chase's car, and she wouldn't get very far at all.

Her heart was jackhammering as she poked the buttons on his key pad again, frantically trying to figure out which vehicle was his—there, a black hatchback's lights flashed on. She stalked toward it, forcing herself not to run as much as she wanted to. Every second wasted meant he could be sounding the alarm and coming for her.

A couple of men leaving a drugstore across the street glanced in her direction. She worried that they might know the black hatchback she'd targeted was Chase's. And maybe recognize the deputy's parka. They saw her bare feet and the bottom part of the hospital gown and could easily put two and two together: wild she-cat who had knocked out deputy was now stealing his parka and car and escaping the clinic.

They'd probably never had this much excitement in the small town of Yuma.

She ran the last few yards, figuring she was on everyone's radar anyway now, and yanked open the car door. One of the men was on his phone, watching her, frowning, and then he and the other men ran toward her, the one still talking on the phone, telling on her, she was certain.

She jumped into the hatchback's driver's seat, started the engine, and began backing out of the parking space, wedged in by cars on either side of her, and one in front. If the men managed to get behind her before she could get away, she was dead in the water.

They looked like they were in the Olympics, attempting to win the gold as they bolted for her. But she managed to get out of the parking space and drove forward, squealing the tires as she saw Chase running out of the clinic, no shirt, no shoes, just a pair of jeans that he was desperately zipping up. She felt really bad about this. She might have run with the wrong crowd when she was growing up, but despite that, she'd never done anything wrong in her life. No traffic tickets. No grand auto theft. Nothing.

But her life was on the line.

She wheeled onto the main road. It was two-lane, three traffic lights, and appeared to be a very small town as she headed for the first red light. She saw a sign for Lake Buchanan at the next street to the right, and that had to mean the wilderness was in that direction, though she was certain that the town was so small that she'd soon be out of the developed area no matter which direction she drove.

She turned right and heard a police car's siren blaring. Her heart began beating triple time. She glanced up at the rearview mirror and saw the car, its lights flashing, turning onto the same road that she was on and speeding up to catch her. Her heart began skipping beats. She wasn't an Indy 500 race car driver, though she loved watching thrillers and car chases. But stunt drivers knew what they were doing when the scenes were filmed. She'd likely get herself killed, or ruin Chase's car. Or both.

As much as she craved reaching the wilderness in the car, she couldn't do it. She pulled down another street into a residential area and roared up into a three-sided carport connected to a one-story brick home. Fumbling with Chase's parka in the confines behind the steering wheel, she stripped off his coat and the hospital gown. She tucked the keys inside the console, and was about to open the car door when the police car, no sirens running now and silent like a cougar, pulled up behind her, ready to ambush her.

The sheriff? His dark brown hair was short and he had

pretty blue eyes that were narrowed at her as he jumped out of his car and rushed the driver's door, rifle in hand.

Naked, she tried to get across the console to reach the other door before he could grab her. If she could open the door in time, she'd shift, jump out of the car, and run.

"Don't… make… me… do it," he said, gruff, commanding, threatening—obey, or else—and she realized he planned to *shoot* her!

And if he caught her? He'd handcuff her to the clinic bed this time for sure. Or… lock her up in a big cat cage.

She didn't want to be shot. She didn't want to be drugged. But she had to risk making her next move.

She yanked open the door, shifted, and jumped out of the car. The sheriff was still on the other side of Chase's vehicle. The carport hemmed her in when she'd thought it was damned clever of her to hide the car there. But he had to have seen her drive up into it.

As soon as she raced for the open end, the sheriff bolted around the car and aimed his rifle at her. He was quick. But not quick enough.

She'd judged the distance, his swift pace, where his footfalls had landed, and she knew she could have escaped, only to have him shoot her in the hip.

So she did the only thing she could do. She readied herself for action, crouched, and pounced.

If she hadn't been so focused on taking the sheriff down and avoiding getting shot, she would have laughed, in a cougar way, at the shocked look on his face. Well, shocked and a glint of awareness that this would not end well for him.

Using all her weight, she slammed her paws against his chest. His shot went wild, echoing off the houses. He fell and landed flat on his back, cursing. She ran, not waiting to see if he was all right, fearing he would reload his rifle and take another shot. Maybe with live rounds the next time.

She had to get off the street as she was certain the word would get out that the sheriff needed backup and men would be all over the place in short order, hunting her.

She headed for a fence and leapt over it, intending to cross the backyard and bound over another fence. But what she saw made her hesitate for a second. A big male German shepherd growled and barked at her, all four feet racing along the ground so that he could reach her. A dog was no match for her claws and teeth, but she didn't want to hurt anyone's pet. And she could leap great distances, so she tore off ahead of the dog and jumped over the fence into another yard just before the dog slammed his body against the wooden slats, shaking the whole fence. Thank God he didn't knock the fence down.

He was making such a ruckus, his barking would alert everyone looking for her just where she'd gone. Not that the shifters couldn't track her by scent anyway.

Thankfully, this yard was unoccupied and she scrambled over the wooden fence into a front yard. Her heart raced as the blood rushed in her ears, and she feared she wasn't going to make it.

She didn't hear the sheriff's car's sirens and that worried her. Was he all right? Or had she injured him like she had hurt Chase?

Now she could be charged with assaulting a deputy *and* a sheriff.

She had no choice but to run along the front yards of the homes here in this residential area—much quicker to reach her destination, the forest off in the distance. Two miles, maybe. The places began to spread out a bit, larger yards, bigger homes, more treed.

She would make it, if reinforcements didn't come in time. She could run there and lose them in the forest. She would have it made.

Until a man ran out of a house with a rifle in hand. An SUV wheeled onto the road she was running next to and headed straight for her. Two vehicles raced along the street behind her.

Change of plans. She did the only thing she could do, ran for another backyard and leapt over the fence. But that wasn't the direction she wanted to head in!

At least the men chasing her would have to regroup.

They had to know she was trying to reach the forest. Which meant she needed to change tactics.

CHAPTER 5

"What do you mean you lost her?" Chase said into his cell phone, not believing this, as he drove one of the nurse's cars to where Dan was waiting.

"Dottie has called everyone on the alert roster who can track down the she-cat. Everyone who is free is searching for her."

"The woman was last spotted at your location?"

"Haverton's backyard."

"Why aren't you there?" Chase was getting a bad feeling about this.

"Let's just say she is one hell of an ambush predator."

Instantly getting the picture and his head aching in sympathy, Chase frowned a little. "Are you okay?"

"I think I feel like you did. I'm getting a ride over to the clinic in a minute. Your vehicle's here, keys in the console, parka on the seat. Got to say she sure is hot to look at. But dangerous. You can go to Haverton's and pick up her trail there. The other guys have lost her."

"Hell." Chase had hoped they were still chasing her down.

"Watch your back. And front. At least she left your car in one piece."

"Thanks, I've got you in sight now." Chase studied Dan

as he held his head between his hands, elbows resting on his knees as he sat on the driveway. He didn't look good, most likely had a mother of a headache like Chase had. Nausea, the whole works. He thought for sure Dan would have already nailed her and been bringing her in. He never expected she'd best him, too.

Another man arrived in a truck. "I've got the sheriff. I'll get him to the clinic," he said as Chase hurried out of the borrowed car.

Chase took hold of Dan's arms and eased him up. "Are you seeing double?"

"Hell yeah. I could have sworn there were two of her when she ran off."

Chase patted his back. "You get better. I'll keep you posted." He handed the keys to the borrowed car to Dan. "Give these keys to Elsie when she checks you into the clinic. I'll take my own car."

"Take my rifle. Catch her before she hurts someone else or someone kills her."

"Will do." At least Chase sure the hell hoped he could. He knew she was plum scared, and he wanted to give her a chance to tell them what was going on, *before* it was too late.

He parked at Haverton's place, leaving the rifle behind. He hoped he could reason with her. No matter what, he wouldn't shoot her again. Part of him was ready to let her go. To just let her fend for herself—but only because he worried that she truly had done something wrong, and he didn't want to be the one to have to bring her to justice. Part of him wanted to take care of her and protect her from whatever she was so scared of.

He opened the gate to the fenced-in yard and took a deep breath. He followed her scent all the way across it. She'd run to the back fence, but she hadn't climbed over it.

She'd raced across the yard at an angle and straight to... *the house*. Hell, she was in Haverton's house. Or had been.

One of the windows was open. He ran to the window and listened. He couldn't hear anyone moving about in the house. He'd been so hopeful she was still here.

He climbed inside the bedroom. Hal Haverton didn't have a wife, so if the she-cat had grabbed some clothes, they would be men's clothes. Packing boxes were stacked everywhere. Which reminded Chase he was supposed to be helping Hal move in a couple of weeks to his new ranch. He guessed that was out while he tried to get one wild she-cat under control.

Chase detected her scent in the underwear drawer and the closet.

Then he heard something in the kitchen. His heart pounding pell mell, he couldn't believe she could still be here. Raiding the refrigerator! And he was damn glad.

He raced down the hall and heard the fridge door shut with a thunk. He reached the kitchen just as the startled dark-haired beauty nearly dropped the glass of milk in her hand.

He saw it coming before she even tossed the glass at him. His instinct would have been to try to grab it, but he couldn't lose her, and he dove for her instead.

His body hit the glass of milk first, the beverage splashing against his shirt as he took her down, and hoped the hell he didn't knock her out.

She fell with an oof and then tried a maneuver to unsettle him, shoving her feet against the floor, bucking, which damn near did throw him off, but he pressed hard against her body, grabbing her wrists, anchoring them above her head.

"Hold... still," he said, irked to the max. "I don't know what kind of trouble you're in, miss, but we'll work it out. As long as you're not wanted for murder..." He saw the subtle change in her wild-eyed look to one of concern, and he feared the worse.

One of their kind couldn't go to prison. She had to have a death sentence on her head if she was wanted for murder.

"I... didn't... kill... anyone," she gritted out, her expression furious. "And I haven't done anything wrong. Get off me!"

"You're kidding, right? You've injured a sheriff, broken in and entered a house, stole a car—mine—stole Hal Haverton's clothes, broken a glass, and littered."

Her grim mouth turned up just a hair at the mention of littering, and damn if he didn't want to kiss her. When she was total trouble. And his prisoner at the moment.

"You're right," she said softly.

"That you've killed someone?" he asked, coming to his senses.

"No," she growled, her golden eyes narrowed in irritation. "That I've... I've done all those other things. But you can't hold me."

He raised a brow. Like hell he couldn't. "If you don't recall me telling you so, I am a deputy sheriff of Yuma Town. And even if I wasn't, I would be perfectly within my rights making a citizen's arrest."

"I don't mean that," she said, sounding exasperated. "You can't incarcerate me. Not when I'm a shifter."

He smiled then. "Sorry, lady. Around here, being that it's a shifter-run town, we have accommodations for our kind, no questions asked."

She was still breathing hard, maybe some of it to do with his body pressing against hers, but he couldn't chance letting her go.

She licked her dry lips and if that wasn't a total turn on.

"I take it that having some of your homemade Irish stew is out now," she said.

He smiled a little. "Maybe I can bring you a bowl to the jailhouse." Hating to do it, wanting to know the truth of what was going on with her, he took hold of her wrists with one hand and reached for his pocket and a pair of handcuffs with his other.

Her eyes widened a bit and she again attempted to unseat him. That had him flipping her over onto her stomach and yanking her one arm behind her back, forcing her to quit fighting him.

"Ow," she said, and he heard the pain in her voice.

He was fairly certain she was being honest with him, but he wasn't giving her a chance to best him again. He cuffed one wrist and then the other.

"You're safer with us, no matter what you've done. Just let me know what your name is and what we're up against." He turned her over so she could talk. She was wearing Hal's gray sweats that swallowed her up, no shoes on her feet. The floor was covered in glass and milk and both of them had the shimmer of glass and wet spots on their clothes.

"Come on," he said, carefully lifting her off the floor so she wouldn't have to walk through the glass. If she wasn't such a handful, he'd clean up the mess, but his priority had to be keeping an eye on her. He carried her into the living room and set her down on the sofa. "Stay."

She scowled at him, then turned away as he pulled out his phone. She was observing the layout of the place, trying to figure out just what she could do to get away, he would guess. But she wasn't going anywhere. Not when she was handcuffed and in his custody.

"Dan, are you okay?"

"Hell… yeah. Doc's got me in a bed, damn it. I'm on

pain meds. What's the news?"

Chase smiled at the woman. "I've got our woman. I'm at Haverton's place. She's made a bit of a mess of his kitchen, but she's fine. Handcuffed on his couch. Not cooperating."

"Resisting arrest?"

"Hell, yeah, resisting arrest."

She jerked her attention to him and scowled.

He smiled. "But she's calm now. I'll bring her into town in a few."

"Whatever you do, don't lose her."

"Gotcha there. See you in a little while." Chase ended the call, then eyed the woman. "Okay, what's your name and what's your story?"

"Ann Osborn is my name."

"Try again."

Her frown couldn't have grown any deeper, he didn't think.

He called another number. "Hey, Dottie, if Dan didn't give you word in case he's too out of it, I've got the woman and you can call off the search."

"Will do. I've heard she's a real wild cat."

"She is definitely that. Call Hal Haverton and let him know I'm in his house with the woman, that she made a mess in the kitchen, and we'll be out of here in a bit, but I just wanted to forewarn him."

"All right. I'll get right on it."

"Thanks. Out here." He sat on the chair perpendicular to the couch and leaned forward. "So if you're not wanted for murder, then what? A psycho stalker is after you? You've committed some other crime worthy of risking your life over? Stolen millions of dollars from a Mob boss? What?"

"I'm totally innocent of committing any crimes."

He raised his brows.

"Before you shot me," she said, scowling at him. "I could have been just on a run through the mountains on a whim. You had no right to shoot me."

"You wouldn't have run away if you hadn't been feeling guilty about something."

"You didn't know I was a shifter and you shot me!"

"Okay, I did. But I told you who I was after that and that Dan, the sheriff, was joining us. You ran again, only you conked out from the drug, and we were able to take you in hand or you would have been gone for good. So why did you run from the clinic? You weren't afraid I was going to press charges. I offered to feed you some of my stew. I apologized for shooting you." He reached out and patted her knee. "Tell me. We'll work through this."

"You can't," she said. "None of you can. Believe me when I say this. The best thing you can do is let me go. Just drop me off in the wilderness, and I'll go far away from your town and out of your territory, so you never have to deal with me again."

He straightened in his chair. "You can't live out there on your own as a cougar. It wouldn't be safe. Hunting season begins in less than two weeks from now. If you leave our territory, you're liable to run into a wolf pack or two, hunters, bear." He considered how thin she looked. "You don't appear to be finding enough food to maintain your weight. Stay with us. With me. My offer still stands. I have cabins up near Lake Buchanan. You can have one of them free of charge. I'll pick up some groceries for you. You can put some meat on your bones, talk with us, get your bearing, and then we'll see where you want to go from there."

"All right. I'll go with you. Just take off the handcuffs and I'll behave."

He smiled. He didn't trust her one little bit. "Or, I can dump you in a jail cell and let the sheriff talk to you when he's no longer seeing double of you."

She closed her eyes, and then opened them. "I had hoped he hadn't been injured like you. But he was getting ready to shoot me. The natural instinct for us is for self-preservation."

"Right. Your choice. My place or jail?"

"You're kidding, right?"

He frowned a little, not getting the gist of her question.

"Your place, of course." She sounded so hostile, he had no plan to take off the handcuffs any time soon.

He called Dan back and informed him he was taking the prisoner to his cabin. Dan was silent.

"I'll talk with her. Learn what I can."

"She'll make a run for it."

"I'll keep her handcuffed."

"It's your call. Not what I'd do under the circumstances, but if you think it will work, go for it. Just let me know what you learn."

"All right. Take it easy, Dan. I'll call you once we're settled." Chase escorted the woman out to his car, helped her in, and said, "Stay." Then he shut the door and headed around to the driver's side, half expecting her to bolt. He really wished he hadn't had to handcuff her, but he knew she wasn't going to cooperate without them.

He was kind of surprised when she stayed put, and he wondered if the handcuffs *had* done the trick.

"We'll stop at the grocery store and grab anything that you'd like to eat and anything else you might need."

"You're going to take me into the store while I'm handcuffed?"

"To me, yes." He wasn't taking any chances.

A few minutes later, they arrived at the store. Ten cars

were parked there, and he helped her out of the car, then unfastened the handcuff on one of her wrists and fastened the cuff to his wrist. Then he took her inside. "What do you want?"

Several of the customers watched them, not just because he was handcuffed to the woman—well, maybe that also—but because they hadn't seen him with a woman here in town ever, so the sight of him with her was catching everyone's attention.

He was certain the news of his injury and his knocking her out had already spread among the shifters earlier also. Then her subsequent escape and the manhunt had to have circulated. Now everyone was as curious as he was to learn who the woman was.

"I can have anything?" she asked, and for the first time he saw something else in her expression. Appreciation, he thought.

"I have sample size toothpaste, hair products, and deodorant. I've got spare toothbrushes, all for guests who forget them at home. So mostly look for any food items you'd like. Meals for breakfast, lunch, and dinner. Snacks. Anything you feel like."

She looked around at the chicken and beef in the meat department, then turned her eyes on him. "I have no clothes," she said.

He hadn't even considered that part of the equation, since she was wearing Hal's sweats, but then he glanced down at her bare feet, mostly covered in the sweat pants hanging in folds, but Chase felt like a heel for not thinking about it sooner. "You're right. After we grab some food, we'll run by a woman's clothing shop a couple of doors down from here. I don't know what she carries exactly, but maybe you can find what you need there."

"I'll have to try the clothes on." She raised her hand

handcuffed to his to emphasize how difficult that would be.

He smiled. He wasn't letting her out of his sight. The vixen smiled back.

CHAPTER 6

If Chase had left her alone for just a few minutes, Shannon would have been out of the handcuffs in a jiff.

But Shannon couldn't believe that Chase would sit with her in the dressing room of the woman's boutique while she intended to try on clothes! Well, maybe she could understand. But he wouldn't even turn away. At least while she was still wearing Hal Haverton's sweats.

"While you're sitting there, I can't leave the dressing room without you noticing. Besides, the woman who owns the shop and three of her patrons are watching this dressing area just in case I knock you out and attempt to escape."

Chase folded his arms and grinned at her.

He really was cute, well, and hot. But for now just... cute.

"I'm not letting you out of my sight. What if you managed to climb over the top and slipped out through the back door? Not on my watch. The handcuffs are off and I'm staying," he finally said.

"Voyeur," she said. Though she had to admit when she pulled off the sweatshirt and revealed her breasts, his cheeks reddened a bit, and then he turned to watch the door to the dressing room, taking his eyes off her. She tried on a bra, and then another, and another. She hated trying on bras. One was too tight. Another too loose. This one…

"Looks great," Chase said.

This time *her* face turned red as she felt the heat creep into it. She tossed the too small bra at him. "Do something useful like watch the door, just in case someone tries to break in. You do realize that other women who might want to try on some clothes will feel intimidated that you're in here with me, and they'll feel they have to wait."

He smiled and she yanked the price tag off the bra she was keeping and tossed the tag to him. Then she pulled on a woman's sweatshirt, the color gray. She thought if she managed to slip away, no one would notice her much.

"The hot pink sweater would look good with your dark hair," Chase said.

"It was too hot pink," she said, though she did agree with him. The color did look hot on her. And she really liked a turquoise blue that also looked great with her coloring, but that's not what she was trying for here. Obscurity was what she needed. If she'd found something to blend in with fall leaves or evergreen pines, that would work to an extent. Except if she reached the woods, she'd dump them and shift into her cougar form. As a cat hiding in the rocks, she blended in completely.

"You need the hot pink—to stand out," he said.

She didn't need him to clarify. She knew perfectly well what he was getting at. She motioned with her finger for him to turn around.

He watched the door while she pulled off Hal's sweatpants and pulled on a pair of strawberry bikini panties, then yanked off the tag and tossed it at Chase. It bounced off his lap, and he leaned down to pick it up off the floor, but not before he got an eyeful of her in the sweatshirt and strawberry panties.

"Nice," he said.

"No commentary necessary," she said, getting what appealed to her and not caring whether it appealed to him or not. He was only the purse for the moment.

She pulled on a pair of jeans. She wasn't used to wearing jeans cut quite that low but she figured she wouldn't need them for long.

"Perfect," he said.

"Aren't you tired of me trying on clothes? Because if you are, you could go down the street and get a cup of coffee at that quaint little coffee shop."

He smiled at her. "Nice try. I'll suffer."

She pulled off the jeans and tried on a pair of gray sweatpants. "You don't look like you're suffering." Not from the way he eyed her while she removed the clothes and put new ones on. "Do I have a dollar limit?" she suddenly asked. She didn't want to be greedy and get too much, or run up a tab too high. Especially since she planned to vamoose as soon as she could.

"Buy whatever you need."

She took a deep breath, guilt washing over her again. "Thanks." She considered the sweaters she'd brought into the dressing room, then pulled off the sweatshirt and began trying them on. "I'll take these two."

"Black and gray." He shook his head.

"I like black and gray." Well, black was okay. She hated gray. Still, she'd feel more nondescript in the gray. "I'll need these socks, and some more panties. And that's it."

"All right. Wear whatever you want, and I'll take Hal's things back to him later. Did... you need something to sleep in?"

She chewed on her bottom lip. "I'll grab something before we leave. I don't have to try something like that on to see if it fits."

She handed him all the clothes, and then slipped into the jeans again, and a pair of socks, black tennis shoes, and the black sweater.

As soon as they walked out of the dressing room, they found ten women standing there watching for their exit, some smiling, some looking a little disconcerted.

The owner quickly divested Chase of all the clothes. "I'll take these so that you can keep your hands free," she said, and glanced at Shannon as if to say that she knew if he was busy and Shannon tried to flee, he had to have his hands free to grab her. "I'll put these on your account and you can settle up later."

"Does she usually put things on your account in here?" Shannon asked, amused. Unless he had a girlfriend, she suspected he didn't come here to shop with or for a woman very often, if ever.

He took hold of her arm and headed for the counter where the owner was ringing up the sales. Shannon glanced at the other women, a couple of whom finally headed for the dressing room with clothes in hand.

"See, I told you, Chase. You scared the women off who wanted to use the dressing room. Oh, and I need to get something to sleep in. And some more panties."

That had all the rest of the women standing there bug-eyed, staring at her.

She would have bought something warm for the winter nights, but because she had a gawking audience of women who would gossip about all this later, she figured she'd give them something to really gossip about. She lifted a sweet pink nightie trimmed with lace off a rack. She could wear the sweats over that. And then she grabbed a handful of colorful bikini panties. She might not want to wear anything noticeable as an outer garment, but for herself, for as long as she was stuck here, she'd enjoy some colorful underwear.

She noted Chase was smiling a little, but his face was a little flushed, too.

"How about a jacket also?"

She hesitated, not wanting him to spend so much when she didn't intend to stay. Then sighed and selected a black hooded, lightweight jacket.

After Millicent added everything to his bill, he carried the bags in one hand, and he had his other locked around her hand. She knew just how to twist her wrist to get free of his hold on her, but she noticed that even while walking out to his hatchback, two people watched them from the grocery store parking lot, another half dozen from a café observed them through the big windows, and two others filling their cars at a gas station, glanced their way.

"Not much going on here, I can see," she said, since she seemed to be the height of entertainment.

"It's not very often that a she-cat knocks out both a deputy and the sheriff like you did, then has an APB put out on her." He waved at a blond-haired man, his hair curly, and she thought he looked like a surfer-dude, tan, muscled, with a pleasing smile. He appeared to be in his late twenties like Chase and Dan, as he headed across the street to intercept them. "Hal Haverton," Chase warned. "Like me, he works part-time as a deputy sheriff. He's also the man who owns the home you broke into."

"His window was unlocked. It was an open invitation."

"Hey, Chase, so is this the little lady everyone's talking about?" Hal looked her over. Then he smiled, showing off dimples. "You could have left her handcuffed in my place, and I would have taken care of her."

"You and who else?" she asked.

Hal laughed. "You're not going to let her get away, are you?"

Shannon didn't think his comment had anything to do with confining her for the crimes she'd committed since she'd come here.

"First chance she got, she would have slipped away," Chase said.

"She wouldn't have knocked me out," Hal said, not taking his eyes off her. He finally turned to Chase. "You're not locking her up at the jailhouse, are you?"

"She's coming home with me to have some of my famous Irish stew. I'll talk to you later. Sorry about the mess she made at your place," Chase said.

"It was all his fault. He startled me," she said.

"She used the glass of milk as a missile," Chase said.

Hal grinned and folded his arms. "Well, if you need me to watch your back on this one, just holler."

"Thanks, I've got it covered." Chase escorted her to his vehicle, threw her packages in the backseat, waved at Hal, got into his vehicle, and drove down the road. "Special Forces buddy of mine."

"You said Dan was also."

"And Stryker Hill, his regular deputy who's on vacation at the moment, is also. We all went into the army together. And when we got out, we returned here."

"So, the other two will be giving you and Dan a hard time concerning me." She thought it was sweet, really. Though Dan and Chase might not think so. "Aren't you afraid I'm going to try and escape from your place?"

"You have no reason to. I'm offering you a place to sleep, shower, and eat. You have clothes to wear, a television to watch, and a beautiful view of the lake and mountains. It's a forested paradise. And you are under my protection. Now, if you really don't want to stay, I'm not going to force you to."

She stared at him in disbelief. He appeared to be

serious.

"Then… then why did you chase me down?"

"You saved that boy at the waterfall, didn't you?"

"He would have drowned."

"Right. Well, the word will have spread that a cougar wanted the boy for a meal. Hunters would have gone after you, or any cougar in the area. You were staying in a cave still close to that waterfall. Beyond that, hunting season starts in less than two weeks. None of our people run as cougars at that time. And you were starving. Besides, I'd tranquilized you. You were in no shape to fend for yourself."

"You think I'm a hardened criminal."

"I think you're running from someone, and I'm here to help you out if you need my assistance. Which, I'm guessing you do. I don't believe your recent crime spree was something you do on a regular basis."

She raised her brows at him, not sure she believed that he really thought that.

He smiled. "I've seen criminals in action. You didn't run after I passed out near the river. You watched over me until Dan arrived. You were concerned for my welfare. A hardened criminal wouldn't have been. You would have been more concerned with getting out of there. You stayed with the boy until help came. That put you at a hell of a lot of risk. You didn't break Hal's window or jimmy it open. You just found that it was unlocked and slipped inside. You didn't ransack his place, just got what you needed—some warm clothes that fit well enough and a glass of milk. That's not the actions of a lawbreaker with a long rap sheet."

He pulled into a treed log cabin resort, each of the cabins connected by a trail to the main one, but pine trees surrounded them, giving each of them privacy. And at once, she loved it. It seemed homey, both to her cougar and human half.

He parked. "So here's the thing. You can stay in one of the rental cabins and we can share meals if you like, or you can do your own thing until you want to talk. You can slip off and run away again. Or you can stay with me."

"Stay with you," she said, not meaning that she wanted to, but she didn't know why he was suggesting *that* as an option.

"That's what you want to do? Stay with me?" He sounded surprised she'd go for that choice.

"No. I mean, why would you suggest that?"

"Because you're running scared. Running from someone. I have two bedrooms. You can take the guestroom, and I can protect you if you need protection. It would make it easier for me to keep an eye out for anyone who might wish to bother you. If you're staying even in the closest cabin to mine, I can't see it from my place."

This changed everything. All that Chase said had merit. She wanted to stay in her own place so she would have more privacy. But she'd been running for so long on her own, isolated from others, and terrified, she'd like to feel she had someone who could watch her back.

"Don't take this the wrong way," she said, "but I'd like to stay with you."

He tried to look ultra-serious, but then he gave in and smiled broadly. "That works for me."

***

Chase had hoped he'd said the right words to convince the lady to stay with him and not want to run off again. In the meantime, he had to learn who she was and what the trouble was that she was facing.

"So, do you have a name I can call you?" he asked.

"Ann," she said this time as she carried the bags of clothes into his cabin and he grabbed the sacks of groceries.

"You're not an Ann."

73

"What's an Ann supposed to be like?" she asked, glancing around his cabin. He was glad he'd picked up the place before he'd had to run after her yesterday.

"Sweet and innocent."

She snorted.

He laughed. "So what is your name, really?"

"Shannon. But that's all you're getting."

He was glad for that much. His phone rang. He set the groceries on the kitchen counter and glanced at the caller ID. "It's Dan. I've got to take this." To Dan, he said, "Hold on a sec." Then he said to Shannon, "First door on the right is your guestroom, bathroom is the second door on the right. Make yourself at home."

"Thanks. Say hi to Dan for me." Then she hauled her bags to the guestroom and shut the door.

Chase pulled the stew out of the fridge, dished it into microwave dishes, and began warming it up. "Shannon is her name, and she's staying with me. I'll protect her at the same time until we know what's going on."

"Who's going to protect you from her?"

"I'll be fine." Chase smiled, then began putting away the groceries.

"Hell, she's liable to handcuff you to your furniture and run off with your money and car. Or leave as a cougar and disappear. Are you sure this is a good idea?"

"Yeah. How are you doing?"

"I've felt worse. But at least I'm home now. Do we have a last name for her?"

"No."

"You think the first name is really hers?"

"I believe so. Not completely sure."

"I've had twenty calls from our people. They want to know the trouble she's in."

"As much as I do." But he worried a little that the

townsfolk were concerned she would bring trouble to them and want her gone. Not that he was changing his mind about this. She was staying as long as she wished.

"They want to help her in any way that they can."

"Good." Chase was truly glad for that. The more everyone wanted to help her, the more he hoped she'd want to stay.

"Some of the single guys called to let me know if she's too much of a handful for the two of us, they'd open their places up to her."

Chase laughed. "Was Hal one of the ones who called you?"

"You better believe it. First one, actually. He said he'd give her a fresh glass of milk and anything else she wanted."

Smiling, Chase shook his head. "I bet."

"Five families said they'd take her in. And a couple of single women said the same. Dottie offered her a home if Shannon didn't mind her twin toddlers."

"Thanks, Dan, I'll let her know."

"Hal didn't just call me though. He dropped by the house to rub it in about the little lady knocking us both out, envisioning she was an Amazon-sized woman with muscles that rivaled Hercules's. Until he saw her in her human form—petite, sweet, and totally innocent looking."

Chase chuckled. "Wait until your deputy returns home from his vacation."

"He already called and asked if we needed backup."

Chase pulled the dishes of heated stew out of the microwave. "He'll do anything to get out of taking a vacation because he's such a workaholic. How did he get word?" Though as soon as he spoke the words, he figured it was Dottie, their dispatcher.

"You know Dottie. She was worried about the woman and wanted all available personnel here to help out."

"You told him we didn't need him, right?"

"Yeah. And Rick and Yvonne Mueller invited the two of you over to dinner, soonest."

"Let me talk with her first."

"Possibly, they can find out who she is through their contacts. It's best if we know as soon as we can what kind of trouble she's in."

"End of the week, Dan."

"Sooner than that. We have to be prepared."

"I'll work on it."

"All right. Hope you know what you're doing. Are you handcuffing her to the bed tonight?"

"No. She's free to go if she feels she has to. But for now, she's staying with me."

"Got another call coming in. I swear everyone in town is going to call me about her. Nearly a dozen women called about the dress shop incident. They told me how you stayed in the dressing room with her. Want to tell me about that?"

"No. Just watching out for her."

"Anything else I ought to know?"

Chase smiled a little. His buddy was fishing. "That about sums it up. We're going to have some stew. You take it easy and I'll call you later."

"She's dangerous, Chase. Just be careful."

"I will. Talk later." Chase started a fire in the fireplace, and then began making some coffee.

Even though he wanted to let Shannon do what she felt she had to do, he was relieved she'd opted to stay with him. If she had stayed at one of the cabins, he figured there would be more of a chance that she would tear off. He couldn't curb the notion that he would be pulling guard duty all night.

Though not to protect her from anyone, but to keep her from running, despite his saying it was up to her. He didn't want her killed. And he knew very well how vulnerable she would be on the run as a cougar.

CHAPTER 7

Shannon put her new clothes away in the dark oak bachelor chest. She still couldn't believe how generous Chase had been to buy her anything she'd wanted in the line of meals and clothes. She tucked her hair behind her ears, walked over to the window, and opened the green curtains. Peering out at the pine trees, she loved the wilderness feel of the place. She should have stayed at one of the other cabins, but she couldn't. She could protect herself to an extent, but she'd been on edge for so long, running as a cougar in the wilderness, and before that, running as a human, that she felt more... vulnerable now that she was standing still.

Despite worrying what Chase and the sheriff might do to her if they learned why she was on the run, she felt safer being here, sharing the same space with Chase. If she'd stay in a different cabin, she would have been jumping at every sound or shadow, just as she had when she was running. She didn't want him to know that was the reason for her staying here, and she didn't want him to think that she wanted to stay with him because she was interested in him. In the end, he could be hurt by all this and she didn't want that to happen.

But for now, she desperately needed a few days and

nights of rest. She would eat some good, nutritious meals during that time and she'd map out a plan. This would work well for her. She couldn't stay long. She was afraid Dan or Chase would learn who she was, or Hennessey would locate her. But she had no idea where she was location-wise in relation to anywhere else. When she had the opportunity, she was learning just where she was and where she could run to next that might afford her relative safety.

She'd felt like she'd lost her humanity for a while, fending for herself, being a loner, surviving—but that wasn't her. Despite the crowd she'd run with when her brother was still alive, she'd always been true to her own nature, honest, law-abiding—but way too trusting. And she'd always had friends, even if they'd been on the wrong side of the law. With Ted, she hadn't been able to have friends, and she realized just how controlling he'd been.

She considered the furnishings in the bedroom: a green leafy bedspread over a double bed, a dark oak nightstand, a soft green chair, bachelor chest, and a tall armoire. They would do.

While Chase was on the phone, she heard the front door open and close. She shut the curtains and moved the heavy armoire, twisting it from side to side until she could push it in front of the window. She didn't want him to know she had moved the furniture because she was afraid, so she was glad he'd gone outside to talk to the sheriff. Though she did have some reservations about him wanting to talk with him in private. Were they planning something? Was Chase lulling her into a false sense of security while they tried to track down who she was? Most likely.

Taking a deep, settling breath, she considered the armoire blocking the window, only a tiny bit of light on either side. She was satisfied that no one could get to her through the window without making an awful racket.

That task done, she wanted to take a bath. She'd swum enough in lakes and streams while trying to catch dinners, and rescuing the boy, that she had bathed often enough in her cougar coat. But the notion of soaking for a long time in a warm, soothing bath lured her in. Thankfully, because of their faster healing genetics, her scratches and bruises from her flight through the wilderness had healed up. She wanted to wash her hair and feel squeaky clean and luxuriate in a bit of self-indulgence. She grabbed the sweats and headed for the bathroom. Chase was still outside talking on the phone.

A handful of photographs hanging on the hallway walls caught her eye—of Lake Buchanan surrounded by the forest wearing its spring green finery, some of the later blooming trees still bare, in autumn with the trees sporting yellows, reds, and oranges mixed in with the evergreen needled pines, the darker green of summer, and the bare branches of winter with a lot of snowfall on the ground. She couldn't help but love the scenes—the same place, but during different seasons of the year.

She entered the bathroom, closed the door, and considered the green marbled walls and walk-in shower, a sauna tub next to it. She smiled. Nice. *Really* nice. After all she'd been through, she was ready to experience a bit of heaven.

Before long, she was soaking in the tub, one of the complimentary bottles of rose mint sitting on the little shelf within reach, the jet bubbles pummeling her back. She knew she had to leave within a few days, but what she wouldn't have given to stay in this tub for a month.

***

Chase considered the woodpile and figured he had enough for a while as he talked on the phone to Dan.

"Listen, that Carl Nelson's been snooping around. You

know the reporter from Denver? While you were being checked out at the clinic, he reported about the cougar and the boy. We had a flurry of reporters down here asking about the cougar after that—had we killed it, had we ever had problems with cougars like that before," Dan said.

"Hell."

"Yeah, I agree. I put out the word that we took care of the cat."

"Took care of…?"

"Killed it. I didn't want a swarm of hunters down here looking to kill cougars. If they figured it was dead, that would be the end of it. But even so, right after he reported it, several more reporters flocked to the area like a bunch of vultures looking for more of a story. They heard about your injury and rumors got out that you were tracking the cougar. We've assured everyone that your injury had nothing to do with the *male* cougar that had pulled the boy out of the water. I swear they're like a swarm of blood thirsty mosquitoes.

"Everyone is being careful about what they say around town, but I needed to give you a heads up. If she's on the run from cougar shifters, hopefully, the reference to the cougar being a male will throw them off. If the story had only run locally, no problem. But a reference to a wild cougar saving a boy to eat him later—well, it hit the national news."

"Great."

"If she's running from humans, no problem. Several of our men scoured the area also, searching for a tent she might have set up somewhere. They followed her recent trail, but they could only find where she traveled for miles. It appears she's been on the run for some time."

"Any clue as to which direction she came from if she wasn't backtracking or meandering a bit to find food?"

"South. Unfortunately, that reporter, Carl Nelson, was in the area when we had the cougar hunt going on in town. Thankfully, there was a lot of confusion since he heard that I was chasing your stolen vehicle and he thought there was a story in that. Then he saw men on a cougar hunt. Everyone he chanced to speak with said the man was crazy. He's calling it a town-wide, conspiracy cover-up. That's all I have now, but don't be surprised if you get a pesky reporter up your way before long."

That's all Chase needed. "Thanks. Good to know."

"Talk to you later."

They ended the call and Chase grabbed a load of wood, walked into the house, and dumped it into the timber box. Then he locked the door. He worried when he saw that Shannon hadn't left the bedroom yet. Was she sleeping? After her ordeal, she would probably need several days to rest up.

Or… hell, had she already skipped out on him? His stomach began to churn with anxiety.

Trying not to panic, he stalked down the hall toward her guestroom, but then heard the jets bubbling in the tub. He smelled the fresh water and the scent of rose mint and suddenly envisioned Shannon naked as soap and water ran down her tan skin.

But what if she wasn't there? What if she had left the jets running in the filled up tub, pretending to be bathing, but she wasn't even in there?

His heart thumped hard as he listened closely at the door, ready to knock to see if she'd answer when he heard the jets turn off, the water draining, and a towel sliding off the rack. He breathed a sigh of relief. Again, the unbidden image crossed his mind of her naked, dripping water, droplets clinging from her nipples when… hell, he had to think of her as nothing more than a very needy guest. What she didn't need was him getting hard with envisioning her wet and naked.

Bathroom cabinet drawers opened and closed.

Not wanting to startle her, but to let her know she was welcome to anything he had, he tapped lightly on the door. "The extra supplies I mentioned are in the bottom drawer."

"I found them, thanks. Hairdryer?" she asked.

"Uh, sorry, no hairdryer."

"No problem."

"Did... you want to watch a movie while we eat?"

"I'd love to."

And just like that, he had the oddest feeling. Like he was on a first date. Which had him shaking his head at himself. First things first. Learn what trouble she was in. And then after that, figure out where to go from there. He was usually good at sticking to a plan. But with Shannon, plans seemed to dissolve into man hunts—or in her case—she-cat hunts.

"Is there a particular kind of movie you're interested in?" he asked.

"Nothing with a lot of blood," she said, and he swore she sounded upset when she mentioned it.

He was right back to believing someone had been murdered. But if she didn't do it, had she witnessed a murder? And the killer was after her?

Hell, he could second guess this all day long. He had to learn the truth.

Then he pondered the movie scenario. He didn't think he had a movie that didn't feature someone who wasn't trying to kill someone. He didn't watch comedies or romance stories. Or animated features. He felt bad that he didn't have anything she might like to watch. He even briefly thought of calling up Dan and asking him if he had anything else they could see, but he dismissed that notion.

Dan liked the same kind of movies that Chase did—thrillers, historical adventures, futuristic drama, survival stories. He wasn't about to leave Shannon alone to go into town to pick one up anyway.

"Not sure I have anything without a bit of violence in it," he said, hating to admit it.

"That's okay. I'll look and see what you've got. Thanks, I'll be out in a moment. Oh, wait, do you have a hairbrush?"

"No hairbrushes, comb in top drawer."

"Okay. Thanks."

For another fifteen minutes, he paced across the wood floor in the living room, waiting for her to leave the bathroom. He couldn't help himself. He wanted to know who she really was and why she'd been running as a cougar in the wilderness. Except for Yuma Town, there wasn't anything nearby for miles. If he had to, he'd agree to Dan's plan to take her over to Rick's place for dinner sometime this week. But he hoped they wouldn't have to dig that deep.

He heard the door to the bathroom close and then Shannon's light footfalls as she walked down the hall. She was wearing the gray sweats. Her wet hair looked nearly black and curled in wet straggles down the sweatshirt, leaving big wet spots.

"We can pick up a hairdryer for you tomorrow."

"That's okay. I often go to bed with wet hair. Hairdryers are harsh on the hair. Is Dan okay?"

"Yeah. He's at home now."

"Good." She took a sniff of the air and smiled. "Your stew smells delightful. Is there anything you want me to do?"

"Ready to serve up." He motioned to the table. "Let's eat at the table and we can watch a movie later if anything appeals." They needed to talk and watching a movie wouldn't be conducive to that.

"All right."

He ladled out the stew, then took a seat across from her and they ate in silence.

"This is really good," she finally said after having finished half of the bowl.

"Thanks. If you need the recipe, I can give it to you."

She smiled a little.

Dumb remark on his part. She was on the run. Why would she need his family's recipe? In the worst way, he wanted to ask her about the trouble she was in so they knew best how to handle this. He was afraid to push her too soon to tell him the whole story. Pressuring her, he imagined would encourage her to light out of here.

But the words spilled out of his mouth anyway. "Did you want to tell me what's going on?"

She didn't look at him and she appeared as though she was going to stop eating. He wanted her to feel comfortable here and free to talk to him when she was more settled, but most of all, to eat. So despite wanting to learn what this was all about right away, he'd let it rest for the night.

"Hey, you want some hot chocolate? Heavy on the whipped cream?" he asked, quickly changing the subject.

That earned him a small smile, and he hopped up to get it. "So what do you think of the place? They've been in the family for generations and are really rustic, even though they've been renovated a number of times over the years. They all have running water, bathrooms, kitchens, et cetera. Not that they have 5-star ratings. But they're comfortable and perfect for outdoor enthusiasts who want more of a roof over their heads at night." He waited for the chocolate to heat up, then poured it into one of the biggest mugs he owned and set it down before her.

"The cabins are lovely. Makes a body feel right at

home."

Her gaze met his and he wondered if she really meant it—that she felt comfortable here, not skittish and wanting to run again anytime soon.

"Thanks for everything."

"You're welcome." He noticed she'd eaten nearly all of her stew. "Do you want some more?"

"I'd love to, but I'm full now."

"Your stomach probably shrank. Are you ready to try a movie now? Maybe I can get something else from town tomorrow."

"Maybe we can skip the movie and call it a night. I'm really tired."

She looked tired, dark circles under her eyes, thin, haggard.

"After all you've been through," he said, "I understand." He'd noted that while she'd been eating, she had been withdrawn—maybe just because she was starving, but she wasn't scarfing the food down, either. He was afraid she was still thinking of running. Or maybe she was worried about whoever was after her. Then again, she might just be exhausted from her ordeal. Maybe she was just shy. Hell, he could try to figure it out all night and never come up with the truth.

"Why don't you go onto bed then, and I'll clean up in here. I might watch something, but I'll keep the TV volume down low." Partly so that he didn't disturb her sleep. But also so he could hear if she was trying to slip out on him.

"Okay. Thanks again," she said, and he didn't expect her next action, but she rose from her chair, approached him, and gave him a quick kiss on the lips.

He knew with every ounce of brain matter he possessed that he should just give as much as he got, a quick unassuming kiss to say thank you back and that was all. But hell, he already wanted more.

He drew her into his arms and kissed her like he'd wanted to so many times before—when he'd been her roommate in the clinic and she'd groaned at seeing him, when he'd pinned her down in Hal's kitchen and she'd been a wild cat trying to unseat him, when she gave him grief in the dressing room and he'd seen her wearing that lacy bra and the strawberry bikini panties, and now this—despite his mind screaming at him that this was so not a good idea. A very, very bad idea in fact. He halfway expected her to jerk away from him, but when she didn't, when she pressed tighter against him and kissed him back, her lips warm and soft against his mouth, her tongue licking his lips and him groaning in response, he felt the whole world shift beneath his feet.

Then she pulled away, gently, as if she had wanted this and was reluctant to stop, but that this was enough for now.

"That... was to say I'm sorry for hurting you and to thank you for all that you've done for me," she said, looking into his eyes, hers wearing the faintest shimmer of tears.

Instantly, concerned she was upset about the whole business again, he hurriedly said, "No problem, Shannon. We're good. Feel free to think of this as your home for as long as you like."

She still had her arms around his waist and their kissing and her continued touch had made his body aroused for her and craving more. Not that he would go that far even if she wanted to. Well, maybe if she *really* insisted. Probably even if she *barely* insisted.

Then he frowned and said, "You're not going to kiss Dan like that for hurting him, too, are you?" He didn't know why he even said it.

She grinned broadly and then brushed a tear rolling

down her cheek and then another quickly away. She shook her head. "Night." She released him and headed for the bedroom.

Hell, his blood was on fire just from that one tantalizingly hot kiss, but he was glad that she had been amused by his comment.

Watching her, he began to wonder what the kiss had really been about and his stomach was bunching into knots with worry. He hated over thinking this, but he couldn't help it when it came to her. She seemed so vulnerable and she needed someone "You're not planning on leaving, are you? That wasn't a goodbye kiss, was it?"

She shook her head, but didn't say anything and continued to the bedroom. She was crying softly, trying not to in front of him, he thought. Ah, hell. He was in too deep already. He stalked after her and placed his hand gently on her shoulder, stopping her.

"Come on. Let's watch a movie. Why don't you see if there's something you might like." He didn't want her to be alone in the room crying. He still feared she would try to slip off in the middle of the night if she didn't feel entirely comfortable or safe here. He felt they'd made somewhat of a connection, and that she was beginning to trust him. "Come on," he put his arm around her shoulders in a comforting way and led her back down the hall toward the couch. "When I'm feeling blue, watching movies helps me to feel better."

She glanced up at him, her eyes full of tears and her face was streaked with tiny rivulets.

He felt bad for her, wishing there was more that he could do to make her feel better. "Yeah, I hate to admit it, but it's true. Sometimes I feel like my whole world has come unglued. I usually get something to drink, and then watch a movie."

"Wine?" she asked.

He smiled a little. "Yeah, I've got some of that." He wasn't certain that she was feeling any better about anything, but *his* whole outlook brightened. He took her into the kitchen, not wanting to let go of her, and wanting to comfort her.

He opened a cabinet and handed her a couple of wine glasses. Then he grabbed a bottle and an opener. He put his arm around her shoulders and guided her into the living room. Once they were seated, he poured the drinks, then he showed her the selection of movies he had.

She was beautiful, her dark hair shiny, her lips a natural red, full and appealing. He meant to give her some room, but he sat close to her, his leg brushing against hers, their arms touching, and he fished out the movies to show her all of them as if he needed to be this close.

"The first one looks good," she said.

He started the fantasy adventure movie.

Risking rejection, he wrapped his arm around her shoulders, hoping she wouldn't mind the intimacy, but in the worse way, he wanted to make her feel secure and reassured. She leaned her head against his shoulder, but soon lay her head in his lap... and fell asleep.

Satisfaction filled him with the knowledge that he had helped her to feel safe enough to sleep. He wondered just how long she'd been running as a cougar, wary, barely able to sleep, constantly on the alert for danger.

His right leg began falling asleep, but he didn't want to disturb her. So he watched the rest of the movie, listening to her steady heartbeat, the way she softly breathed as he stroked her silky hair, and told himself that this couldn't go any further. That whatever mess she was in could be resolved or not, and she may never be able to stay here and start a new life. Though he was already hopeful she would.

And he knew how crazy that sounded without knowing anything about her. Still, here, she could find a life where others of their kind lived, helped each other out, cared about one another. And he sure hoped she could stay. He didn't want to feel that he was the law and she was wanted, in a criminal sort of way.

When the movie ended, he turned off the TV and carried her to bed. She was warm and soft against him, her eyes closed in sleep and in that instant, she looked so innocent and sweet. Which made him smile, considering the way she had snarled at him with her cougar canines when he'd pounced on her in his cat form yesterday.

After covering her with the comforter, he glanced at the armoire sitting in front of the window, his jaw hanging for a second. Hell, that thing was heavy. He thought he'd get a hernia moving it. He couldn't believe she did so on her own. It reminded him just how much she feared for her life. He closed the bedroom door, then returned to the living room, grabbed the wine glasses, and put them in the dishwasher.

He had really enjoyed watching the movie with Shannon. Not that she had watched it much as she'd fallen asleep fairly quickly, but he liked that she had finally relaxed at his place and with him. Cuddling with her had been so unexpected, and… nice. He had thought that being alone suited him fine, but now… Hell, even the thought that she wouldn't be here in the morning, or sharing another night like this with him tomorrow bothered him. If it helped her to feel comfortable here, he was all for continuing with the movie nights.

He sat on the couch and called Dan. "Have you got any… *non*violent movies lying about your place?"

"What?" Then Dan asked, "Are you *kidding*?"

Chase figured as much. "I just thought maybe you had

something that was more suitable for Shannon to watch."

Dan didn't say anything for a minute. Chase knew he was coming to some conclusions of his own as to why Chase would be doing all that he could to make Shannon feel welcome—and it didn't have all to do with wanting to ensure she stayed here so she'd be safe.

"No. I'll ask Dottie. Anything else you might need?" Dan asked, sounding a little amused.

"Hairbrush, hairdryer. I can pick those up later."

"What is she doing? Did she talk to you? Tell you anything we can go by?"

"She's asleep. Exhausted. I don't blame her."

"Do you want some company?"

"Sure, come on up. Are you feeling good enough to drive?"

"Yeah, I'll be there in a few."

Chase checked the news on his cell phone, but didn't see anything that featured a woman wanted by the law that had hit national news, anyway.

Twenty minutes later, Dan was at his door with a handful of movies. "I borrowed them from Dottie. She said that Shannon might like them if she doesn't want to watch the kind of movies you've got. She also had a spare hairdryer she had for trips that she's not using and a hairbrush that she bought for her daughter that she hasn't used yet. She'll get another."

"Tell her thanks." Chase looked through the movies. "Romances."

"Yep." Dan chuckled.

Chase set them on the coffee table, then went into the kitchen and grabbed a couple of beers. "You know, in all the years I've done the rough stuff, I've never had a woman nearly knock me unconscious. You either."

"Don't tell me that's why you're interested in her." Dan

shook his head and took a swallow of his beer then took a seat on the couch in the living room.

"I'm not interested in her."

Dan raised a brow that said he didn't believe it for a minute.

"Okay, so yeah, she appeals." It was a damn good thing she hadn't been wearing lipstick when they'd kissed. "I mean, hell, she's tough, living alone in the wild, and nearly knocked me out. I have to admit there is some appeal to that."

Dan chuckled. "I want someone warm, soft, and cuddly, and nurturing. Not someone who nearly kills me, then forces me to chase after her for miles while I'm suffering from a head injury to get her concession just to save her ass."

Chase grinned at his friend. "Like hell, you wouldn't. You're just wishing you hadn't sent me to search for the she-cat and located her first." Although she was warm, soft, and cuddly, too. And nurturing—when it came to her saving the boy's life and warming him overnight.

"Yeah, right. I'm serious. Watch yourself with her. She's in trouble and she's reluctant to say why. Has she told you anything?"

"She's running scared. I'll ask her again tomorrow when she's had some time to rest up though."

"You think she'll still be here tomorrow? That she won't sleep some and then when she feels she's had enough rest, she'll slip out while you're still dead to the world?"

Chase shrugged. He hoped she'd still be here, but if she wouldn't let them help her, there wasn't a whole hell of a lot he or anyone else could do about it. Even though he knew that if she took off, he'd be hunting her down again.

"I want to know what we could be up against." Dan

tossed back the rest of the beer. "Have you got anything of hers that she's touched that I can run fingerprints on?"

Chase should have known this wasn't just a social call. And if he wasn't already getting in over his head on this, he would have already bagged something she'd used. Instead, he'd put the dishes away and hadn't given it a thought.

Or maybe subconsciously he had—and hadn't wanted to learn anything bad about her.

"In... the dishwasher." Chase led him into the kitchen. He glanced at the silverware basket, but it was full and he had no idea which of the utensils she had used. He pointed out the two wine glasses. "She used one of those, but I don't remember whose was whose."

"And you handled both, or did she put the glasses in the dishwasher?"

Feeling a little defensive, Chase let out his breath and folded his arms. "I did. She had already gone to bed."

Dan smiled a little and shook his head. "You're already way over your head on this one, buddy." He bagged the wine glasses separately. "I'm calling it a night. If you have any trouble, anything at all, call me. And I'll let you know if we lift any prints off these---*besides yours*—and find a match in the database."

Chase saw him out to his vehicle.

"Oh, and I almost forgot. We have an invitation for dinner tomorrow night at the Muellers' home. You know them," Dan said. "As soon as they heard of her plight, they began looking into it. It's better for everyone concerned if we know the truth sooner than later. So it was their idea, but I'm in total agreement. Just ask her."

"All right," Chase said gloomily. He knew Dan was right and in truth, he wanted to know what was going on, too, and soonest. But he didn't want to pretend to Shannon that this was all just a friendly get together, when it wasn't. Not that the Muellers weren't friendly, but they just had a hidden agenda. And Chase was still trying to earn Shannon's trust. "If she's feeling too exhausted, we'll have to make it another time."

"Give us enough notification, will you, if she says no. All right?"

"Yeah, sure." Chase wanted to tell Shannon what the Muellers' former occupation was, but what if she decided to run? He didn't want to put her life in jeopardy by scaring her into running, either. Nor did he want to have to hunt her down again.

Dan glanced at the guestroom window. "Looks like the light's on in the guestroom. Are you sure she's asleep?"

Chase considered the curtains covering the window, the dark object—the armoire sitting in the center—and a scant light on either side showing. "Maybe we woke her. I'll check on her. Thank Dottie for the movies and everything else."

"Will do. Night, Chase."

Chase watched as Dan drove off. Again, he studied the curtains in the window where Shannon was supposed to be sleeping and shook his head. Would Dan discover a long rap sheet on the lady? Chase sure hoped he wouldn't find anything. At least nothing bad.

***

As soon as Shannon heard men's voices in the living room, she'd awakened. Fear had sliced through her, and she had quickly climbed out of bed and pressed her ear against the door. Then she'd heard Chase and Dan speaking low about movies that Dottie had loaned to Chase. Shannon was relieved to know it was just Dan and not someone else who was looking for her.

Their voices had dropped lower and she was certain they were discussing her. But no one was coming to arrest her, so she thought they still didn't have a clue as to who she was. She gave up on listening, tired, not able to hear anything anyway, then turned on the light, not wanting to be surrounded by the dark.

Sure, she could see in semi-dark like her fully cougar cousins, but she felt comforted here in Chase's cabin with the light on in her room. She climbed under the big fluffy comforter on the guest bed, needing to sleep.

But now that she wasn't trying to find a safe haven for the night, her thoughts turned to Hennessey and how he might find her at any time and she'd be dead—unless she could kill him first.

CHAPTER 8

Chase took a warm shower, but when he left the bathroom, he heard the curtains moving in the living room and found Shannon wearing her gray sweats now, peeking out through the drapes at the dark night.

Had she heard something—someone? He cleared his throat so as not to startle her. "Can't you sleep? I saw the light on in your room."

She jumped a little and turned quickly to face him. "I was dozing," she said, her voice a little anxious. "I thought..." She shook her head.

"Is the light disturbing you too much? Would you prefer a night light?"

"No, thank you. I'm fine, really. I just... I just heard something. I thought it was... a bear outside and I... I had to check it out. But I didn't see any."

He wondered if she worried it was something else. Maybe someone who had been chasing her. "All right. Do you want anything? Some milk? More hot chocolate? Would that help?"

She shook her head. "I'll be all right. Thanks."

Chase pointed at the oak coffee table. "Dan brought some movies up for us to watch that you might like better. Compliments of Dottie. She also sent a spare hairbrush and hair dryer. Dan also asked if we would like to have dinner with a couple in town tomorrow night."

Shannon eyed Chase a little warily.

"We don't have to go if you don't want. It was just an offer, but we're under no obligation."

"All right," she said. "We can go."

He thought his saying they were under no obligation to go was what made her agree. He would have to remember that if they got any more invitations, and knowing everyone like he did, he suspected they might.

***

Now this was awkward. Chase was waiting for Shannon to return to her room, but he stood near enough to her door that when she opened it, he would see that she'd rearranged the furniture. She didn't want him to believe it was because she was scared. When she just stood there, hoping he'd move along to his own bedroom, he finally reached around her and opened the door to her room for her.

He paused for a moment, considering her, not the room, and then he suddenly said, "Wait, let me get you something." He stalked off down the hall to his bedroom.

When she saw the cell phone in his hand, she was hopeful that she could look up the news on the Internet.

"I want you to take my cell phone. I've got another that Dan assigned to me for police work. My number is listed under contacts in my phone. When I'm out working on the cabins or anytime you want to call me, feel free."

He had no intention of monitoring her every move? She felt a sense of liberation in that instance and she really appreciated him for that. Though she was a little surprised he really was giving her free rein to do as she pleased. "Thanks," she said, "for everything."

He glanced at the armoire she'd had a devil of a time

moving against the window. The bedside table was next to the door, so he might have assumed she had shoved it against the only door to the room before she went to sleep. Which made her seem paranoid.

"Good night. If you need anything at all, just come get me. For breakfast, I'll fix us some ham and cheese omelets."

She was grateful he didn't mention anything about her moving furniture when she had really expected him to. But then she realized that he must have carried her to bed earlier and already seen that she'd moved the furniture!

Then he gave her a quick kiss on the forehead. She couldn't figure him out. He was so good to her when he didn't know her at all.

"Did… you want to sleep with me instead?" he asked. When her jaw dropped a little, he quickly added, "If you thought you could sleep better because you felt safer."

Then she laughed. "Yeah, right."

He gave her one of his charming, dimpled smiles, and he looked absolutely delighted that he'd made her laugh. "Are you sure? If you're having nightmares—"

"Thanks, I think I'll be safer in my own bed. But I really appreciate the offer." She smiled a little and stepped into the room. He closed the door for her. She had to admit she would have felt safer in his arms, at least as far as worrying about anyone breaking into his place and trying to kill her. But on a purely physical level, sleeping with Chase would not be safe.

Not with the way she was already attracted to him. Just the way they'd wrestled on the kitchen floor of Hal Haverton's house and she'd felt the way he'd become aroused and she hadn't been able to hide hers any more than he could his, and then the kiss she and Chase had shared that hadn't been exactly chaste—she couldn't see sleeping with him as anything more than asking for trouble.

She moved the bedside table in front of the door and then climbed into bed. With the light on and the covers tucked under her chin, she stared at the ceiling and wondered where Hennessey and his brother and uncle were now if all three of them were after her. If all three were involved in the illegal stuff that Ted was into, she figured that his brother and uncle would want her dead just as much. Were they tracking her as cougars? She had believed they would, but then how would they be able to get to her if she did end up doing this? Rejoining the human population?

Unless they were waiting for word of her suddenly showing up somewhere as a human again.

Eager to learn if her picture was plastered all over the news as a person of interest in the murder of her cop boyfriend, she opened the phone and frowned at it. The cell phone was an older model, which meant? No Internet!

***

Early the next morning, Chase was torn between wanting to wait for Shannon to wake and serve her a hearty breakfast, worried if he didn't, she wouldn't eat enough, and wanting to ensure she was okay with him leaving her alone while he worked on one of the rental cabin's roofs. He hoped she was having the best sleep of her life. He knew she needed it more than anything else right now after what she must have endured.

Unable to quit worrying about her, he tried to peek into the room to see if she was still in there. The door was locked. Not that he was surprised. He went outside and surveyed the window. The armoire was still blocking it.

Believing she wasn't going to get up anytime soon and attempting to set aside his concern, he fixed himself a piece of toast and honey, then headed out to work. He was just ready to climb onto the roof when Dan called. Immediately,

Chase was apprehensive.

He hated that every time his friend phoned him now that Chase would think the worst. That Dan had learned some horrible news concerning Shannon, and they'd have to arrest her. And he was already contemplating how he was going to hide her away.

"Yeah, what's up?" Chase asked.

"We couldn't lift any prints off the wine glasses. They were too smudged. We'll have to try at the Muellers' dinner. Or you can make the attempt again at your place. We're still looking for any clue as to who she is and what trouble she's in. Anything from your end?"

"Not yet," Chase said. "I'm going to work on some repairs to a roof. She's sleeping right now."

Pause.

"You still there?" Chase knew Dan thought he should keep an eye on her every minute of the day, but he still felt the best way to learn who she was and what was going on was to earn her trust.

"Do you think that's wise?"

"She's exhausted with all the running she's done. She needs to take it easy. I figure she'll talk about it when she's ready."

"Which may be too late."

"I know. That's why I'm trying to ease her into it. Trying to be her friend first."

"Just be careful you're not thinking with your heart instead of your head," Dan warned. "It is a go on dinner with the Muellers, right?"

"Yeah, she was good with it. I've got to get to work on the roof. The sooner I get to it, the sooner I'll be back at the main house. Let me know if you learn anything later."

"Will do."

Chase tried not to think of Shannon while he

concentrated on the roof, or he could take a misstep and end up landing on his backside below. That's all he would need—to injure himself when he was supposed to be protecting the lady. But he couldn't quit thinking about her. About the way she was so scared—not just from the way in which she had rearranged the furniture, which had been telling enough, but leaving a light on in the room, as if to warn anyone away who might think she was asleep, and then peeking out the living room curtains when she heard noises outside.

She'd seemed to sleep well when she was cuddled with him on the couch, and that got him to thinking again about her sleeping with him in his bed. After the kiss they shared? Not a good idea.

And yet, he couldn't quit mulling it over. Between listening for any sign of anyone else approaching the cabins, and wary that she might decide to sneak out, he really was having a devil of a time concentrating on his work.

He was just finishing up the repairs on one section of the roof, when his phone rang. He fished it out of his shirt pocket, sure Dan had some devastating news if he was calling again this soon. For a second, he saw his name and cell phone number in the caller ID, confusing him, and it took him a minute to realize Shannon was calling him. He smiled. He didn't know why it pleased him so much to get a call from her, but it did.

"Hey, did you finally get a good sleep?" he asked. He sincerely hoped so.

"I've been awake for a while, but I saw you headed to one of the cabins with roofing materials in hand, and I didn't want to distract you when I know you have work to do. I wondered if you'd like for me to fix you something to eat for lunch when you're at a good stopping point."

"I'll be there in fifteen minutes."

She laughed. "You must be hungry. What if I make something that doesn't appeal?"

"I'm starving. I'll love it, whatever it is."

Within ten minutes, he headed back to his cabin. He really was trying to give her more time, but he was at a point that worked well for him to quit, he *was* hungry, and he was thrilled that she seemed to want to stay put for the moment. Not wanting to alarm her, he unlocked and opened the door, calling out, "It's just me."

The fragrance of chocolate baking in the kitchen filled the air. "Hot damn, now this is the way I wish my cabin always smelled when I finish some repairs on the cabins."

She chuckled.

His stomach began rumbling as he walked into the kitchen. Shannon smiled at him. She looked ravishing, her dark hair cascading softly over her shoulders in silky curls. Her golden eyes were bright and her smile contagious.

The aroma of roasted chicken made his mouth water. "Besides the chicken, which smells divine, I smell chocolate," he said, wondering what she was making.

"I baked a cake for tonight for when we go to your friends' house." She motioned to the cake cooling on the slate counter.

He felt guilty all over again knowing some of the reason the Muellers wanted to see them was to lift her prints off something she used while at their home, if they could. "They'll love it, though the cake might not make it out the door."

She smiled at him again, and she seemed to be much more rested today. She was wearing the black sweater and the jeans again and though she looked good in it, he was thinking about that hot pink sweater and how much he'd like to see her wearing it.

Then he got to thinking about her comment that she'd

seen him head over to the cabin to work on it, and he wondered if she had slept much at all. He had hoped she'd been sacked out all this time. "Did you finally sleep well?"

"Much better."

"Good."

"So how's the roofing going?" She served up the chicken and baked potato and carried it to the dining table.

He grabbed glasses of water and set them on the table, and then returned for the bowl of salad. "Good. Another couple of hours and I'll have the cabin's roof patched. Did you need anything before I go back over there and finish it?"

They took their seats. She shook her head. "Just resting up."

"I take it if you're making cake for tonight, you feel all right about going over there." He shouldn't have said anything more about it, but he didn't want her to feel pressured into going.

"Yeah. I've been running for so long and avoiding people—natural instinct when running as a cougar—but after shopping yesterday, I must have met half your townspeople, so I figured what's the difference if I meet one more couple?"

All the difference in the world, if they got lucky and could identify who she was and what had happened to make her run. He wished he could quash the guilt he was feeling. But they had to know how to help her if she was in danger. And it appeared from her every action that she was. He would be perfectly upfront with her, if he wasn't afraid she'd feel the need to run. Instead, he worried what little trust she had in him would be shattered once she learned the truth.

***

At dinner that night, Shannon met Yvonne and Rick

Mueller, both blond with blue eyes and the friendliest smiles. They, and everyone else in town, had been so genuinely eager to meet her. Though she suspected a lot had to do with wanting to know in the worst way why she'd come here the way in which she had. But everyone was being ultra-polite in not asking the question straight out. And she appreciated it more than they could ever know.

She was somewhat apprehensive to see the sheriff's car there. The last time she'd seen him, she'd assaulted him, knocking him flat on his back. But he never had said anything about charging her with it, so she finally relaxed— a little. She still felt she was under a magnifying glass since Dan and Chase were lawmen. No matter how much she wanted to see Chase as just a nice and helpful guy, she had to remind herself he had a badge, her cop boyfriend was dead, she would be a murder suspect, and cops stood together when it came to one of their own.

They'd talked about the weather and all kinds of inane subjects and Shannon finally asked, "So do you have any hobbies?"

Everyone just looked at her and then at each other. She didn't mean for it to be such an abrupt conversation stopper. She shrugged. "I used to do a lot of photography— for a hobby. I'm not a professional photographer or anything."

"Photography," Yvonne said. "Now I can get into that. Love to do it, but like you, just a hobby."

"Fishing," both Dan and Rick said.

"Me, too," Chase said.

Silence.

"I love reading. Haven't done any in a while, though," Shannon said.

"We have a nice library," Yvonne offered.

"We can run by sometime this week and get you a

library card," Chase said.

She smiled a little. She wasn't setting down roots. She didn't even have any ID, though she suspected that the local library would still give her access to the books if the sheriff and his deputy vouched for her. She guessed no one read much, so she didn't mention what she liked to read.

Silence.

"We're glad you found your way here. It's the perfect place to raise one of our kind," Yvonne said.

As if Shannon was ready to have kids even. "I won't be staying," Shannon said. She couldn't lie about it.

Yvonne looked sympathetic. "We'll look out for you. Believe me. You have no need to worry about anything. Truly."

She swore Yvonne was trying to tell her that no matter what the circumstances surrounding Shannon's flight, they were behind her. But they didn't know her boyfriend's family.

Even so, at the thought that Yvonne and the others would take her in like that, she couldn't help the tears forming in her eyes. "Thank you. I... I believe you're sincere. All of you."

"But?" Yvonne asked.

Shannon shook her head. She didn't want to cause trouble for these people. Hennessey was sure to come after her here eventually. She suspected Hennessey, his brother, Roger, and their Uncle Murphy were all getting kickbacks on whatever illegal business they were involved in as close as they all were. And they most likely all had a stake in Ted's death.

Then suddenly she thought—what if they believed she knew all the details of their criminal activities? Maybe they knew her background. That her brother had been in trouble with the law and they felt comfortable that she hadn't come from a law-abiding family. But then they worried that she knew too much. Well, besides that Hennessey murdered Ted in cold blood.

Yvonne patted Shannon's shoulder. "We'll protect you."

Shannon immediately was drawn out of her worrisome thoughts and at once felt self-conscious as everyone watched her reaction. She didn't think they could protect her. Not always.

Then Dan began talking about the cougar hunting season coming up and how dangerous that was for their own kind.

She swore they were discussing it to remind her how dangerous it could be soon if she decided to run as a cougar. Not that some hunters didn't illegally kill cougars— or other animals—out of season.

She enjoyed the delightful dinner of spicy spaghetti, Italian garlic bread, and a salad while the conversation switched to the weather and fishing and then the chocolate cake was served up. She was amused to see both Rick and Chase take second *large* helpings and she was pleased they'd enjoyed it so much.

To Shannon's surprise, Rick talked about a mission that the three men had been on while in the army. She hadn't realized he'd been a military man also. Unlike Chase and Hal's, Rick's hair was cut shorter, more military style like Dan's was.

She remembered her father talking with her brother when they were little about having served in the army, and she wished that her father had known how proud she'd been of him for having done so.

"My father..." As soon as she spoke the words, she abruptly stopped and felt her face heat as all eyes were upon her. They were waiting anxiously, trying to appear not to be, while she gave them some hint of who she was. She was becoming too free with her words. Drinking the wine, eating the good food, having a nice conversation, and being so comfortable with everyone as friendly as they were, she almost forgot to keep her guard up. "Have any more of the men in the town served in the military?" Shannon asked, changing the subject.

There was a pause. They had to know she wasn't about to say anything more about herself.

"Over the years, many have served in all of the major wars," Dan finally said. "Every year, in honor of our military, we have a grand celebration for the 4th of July and Armed Forces Day."

"Oh, speaking of celebrations, Thanksgiving isn't that far off," Yvonne quickly said. "We haven't really discussed it, but usually Dan comes over, and we've asked Dottie if she'd like to come and bring her two children. We'd love to have you and Chase," Yvonne said to Shannon.

Shannon wondered then what Chase normally did for Thanksgiving. Surely, he didn't sit at home alone. "I'm sure that I'll be gone by—"

"We'll have to decide a little later," Chase said, coming to Shannon's rescue, or maybe he was just rescuing himself from the holiday fare.

When the meal was through, Shannon offered to help clean the dishes, but Yvonne shook her head. "Thanks so much, but I have my own way of doing things. Takes just a second."

Shannon glanced at Chase, silently telling him she wanted to leave, but she didn't want to appear ungrateful. Even though she'd wanted to mix with their kind, she hadn't realized how wearing it could be.

"We need to go, and we'll definitely get back to you about Thanksgiving," Chase said, sounding as if Shannon was staying that long, when there was no way that she could.

"It was so good to meet you, Shannon. I hope you are here for the holidays," Yvonne said. And then she, Rick, and Dan walked them out to the car.

After saying their good nights and thanking Yvonne for the meal again, Chase drove Shannon back to his place.

"What was that all about?" she asked, feeling a little wary.

"What do you mean?" Chase said, sounding cautious.

Shannon didn't say anything for a few minutes as he drove down the dark road through the woods to his cabin resort as she tried to think of what to say without sounding like she was being totally paranoid. "I… I feel like this is *The Stepford Wives'* town, except that everyone is too nice. Too caring. Too eager to be my best friend. Not just the women like in *The Stepford Wives*, but *everyone*."

"We're a friendly town—toward everyone—human visitors, cougars—but believe me when I say that a female cougar traveling alone the way in which you have has rallied everyone to want to take care of you. No secret agenda. Everyone wants to help you out, Shannon. We understand what it's like being a shifter in a human world. We know how dangerous it can be for one of us who has no support system. We want to provide you with that support system. No strings attached."

"All right. Thanks. I'm… sorry if I sound suspicious of people's motives when they don't know anything about me."

"I understand. We won't put you at risk."

"Which means practically your whole town, right? Or someone could accidentally mention me to others." She couldn't help worrying that someone would blog about her or put the story on Facebook, something that might alert

Hennessey as to where she was.

"Our whole town. We work together, play together, take care of each other. If we didn't, who else would?"

Shannon sighed. "Sorry. It's just... so hard for me to trust anyone after all that's happened."

"I understand. You'll be all right here, Shannon. One thing about the people here is that everyone is aware of your dire circumstances. If anyone hears of anyone asking questions that could pertain to you, this information will be reported right back to Dan. He'll get in touch with me at once."

"Thank you," she said. Though she didn't entirely trust everyone. What if they learned the real trouble she could cause them and decided being one of them just wasn't good enough?

CHAPTER 9

Later that night, Shannon was half dozing in the bedroom when she heard something—outside, she thought. She wasn't sure what the noise had been.

A scratching? She thought that once she was inside a cabin like this, she'd sleep better than when she had to attempt to sleep in the wilderness, fending for herself.

She got up and moved the table away from the door, then opened it. In the dark, she made her way into the living room and heard something bumping into something outside.

A trashcan?

Her heart racing, she peeked out the living room window curtains and saw a black bear trying to get into a bear-proof trashcan. She took a calming breath. She was safe, she told herself. Not like when she was running in the wilderness as a cougar. But her heart was still beating a million miles a minute.

A gun went off—a crash, and she made a small cry of distress. Not meaning to. She just hadn't expected the gunfire and it had scared her—the thought flashing through her brain that she could be the one being shot at and the reminder that Chase *had* shot her.

The bear quickly took off and Shannon saw Chase with his rifle at the ready, then he moved back into the shadows of the woods and disappeared.

For a long moment, she just stared out the window, then coming to grips with the fact that the bear was gone for good, and Chase would be all right, armed as he was, she returned to bed and closed her eyes, grateful again for everything Chase and the townspeople had done for her. If only someone could put Hennessey down, prove he had killed her boyfriend, and remove her from the family's hit list. Then... well, she could even stay in a place like this. With someone like Chase. And raise a family of her own. And then she drifted off to sleep, dreaming about making love to Chase and creating those babies with him when Hennessey's knife-wielding figure transformed her dreams back into nightmares again.

***

Dan called Chase right after he'd scared the bear off. He'd seen Shannon watching out the living room window or he would have called her and told her it was just him and he'd been chasing off a bear. That must have been what Shannon had heard last night, too. But Chase had gone out, just in case, to ensure it truly was just a bear and not someone skulking around.

"Yeah, Dan?" Chase said, locking up the place again, and then locked his rifle away in the gun cabinet.

"Yvonne and Rick sure wished Shannon had said which branch of the service her father had been in. And wished we knew his last name. I'm sure she saw how much it killed us not to know as she nearly made the slip. But they'll use their resources to learn what they can about her. They said that the utensils she used and the wine glass were still too smudged to get any clear prints off."

"All right, but I wished we could just let her tell us what was going on for herself."

"I'm afraid we don't have the luxury of time. We might,

but if someone is after her who can track her, they'll learn where she is eventually. Not that any of our people will give her location away, but if whoever is after her smells her scent, he'll know."

"She has trust issues."

"I understand, Chase. But we have to know what this is all about. We have to learn what we're going up against. Listen, several of our people have started making up a cover story for her also."

"So it sounds like she's lived here always?"

"Right. Only... well, the word that is getting out is that... she's your wife."

Chase stared at his living room floor, not really seeing it as he couldn't believe what he was hearing. "That won't work. You know it won't. She's not about to go along with it."

"Okay, look. I didn't figure you'd like it. But think of it this way. If she's your wife, that's going to look a lot less suspicious than any other scenario we could come up with. A single woman staying at one of your cabins, who's the age that she is, automatically calls suspicion to the situation. Everyone else in town either has a mate, is too old to fit the bill, a lot too eager, or too young. And you have the military and police training to keep her safe. Besides, she's already staying with you and you're my deputy sheriff."

"Part-time."

"Right. Which is perfect because you're free to watch over her. If I need extra help, I'll call Hal or Rick. Besides, she already trusts you."

Chase ran his hand through his hair. "What if this scares her into running?"

"I'm certain you can convince her how sound the plan is. As long as *you* are all right with it."

Chase knew his friend was worried about him being

okay with it because of having lost his wife and baby daughter. He would never forget them and often thought of them, but he didn't have a problem with this. He just worried that Shannon would.

"I've considered every possible candidate and unless you're completely against it, or she is, I really think it's for the best. You know Hal would jump at the chance, but he's moving to that ranch and he's got a lot on his mind right now. My deputy would, too, but he's got to keep his mind on business. He has a job to do. You're free up there at your cabin resort to protect her 24-7."

"I'll speak about it to her tomorrow. If she's agreeable, we'll do it. But we need to learn what this is all about."

"Agreed. And tell her Dottie has a birthday party for her kids tomorrow afternoon, and she wouldn't want Shannon to miss it."

"I thought her kids' birthdays were closer to Thanksgiving."

"She's having it early just in case Shannon decides to leave."

Chase suspected that meant Dottie was going to try and learn something about Shannon in a woman-to-woman way. Then he thought about the party for a moment. "What if she's not into kids?"

"Just ask her, all right? The Kretchens's thirtieth wedding anniversary is the night after that."

Chase smiled. "And the day after that?"

"Their wedding anniversary *is* at that time."

"All right." Leave Chase to have forgotten the date.

"We're still trying to come up with something for the next day."

Chase chuckled. "Remember, she's tired."

"She needs to feel as though she's part of the community. The more she can be around our people, socializing and making a connection with them, the more she'll fit in. She won't feel she's an outsider and hopefully she'll stay and trust we'll help her out."

"Then maybe she'll want to stay through Thanksgiving and beyond." For the first time since he'd moved back home, Chase thought spending Thanksgiving with Shannon at the Muellers' place had real appeal.

"Right. We'll have to determine why she's run, but yeah, that's the plan. She's a cougar shifter without a home. We're ready to take her in. All of us. If she's free and available, someone's got to be just right for her."

Chase shook his head. "Which is another reason to encourage her to attend all of the social gatherings." He wanted to say that if Dan started to invite her to single cougar gatherings, *he* wasn't going for it.

"Right. I'll talk to you tomorrow," Dan said.

After they ended the call, Chase thought Dan's plan had merit. But he wasn't sure that Shannon would agree.

***

Every little sound woke Shannon that night. She thought the bear had come back and was snorting around outside in the middle of the night. Just about the time she had drifted off to sleep, something screeched in the distance. Much later that morning, Shannon climbed out of bed and headed to the kitchen for a glass of milk.

The house was quiet, Chase's bedroom door standing ajar, and no sound of him moving about in the living room or kitchen. The phone rang in her pocket, startling her, and she fished it out and checked the caller ID. She was glad to see it was just Chase. She wondered then if he'd told everyone to call him on the police phone and not this one. "Hello?"

"I need to talk to you. I'm just finishing up some painting I'm doing in one of the cabins. Are you ready for me to make us those omelets for breakfast?"

"What's wrong?" she asked, instantly wary when he sounded like he needed to talk to her about something that could be trouble. No good morning, no—how are you this morning, did you sleep well? But—he had to talk with her.

"Nothing's wrong. Dan had a suggestion that might work and I wanted to talk with you about it."

She still didn't think it sounded good. When people had to speak face-to-face, that usually meant trouble. "All right. I just got up. I'm grabbing a cup of hot tea."

"Another bad night?"

"I thought I heard the bear prowling around again last night, and... I just kept waking for other reasons." He didn't say anything for a moment and she frowned, thinking they had gotten disconnected. "Chase?"

"Yeah... you're not... feeling like you would be more comfortable at someone else's place in town, are you?"

He sounded so anxious that she might say she would prefer staying somewhere else that she smiled. "No. I love it out here." She swore she heard him sigh over the phone. She couldn't let him know the reasons that she wanted to stay out here though—that his place was in the wilderness and she could easily take off at any time, but she also felt he could protect her *and* himself better if they did have trouble.

"Okay. I'll wash up the paintbrushes, and I'll be right over. Ham and cheese omelets all right? Or do you want something else? French toast? Pancakes?"

She smiled. "Omelets would be great. But I can fix them."

"Nothing doing. My treat."

Now how could she say no to that? She wasn't used to being pampered like this and she wondered if he was always this way or if he was only trying to make her feel more comfortable so she'd tell him the truth.

When he arrived, he was all smiles as if seeing her waiting for him was the best thing ever. He wore jeans, boots, and a red plaid flannel shirt and looked as sexy as always. His eyes were bright and his smile just as cheerful. And that worried her a bit. What if he hoped to encourage something more... permanent between them? When she knew it couldn't happen—not given her current circumstances.

He headed into the kitchen and began banging around in a cabinet for a pan. "First, Dottie invited you to her kids' birthday celebration. It's a little earlier than usual, but I guess she really wants to make sure you're going to be here and can attend. It's in a couple of hours. I certainly would understand if you don't want to go." He looked hopeful that she would say yes.

"That would be fun as long as you're going," Shannon said, looking forward to it. She didn't know why she said the part about him going. That made her sound horribly clingy when she wasn't normally like that.

He smiled a little at her. "I wouldn't miss it for the world."

Because he was dying to see the kids, or because he wanted to stick close to her at all times? Then she realized she had no money for gifts.

"No gifts expected," he said, as if anticipating her next comment.

When he served up the omelets, she brought over a couple glasses of milk. He seemed so serious now, and she wondered what was up. She suspected something else had happened that he hadn't wanted to talk to her about over the phone. And it wasn't about going to a kids' birthday party.

"Okay, the other thing Dan called me about last night

was a suggestion, really. In case anyone's looking for you," he said.

She began eating some of her cheesy omelet and thought she was in heaven. Especially after having to catch her own meals in the wild. And not being very good at it. "Hmm, these are *so* good."

He smiled, but he still looked concerned. "Well, he had the idea that we'd have the cover story that you've lived here all your life."

"Okay." That would work for her. She had no problem with that. She lifted her glass of milk and took a sip.

"And... that you are my wife."

She practically choked on her milk.

"It would look *less* suspicious if you were married and had lived here all your life than if you were a single woman who suddenly just showed up in our town, should anyone come looking for you," he said quickly as if trying to convince her what a good idea it was. Then he paused and said, "So... will you be my wife?"

***

She'd had three boyfriends, all dead now, and not one of them had ever asked Shannon to marry him. Though she knew it was all pretend with Chase, she almost wished it was for real because she couldn't think of any man she'd ever met who could be more ideal. Chase had finally—and she thought a bit reluctantly—told her just how many people, single males included, had wanted to take her in. How could she not love it out here with the beauty of the forest, lake, and mountains so close at hand? And being with him. He was a dream come true. But didn't all dreams come to an end?

For her they did. And then the dreams turned into nightmares. She had three dead boyfriends to prove it, too.

"It was just a thought," Chase said, and began to pick

117

up their dirty dishes, looking a little hurt.

Even though this was all a ruse, she guessed even for pretend, a guy getting turned down could feel—rejected, and she hated to see his hurt expression.

"It was just such a shock," Shannon said, helping him to clear the table. "I've... I've never been asked before." She hated to admit it, but it was true. She seemed to hook up with guys who hadn't had the marrying gene. Which, considering what had happened to them, was for the best or she would have been a widow three times over. Maybe with kids to raise as well.

Chase's gloomy expression quickly brightened. "Hell, Shannon, what kind of idiots have you been dating?"

Criminals, she thought morosely. Even Ted, who was supposed to have been upholding the law.

Then she gave Chase a small smile. "I'd love to be your wife. Where should we take our honeymoon?"

He smiled right back, only his smile was much broader, his eyes sparkling with pleasure. "Hmm, I don't know. Where would you like to go?" He finished loading the dishes and silverware into the dishwasher.

"Fiji Island? Grand Cayman? Virgin Islands?" She slipped her arms around his waist as if this was for real.

He rubbed her shoulders, smiling down at her, a good sport about playing the game. "One of the islands, it is." He leaned down then and kissed her as if sealing the bargain, and she realized this was another reason she wouldn't have considered staying with anyone else.

She loved this, their movie night and the promise of more, their... well, just being together. It felt good to be with him, around him, talking to him, or just sitting quietly beside him.

He broke off the sweet kiss and cleared his throat. "I've got something for you."

He couldn't have picked up a ring, or intended to loan her his dead wife's ring. She tried not to stiffen at the notion.

"I'll be right back." He left her quickly and headed for his bedroom.

She attempted to put on a cheery face, no matter what, after all he'd done for her, but she couldn't help feeling apprehensive. She didn't want him to get the notion she was staying.

When he returned, he was carrying a pink box with a bright pink bow on it, a clothes box, not a jewelry box and she breathed a sigh of relief. "It's the toddlers' birthday celebration today. Not mine," she reminded him, but she was dying to open it, even if she shouldn't have been.

She hadn't gotten a gift in forever. Even when her on-the-lamb boyfriends had given her the rare gift, she always had to ask if they'd bought the item and hadn't stolen it. So she had much preferred they didn't bring her anything in the form of a gift or she could have been charged with receiving stolen goods.

Chase smiled as he handed the box to her, looking eager to see how she liked what he'd picked up for her. She wondered when he'd done so. Before she'd awakened this morning?

She felt some trepidation, afraid of what it could be, that it might be something too personal. With trembling fingers, she unwrapped the bow, then handed it to him. She opened the box and saw something pink vaguely hidden beneath the pink tissue paper.

Her heart was thumping harder in anticipation and a little thrill of expectation building. She pulled the tissue open and smiled to see the hot pink sweater she had admired at Millicent's Dress Boutique, but wouldn't have gotten for herself in a million years.

"I thought for the party you might like something a little more... colorful," he said, sounding like he truly hoped she liked it.

But she also thought he'd gotten it for her to ensure she didn't blend in so much that he could lose her in a sea of people. "I'd say this is the nicest thing you've ever gotten for me and I adore it, but you've done so much for me that everything—well except for the tranquilizer dart in my shoulder—that you've given me, I've truly treasured."

He smiled a little at the mention of the dart.

Then she gave him a hug that said she loved him. Not in a "forever, I'm marrying you kind of way," but to say she really, really loved the way he had been so good to her. But then she felt guilty again about not telling him what was going on with her.

He'd want to take everything back, his deeds, his gifts, everything and turn her out before he was a target next.

"I love it, Chase," she said, and kissed him full on the mouth, breasts pressed against his chest, the whole nine yards, wanting to be about as close as she could without getting herself in over her head.

His arms went around her again and he kissed her back. She felt his arousal, knew she'd incited him too much already, but she wanted this for the moment. She loved their sweet intimacy.

He finally broke off the kiss, his heart pumping as fast as hers, his eyes lusty and dark, his breathing hard. "As much as I regret having to say this, if we want to make it to the birthday party—"

She figured he was the kind of guy who was never late for anything. But if she'd pressured him to take this further, would he have skipped the party? She wouldn't have done that to him or to Dottie, yet the devil in her wanted to see if he would.

"If it's all right with you, can we stop to get the kids a gift each?" she asked.

"Just the thought I had. Which is why we need to leave a little early." He sounded as though he truly regretted that they had to leave so quickly.

"I'll just change." And then with tears in her eyes that she tried damn hard to hide from Chase because at every turn, he'd been so good to her—but she was certain he saw her tears anyway—she slipped into her bedroom and closed the door.

As soon as she took off the gray sweater she'd been wearing and put on the hot pink one, she saw the transformation right away from a gray look to bright and vivacious. She thought she looked good for the first time in over a month.

When she left the bedroom, Chase was waiting for her in the living room, his mouth curving up in a generous smile. His appreciative expression stated how much he liked her in it and made her feel like she was rocketing to the moon. "I told you that you'd look hot in that."

Maybe he hadn't been just interested in the sweater to make her stand out in a crowd, but because he thought he'd truly like the color on her.

She smiled. "Thanks again. It's beautiful."

"You're beautiful," he said, kissed her cheek, and then before they could get distracted and take this further than prudent, they were on their way to town to pick up toys at a department store first, which caused all kinds of speculation that she hadn't expected.

"For Dottie's kids' birthday party," he told the clerk, who was eyeing them *way* too much, along with four others in the store.

As soon as Chase and Shannon were again on the road, she asked, "The word isn't also being broadcast that I'm already pregnant with your child, is it?"

He chuckled. "No telling. If they think that will protect you, they'll say it."

He didn't seem to be bothered by the notion and for that she was grateful. She'd thought about having kids, but not with the boyfriends she'd had, who had been working outside of the law. She knew nothing good would ever have come of it. And not with Ted, who had told her right upfront he wasn't interested. But for some inane reason, she was thinking about having Chase's babies. Only because of the way the women had been eyeing them with the toys in the store. And maybe because of how nice he was to Shannon and since he'd already had a baby and he'd cared deeply about her—it just seemed natural to think about it.

"If you want to leave the party at any time," he said, "just let me know. Dottie will understand."

And that was another reason she really cared about him. He always was so concerned about how she felt.

She nodded and enjoyed seeing the area as he drove her out of town to Dottie's place. The forest. The flutter of birds in the trees. She was surprised she didn't feel the urge to run at the moment. For now, she was just relishing this.

Dottie's place was out a ways, in a different direction than Chase's place, woods were all around her one-story, brick home, and several cars were parked outside already. But the sheriff's car caught Shannon's attention.

She worried about the reason he kept showing up at all the things that she and Chase had invitations to as if Dan was there in the capacity of sheriff, observing her every move. Seeing his car here now, she felt a little apprehensive. Chase escorted her inside and she was a little overwhelmed to see all the kids, moms, Dan, even Rick and Yvonne Mueller, and Hal, which surprised her the most. She would never have had thought a bunch of eligible bachelors would be at a kids' birthday party. He winked at her and she felt the heat rise in her face. Like with Chase, she didn't think he looked like a rough and tough military type. When they ditched their uniforms, they'd ditched their military haircuts, too.

Why would a single guy be here at a toddler's birthday party? But then again, she'd learned he was a deputy sheriff part-time so he undoubtedly was there to listen and learn about her also if he could. Maybe they were all there to ensure she didn't slip away and flee.

When she saw Dan and he caught her eye, he arched a brow at her and Chase, a glint of humor in his blue-green eyes, a tiny smile touching his lips.

A harried-looking woman hurried over to greet Shannon and drew her away from Chase and the crowd of women and kids.

"I'm so glad to see you. I've heard so much about you. I was dying to meet you in person. I'm Dottie Brown, dispatcher at the sheriff's office and those are my birthday kids, Jeff and Trish."

"They're adorable," Shannon said, watching the toddlers dressed in jeans and sweaters—blue for him, pink for her, their socks dangling off their feet as they chased other kids around the room. Both had blond ringlets and beautiful blue eyes.

"Are you okay, Shannon? Do you need anything? I'm just a call away and if you ever need anything, please feel free to ask," Dottie said.

"I'm fine. Thanks for the movies and everything."

"You're so welcome."

Two other moms were serving up cake and ice cream to the kids of all ages from two to sixteen.

"Some teens blew up the balloons and will help with games and prizes."

Which totally surprised Shannon. She realized then that the people living here really did bond together and help each other out.

"Is everything working out at the cabins?" Dottie asked.

"Yeah, Chase has been wonderful about making me feel at home. I'm really fine." *If* Shannon could quit having nightmares. She had thought it was only the bear and other wildlife noises that had intruded on her sleep, the memory of the nightmares eluding her once she woke the following morning. But she realized that was another reason she wasn't sleeping well—nightmares of Hennessey killing his brother and then coming after her with the bloody knife. Nightmares of him attempting to rip her to shreds with his cougar's teeth and her fighting back.

Dottie smiled. "I can't think of a better 'boyfriend' than Chase." She paused. "Did... did he talk to you about the wife situation?"

Shannon shouldn't have been surprised when Dottie asked her, but she'd never been in a place where everyone seemed to know everyone's business. She wasn't sure why she said what she did in the way she did it, but she smiled and said, "Oh, yes. He asked me if I'd be his wife."

Dottie stared at her in surprise, her eyes round. "He did?"

Shannon laughed. "For pretend, sure."

Dottie let out her breath. "I thought he'd done it for real." She chuckled, then she sighed. "Even for pretend, you couldn't do better. He hasn't dated but a couple of times since he moved back here. After that, he clammed up again and went back into seclusion at his resort—as far as dating went. He's always visiting with folks. I don't mean to say he's a recluse or anything. But when it comes to dating women, that's another story. I think he just couldn't deal with seeing other women yet. Or they just weren't right for him. But he seems to be all right with you. Well, better than all right. You're the talk of the town—in a good, happy way. So I think the two of you just might be the best for each of you right now. Well, until we can sort this all out."

"Truthfully, I feel safer staying with him, and maybe I can get a few good nights' sleep for a change. I haven't had that in a very long time."

"I can't imagine how hard that had to have been for you. How long were you in the wilderness on your own?"

Shannon had chanced to see the cougar calendar on Chase's kitchen wall and couldn't believe she'd actually been running for so long. "Four and a half weeks. For a while there, I didn't think I'd ever be able to be human again. It's weird. I kept thinking that if I was a cougar long enough, I'd feel more in tune with the wilderness. But we're too human to be a cougar always."

"I can't imagine how awful that must have been for you. I doubt I would have lasted as long as a week. Most women around here couldn't have. Even some of the men might not be able to manage for that long. Real cougars, or cougar shifters, can have a dangerous time of it out there. I've taken the kids into the woods really close to the house a few times. It's important for them to get used to being in the woods, but I'm not comfortable going very far with them yet. And I really don't need to until they're older. We're so glad you're here with us now."

"When Chase shot me, I didn't believe I was lucky at all."

Dottie chuckled. "The word spread like wildfire that we had a real wild cat in our midst. You can't believe how much everyone wanted to take you in and offer to protect you."

"Everyone's been very kind."

Dottie leaned closer and whispered, "I hadn't expected

so many of the ladies to show up at the kids' birthday party, but I think they heard you were coming and wanted to get a look at you."

Shannon wished she hadn't become such a celebrity. She wanted to blend in and just pretend to be one of them for the day, to enjoy being around people, to hear them talking and laughing and having fun. When she was running as a cougar, if she heard people's voices, it meant she had to run away as fast as she could. It was an eerie feeling from normally being accepted as just another human to suddenly being vilified as one of those man-eating cougars.

"I love that hot pink sweater on you," Dottie said, glancing down at it. "Really looks great with your coloration."

Shannon could just imagine the speculation running rampant when Chase had bought it for her. She was certain that Millicent would have told everyone she knew that she had even giftwrapped it for Shannon. She still couldn't decide if it was because he liked her or he wanted her to stand out at the party and not disappear.

For a few more days, she wanted to enjoy herself and visit with some of her kind, then she was out of here and back into her cougar existence and total isolation.

"Chase has told us nothing about you at all. Do you have any siblings?"

"A twin brother, but he's dead." Shannon figured no one would discover who she was based on that information. Without names to go on, they wouldn't have a clue.

"Oh. I'm so sorry. I don't have any siblings. I'm an only child. It's unusual for us not to have a twin or triplet brother or sister, but..." Dottie shrugged. "What about your parents?"

Shannon shook her head. Again, same thing. With no one left in her family, she was orphaned and they had no one to search for.

"Me, either. Mine died some years back. When I had the kids, I sure would have loved it if my mother and father were here to enjoy them. My husband ran off and there I was left with two little toddlers."

"I'm sorry. Now to me, raising twin babies all on my own would have been just as grave a hardship as running in the wilderness all those weeks."

"Not hardly. It was a terrible hardship to begin with, but I wasn't worried about losing my life."

Dan was playing pin the tail on the cougar with the kids. Shannon was surprised to see him playing with them. She just hadn't envisioned him to be a kid kind of person, and she really thought he was here just to watch her.

Chase stood nearby, cup of pink punch in his hand, talking to Hal while he observed her. She felt her whole body warm. She was certain that everyone was kind of watching her, looking her over, putting her face to the she-cat who had caused the sheriff to call up the emergency alert roster—*twice.*

But she hadn't expected Chase to be so obviously observing her. Why wouldn't he though? She was certain he wasn't about to let her out of his sight, despite telling her she was free to leave anytime she wished. Not because he thought she was some deranged killer they had to keep their eye on, but more that he truly worried about her safety.

"He sure does like you,"' Dottie said.

Shannon glanced at her, wondering if Dottie was talking about Chase.

"Chase. Believe me, he wouldn't have taken just anyone into Millicent's Dress Boutique and bought her a bunch of clothes—and stayed with her in in the dressing room. He has a reputation to uphold. Since his wife and baby died, he's really been careful about who he sees and keeping it private. Then here you are, and he's blatantly showing you off as if you're his already. You can't know how much we're glad for it. We really worried about him in the early days after he moved here."

Shannon wondered what had happened concerning his wife and baby, but she felt uncomfortable asking. She sipped some of her water. "He was making sure I didn't run off again. He had removed my handcuffs." She wanted to ensure that everyone knew the reality of the matter, and she figured Dottie would help spread that truth.

"Is that what he told you?" Dottie asked. She laughed.

Okay, so maybe Dottie wouldn't help Shannon dispel *that* rumor.

Shannon liked Dottie. She couldn't imagine raising twin toddlers on her own and working as a police dispatcher, too. She really admired her for that.

"Believe me, if he had worried about you escaping, he could have had Millicent go into the dressing room with you, and he could have stood outside of it. And he *would* have, if he hadn't already been fascinated with you."

"I was *dangerous*. I'd knocked both him and Dan out once already. He *couldn't* risk it."

Dottie chuckled. "I think that's why he was so intrigued with you. And… maybe feeling a little bad that he'd shot you first. In any event, neither Dan nor Chase will ever be able to live that down. I have to say that you have sure livened things up around here."

The kids finished their treats and began playing more games.

"Have you thought about getting a job here? Millicent could use some extra help over the holidays at her dress shop. The coffee shop on Main Street is looking to hire a new waitress. The bank could use another teller. We've got plenty of work opportunities here if you're interested."

Shannon thought it was sweet of Dottie to want her to set down roots, but she couldn't. Then again, she wondered if Dottie was digging to see what kind of work Shannon had done before.

"If Dan hadn't given me a job as a dispatcher, well, I don't know what I would have done. I felt like knocking off a bank or something. Maybe even borrow money from one of those loan sharks, if we'd had any around here, just to ensure I didn't lose my house and that I could still feed my babies."

Shannon frowned at her. "Surely everyone here would have come to your aid." Just like they had done for Shannon. And *she* could be wanted for murdering her boyfriend! But Dottie had lived among them and had babies to raise.

"Sure, but I didn't tell anyone what had happened for a long time. I was ashamed that he ran off. I kept thinking my deadbeat husband would return before long. Or at least I hoped he would. Then the bank notified the sheriff that I hadn't paid my loan in three months, and he came out to see me. I was so afraid when he pulled into the drive that he was going to serve me an eviction notice. That's when he learned I was close to losing everything, and he gave me the job."

Shannon wanted to know if Dan and she were a couple, but she didn't want to pry. "He seems to be a good person." Especially since he hadn't arrested her for assaulting him while he was performing his duties as the sheriff.

Dottie's kids began opening presents. And other kids got into the act to help them. Now that she saw all the presents the kids were swimming in, she realized they hadn't needed to buy them anything more.

"Dan's the best. Most folks around here are. I should have shared what was going on with my finances with someone long before that. Everything worked out fine in the end. But I was living in such a state of despair when I hadn't needed to. Now, some of the ladies take turns watching the toddlers and teens babysit them in the afternoons. Dan lets me off early whenever he can so I can be home with the kids."

"That's wonderful."

"What I'm trying to say is that sometimes you can have the worst trouble that seems insurmountable, but others can help you to cope and all of a sudden nothing is quite that bad."

Shannon realized Dottie was talking about her—about how she just needed to reach out, and they'd all be there for her. But being wanted for questioning in the case of murdering a police officer wasn't the same as financial difficulties. "I agree." With Dottie's situation, not her own.

She wasn't about to share what was going on with her with Dottie or anyone else. She wondered then if this was a way for Dan and Chase to convince Shannon to spill the truth—by having Dottie speak with her—since they hadn't been able to learn anything from her on their own. Or maybe it was just Dottie being Dottie.

Shannon understood. Really. Everyone wanted to help her out. But if she told everyone what the police wanted her for, what would the local residents do? Right now, they didn't know they were harboring a possible fugitive running from justice, even though *she* knew she was innocent. If Hennessey managed to pin the crime on her, then everyone here could be guilty of the crime of harboring her.

"I think you're innocent," Dottie said, studying her. "We all do."

Shannon instantly felt panicked. Then she thought they

didn't know anything—just suspected she was running from the police. But still, Dottie could smell her fear and that was just as telling.

CHAPTER 10

"I don't blame you for not being able to take your eyes off her," Hal said to Chase as he observed Shannon while Dottie talked to her.

Kid's music was playing in the background while the kids were playing a game of mouse hunt—toy mice with each child's name on it had been hidden somewhere in the living room. First one to find the correct mouse with the child's own name on it won as the best cougar hunter among them.

"Do you think Dottie's getting anything useful out of her?" Hal asked.

"It appears Dottie is doing most of the talking," Chase said, barely taking his eyes off Shannon the whole time they'd been there. If she'd given any indication she wanted to leave and return to his cabin, he would promptly rescue her.

He hated seeing how uncomfortable Shannon looked. She'd said she wanted to come and he was glad to bring her there—to see her make new friends. But every time the toddlers squealed in delight, he saw her flinch. Dottie had been talking to her nonstop and Shannon had barely said a word. He'd be surprised if Dottie learned anything at all.

He hoped that Dottie wasn't pushing her too much to

learn the truth. He knew that Dottie only meant well and wanted to help Shannon. He didn't think that forcing her was the way to get her to reveal what was going on, though. They'd have to uncover the truth themselves and then show her that they were still there for her and would do anything they could to protect her.

Rick and Yvonne were playing hide and seek with the kids and Rick got caught right away. Shannon laughed. Everyone else did also, but seeing Shannon's face brighten with laughter really cheered Chase. He felt a modicum of relief then that she was having a good time. She was eating some of the pink-frosting decorated cake and peppermint ice cream, and he was glad to see that, too. She was looking better, not so thin, her cheeks rosier than they'd been in the beginning.

Hal folded his arms. "She's a keeper."

"She's in trouble with the law. She has to be," Chase reminded him.

"She's *still* a keeper," Hal said, as if he had to tell Chase that. "Dan said you told him that she was free to go if she wanted. You can't be serious."

Chase smiled just a little.

Hal shook his head. "I told him I didn't think you were serious. I'm not sure I would have been that brave to risk that she'd trust me enough."

Chase chuckled. "You'd do whatever you could to make her feel welcome."

Hal sighed dramatically. "I've already given Dan hell over calling you up to hunt her down first and not me."

Chase laughed.

As to watching her? Chase had to admit he didn't want her to slip away from the party in all the excitement and confusion. He figured enough people were probably watching her at any given time, but he still didn't trust that somebody else would notice if she attempted to steal away. She looked damned hot in that vivid pink sweater just like he knew she would. When he got it for her, he really wasn't sure she'd wear it because she'd been reluctant to have him buy it for her in the first place. But he was glad she had. And it wasn't just because he wanted her to stand out in it. He wanted to see how pretty she looked when she wasn't trying to hide away in grays and blacks.

Dottie's daughter, Trish, ran over to show her mom a toy and Dottie spoke to her and the toddler looked up at Shannon.

She smiled and crouched down in front of Trish and showed her how to play with the toy. All smiles, Trish ran off and joined the others. He thought again about Shannon taking care of the boy who would have drowned in the waterfall pool. She appeared to be a natural with children.

When the party began winding down and moms were taking their cranky little ones home, fussing because they didn't get to take the birthday kids' toys with them, Chase said, "Looks like it's time to go."

"Yeah, back to the ranch," Hal said.

"I was supposed to help you move in a couple of weeks."

"I think you've got your hands full. Unless Shannon would like to see my spread." Hal smiled.

Chase shook his head. "I'll ask her if she minds." Though he was afraid she would attempt to run again—based on what she'd said at the Muellers' home—well before that. "See you later."

"Watch your back."

"Will do."

***

As soon as Chase and Shannon were headed back to his resort, she was ready for a nap. But the first thing Chase said to her was, "We have an anniversary party to go to tomorrow night." This time he didn't ask. Just took it for granted that she'd want to attend it.

She groaned.

"You don't like anniversary parties?"

"Right this instant, the thought of going anywhere wears me out."

"It's not until tomorrow night. We can relax this evening, watch a movie, have some shrimp pasta, and then tomorrow you can spend the whole day just chilling until we go over there."

"You really want me to go?"

"Yeah, I do. He's retired army and because of all the war stories he used to tell us when we were kids, he was the one who influenced us to join up. They're a really nice couple. Besides, how would it look if I showed up without my wife?"

She laughed and shook her head. "I haven't gotten used to *that* idea yet."

He tapped his fingers on the steering wheel. "Now that we're married…"

She raised her brows as she considered him.

He smiled at her. "Sorry, I really can't keep a straight face about this. But I was wondering if you want to sleep with me."

She laughed. "No," she said, without hesitation.

"Not because we're pretending to be married, really," Chase said, watching his driving. "But because you're having such a time sleeping."

"You think if I slept with you, I'd sleep better?"

His lips parted as he was about to answer her, and then he clamped them shut. He took a deep breath and let it out. "Maybe not. But you did sleep soundly on the couch when we were watching a movie."

"I think being in bed with you would make a difference."

He glanced at her. Was she feeling the same thing that he was feeling between them?

"What do Yvonne and Rick do for a living?" she asked, quickly changing the subject.

He guessed not then, or she wasn't ready to admit it. "Both of them work at the bank as financial advisors."

"I was surprised to see them. Well, and Dan and Hal at the kids' birthday party, considering none of them have kids."

"Dan has kind of a thing for Dottie. Don't tell him or Dottie I said so. Okay? He's in total denial about it. But as soon as her husband ran off, and Dan's dispatcher up and retired on him, he hired her. He encouraged her to file for divorce right away. Her ex-husband has been gone for two years and Dan has attended their birthday parties since then. Then again, he's a nice guy and he might just be feeling protective of her, partly doing his job as sheriff."

Shannon smiled. "So that's why he didn't offer to be the one to protect me. What about the full-time deputy?"

"Stryker? He would be in shock when he returns home from vacation and learned he had become a husband while he was away. Dan has a hard enough time talking him into taking vacations during the year. He's a real workaholic."

She chuckled. "Yeah, I could see how that would be a shock. But you're okay with it?"

"Better than okay with it. You love my cooking. That says a lot."

"I hope it's not too... unsettling for you."

"No, Shannon. It feels right. We'll have the best cover, guaranteed. So tomorrow we have the invite to the Kretchens' wedding anniversary celebration, and I'll work during the day on some painting projects I need to get done."

"Don't tell me their wedding anniversary is being celebrated early also."

"No. It really is at this time, so Dan assured me. Anyway, if you're okay with it, did you want to go?"

She sighed. "Okay, sounds fine with me."

"And then in a couple of weeks, I was supposed to help Hal move to his ranch. He specifically wanted to show you his spread."

Shannon smiled a little. "Does he act that way toward all women?"

"No, actually he doesn't. I think he does with you because he's really impressed with how you knocked Dan and me out."

She laughed.

"You've got to remember we're all Special Forces. It takes a lot to catch us off-guard."

She was still grinning when they arrived at his cabin.

But as soon he parked, a pickup drove in behind them and Chase pulled a gun from his belt, shocking the hell out of her. She had never noticed he'd put a shoulder holster on under his jacket. "Wait here," he said. "You got my phone handy?"

Her heart beating wildly, she pulled the phone out of her pocket.

"Dan's number is listed under contacts. Call him if this gets ugly."

She didn't recognize the truck, but it didn't mean it wasn't Hennessey or his kin.

"Reporter," Chase said as the man got out of his truck and Chase holstered his gun. "Why don't you go on inside, and I'll take care of this. Pull up your hood in case he tries to take a picture of you."

She did as Chase said, glad it wasn't Hennessey, but

afraid if the reporter snapped a shot of her and it was on the news, Hennessey might see it.

She started to open the car door and Chase said, "Wait a minute."

She hesitated, her hand on the door handle.

"Okay, go!"

She opened the door, got out as quickly as she could, slammed it shut, and headed to the house.

And realized she didn't have a blasted key. She headed around the back of the cabin, and she was afraid Chase would worry she was going to run off. But she really couldn't do anything else but move around to the backside of the house and out of the reporter's view, unless she broke a window to get inside.

Chase swore under his breath when he saw Shannon head around the back of the cabin. He really worried she was planning to run, afraid the reporter would spread the word she was up here, even though Chase had remembered too late that she had no way to get into the damn house.

He quickly got out of the driver's seat and intercepted Carl Nelson with his notepad and recorder in hand.

"I'd like to ask you some questions about your injury the other day in the woods," Carl said. "Sheriff Steinacker said you were hunting a cougar down, but that he didn't injure you. He wouldn't say how you got hurt. But you were kind of out of it at the time, so I figured that was the reason why the sheriff didn't know the facts. So I wanted to get it from the horse's mouth. Oh, you don't mind if I record this, do you? To make sure it's accurate?"

Chase didn't mind reporters when they could help in a police investigation, but in this instance, the man could very likely endanger Shannon. He had to walk a careful line—not give Carl a reason to want to try to dig up more of the story if Chase gave the impression he was being too elusive. At the same time, it really was none of the reporter's business.

"Nothing to report," Chase said. "Just an accident."

Carl looked at the cabin. "I heard some rumors that you went and got married. Congratulations."

"Thanks. If you don't have any other questions..."

"After you left the hospital, I heard you were chasing down a cougar again. I understand it was running through Wildwood Estates. Sheriff said the male cougar that had pulled the boy from the waterfall pool was shot and killed. So this couldn't have been the same one. Was it a female or male?"

"I don't know. I was tracking its last known whereabouts, but I never actually caught sight of it."

"Did anyone ever catch it... or kill it?"

"No. I'm sure with all the commotion in the area, it learned not to go around there again."

"I heard you made an arrest that same day—a break-in of one of the homes in that same development."

"Nothing to report."

Carl smiled a little and Chase was afraid he'd been in the area and actually witnessed something firsthand. Like having a woman handcuffed to his wrist at the grocery store.

Carl glanced at his notebook and flipped through a few pages. "You were spotted with a woman handcuffed to your wrist at Save Right."

The grocery store.

"Nothing to say about it," Chase said.

"You... were seen taking her to Millicent's Dress Boutique after that and came out with a lot of packages and the two of you were no longer handcuffed. Then you came back here with her." Carl raised a brow.

"If you know everything, why are you asking me?"

Carl shrugged. "Just want to get my facts straight."

Chase wanted to punch the guy's lights out. He wanted to threaten him to leave her out of the picture, but he knew Carl would treat it as if he'd just been tossed a bone. And Chase damn well wanted to see to Shannon, get her into the house, and ensure she hadn't stripped, shifted, and taken off.

"Is that all you wanted to ask?"

"Unless you've got something more interesting to tell me." Carl again glanced at the house.

"Talk to you later then," Chase said dismissively and headed for the cabin.

"Mind if I have a word with your wife?"

Chase ignored him and unlocked the door to the house. He stepped inside and fought slamming it. At a run, he headed for his bedroom, figuring until Carl left, he had no other alternative but to let Shannon in through the window. He opened the curtains and slid the window open. But when he didn't see any sign of her outside, his heart began pumping faster. He couldn't quash the fear rushing through his blood.

What if the damned reporter had frightened her so much that she *had* run off?

His heart pounding furiously, he climbed out the window. He had his cell in hand, ready to call Dan and have him alert everyone when he headed for the woods. But out of the corner of his eye, he saw something pink and turned. Shannon was crouched behind the woodpile, her arms wrapped around herself, trying to keep warm. He was so relieved to see her there, but so angry that she'd had to hide out there in the cold. She watched him, her concerned expression turning to relief.

"God, Shannon, I'm so sorry," he whispered to her.

She was shivering and he instantly pulled her up from the cold ground and gave her a hug.

"I haven't heard him drive off yet," he told her in a hushed voice and hurried her back to the bedroom window. He lifted her partway, and she climbed inside. Then he joined her and closed the window and pulled the curtains shut.

The relief he felt in having her safe here with him had been instantaneous.

But her eyes were wide with concern. "I was listening. I heard everything."

"He doesn't know anything. He hasn't a clue what's going on between us."

"What if he digs further for the truth?" she asked.

"Oh, I'm sure he'll try, but what will he find?" Chase wanted to say that even *they* didn't know who Shannon was, even though they were using every resource they could to learn the truth about her.

But when he looked into her golden eyes, he realized just how concerned she still was.

"He won't discover anything."

And then he was kissing her and she was kissing him. She was cold, like he was, but the next thing he knew, she was pulling at his parka to remove it, their lips still pressed together, tongues touching this time.

He quickly jerked his parka off and tossed it, and then began to unbutton her jacket as if their clothes were on fire. His blood was on fire, just from feeling her mouth pressed against his, the way she tangled her tongue with his, the way she so eagerly was trying to remove his clothes.

They shouldn't be doing this. Not in a million years, they shouldn't be going there. But he couldn't quit it unless she said she didn't want it, and she didn't look like she had any intention of stopping where this was going.

She tugged at his belt and he lifted her onto his bed and pulled off her hot pink sweater. For a moment, he just stared at her lace-covered breasts and the hint of dusky, aroused nipples that already poked at the lace. He crouched down to pull off one of her tennis shoes and then the other, vowing to get her a pair of snow boots next time they went into town together. She wasn't leaving him. She wasn't going anywhere. She belonged there... with him.

He slipped off her socks, but then she tugged again at his belt, as if she wanted him to strip as much as she had already. He hurried to unbutton his shirt as she started unfastening some of them, too. Her fingers brushing against his chest, her helping to undress him aroused him all the more.

She slid his flannel shirt off his shoulders, then kissed one, and then the other, her mouth on his skin hot and erotic. But then she was again frantically attempting to pull off his clothes as if she was afraid she might change her mind about this, or he would.

He wasn't about to. Every bit of him said he wanted this as long as she did.

He pulled off her jeans, and then removed his boots, socks, and his own jeans. Winter weather meant way too many clothes. He was already thinking what it would be like come summer and seeing Shannon in fewer clothes.

Before he could pull off his briefs, she slowed down, running her hands over his taut abs, the feel of her fingers skimming over his skin, making every inch of him sizzle with heat. He took her face in his hands and began to kiss her, slowly and gently, wanting to make this last. Her hands slid down his waist and as soon as he felt her thumbs slip under the waistband at his hips, he knew he was going to have a hell of a time going slow.

She pulled the briefs down, freeing his erection, her cheek brushing down the length of his cock as she slid the briefs all the way to his ankles. Stepping out of them, he reached behind her to unfasten her bra and struggled to unclasp it as their mouths again sought each other, kissing, pressuring, her lips warm and soft against his. Her bra undone, he slid the straps down her arms and gazed at her luscious breasts, heavy, the nipples aroused. He cupped each in a hand and enjoyed the feel of her soft flesh. She ran her fingers through his hair, her nails gently scratching his scalp, as he took one of her nipples in his mouth and teased it with his tongue, licking, sucking, making her collapse onto the bed.

He smiled, then pulled off her panties, and she moved farther onto the bed, her head on his pillow. Somehow, seeing her dark hair stretched out over his pale blue flannel pillowcase made him feel as though she belonged there, in his bed, just like that.

She was smiling at him, her eyes dark with desire, the curly dark hair at the apex of her thighs dewy, her nipples begging him to sample them again. He couldn't help that he wished to admire her beauty before he joined her, but when he looked up at her face, he found her eyeing him in the same appreciative way. That had his erection jumping.

She smiled. And then he was beside her on the bed, kissing her, his hand on her breast, the nipple poking at the palm of his hand. She smelled of the outdoors, the pine, hot, and sexy cougar. She tasted of pink fruit punch and sweet sugary birthday frosting—a sweet confection that was all his.

He swept his hand down her soft belly, lower until his fingers found her swollen feminine bud. He began to stroke her, not believing it would come to this. Despite knowing he shouldn't be doing it, being with her like this felt right.

He continued to stroke her as he kissed her mouth. She held his face and kissed him eagerly back until he felt her tense, and then she let out her breath in a happy exhalation, before she forced him onto his back, surprising the hell out of him.

He wasn't sure she'd want to go all the way, but when she lined herself up to impale herself on top of his rigid cock, he managed to use his other brain and said, "Wait, let me get a..."

"Implant—three year birth control," she said, and he was glad she was protected, given her current circumstances.

She finished the move and he felt like he was in heaven as his cock pushed deep inside her. He reached up to cup her breasts as she rocked on top of him, her own muscles clenching tight around his erection, still pulsing with her orgasm when Chase's damn phone rang.

Ignoring it, he placed his hands on her hips and worked her up and down as he watched her exquisite breasts bounce with their moves. He thrust into her, loving the way his cock was surrounded by her dark curls as he pumped into her.

He was on the verge of coming when she began to slow down, and if she stopped now, he swore he was going to die.

Shannon had never felt so wild with abandon as she did with Chase. She didn't know why she felt that way with him when he was the nicest man she'd ever met. But something about him made her take risks that she normally wouldn't take. Like making love to him when she had no business doing so. She told herself it was okay because she really wasn't a criminal. But the truth of the matter was, she could get him killed. And he certainly didn't deserve that.

Then she felt another climax coming and she slowed down to savor it, to allow it to build, to feel herself rising above the world and ascending to heaven when it hit. "Oh... my... God," she said, but as much as she was totally boneless and tired and felt like the whole world was at her command—after she took a nap—she knew Chase wasn't quite done.

His face was hard with concentration, his eyes lusty, the smell of the all big he-cat, musty, sexy, and hot, hot, hot. He groaned as he came, and yet he still rocked into her, still pumping hard until the last. And then he grabbed her arms and pulled her against him, his hand on her back, his other sliding down it in a soothing caress.

They didn't say anything, just listened to each other's heart beating way too fast, their breathing heavy, and she felt totally satiated.

She snuggled against his chest, when he pulled the covers over them to keep them warm, though the heater was on. He was still inside her, as if he intended to take a cat nap with her just like this.

Then she recalled the phone call, and she wondered who had called. And she wondered if Chase was thinking about it, too. He didn't say anything about it though, just stroked her back and held her close as if this was the most natural thing for the two of them to be doing. And in a weird way, it felt right, as if they were living the lies that everyone in town was already saying were true—that they were married, she had lived here forever, and this was her home.

That was the last thing she remembered thinking before she fell asleep.

Chase held onto Shannon, torn between wanting to stay here the rest of the day and night, and knowing he needed to check on the phone call. But Shannon was sound asleep and despite that, just her breasts pressed against him, her light, warm breath tickling the hairs on his chest, and the way she was straddling him as if she'd claimed him was making his cock stir inside her.

He wasn't about to move an inch, had no intention of unsettling her, not when her being with him allowed her to feel safe. He snorted. Hell, safe from whoever was out there, but what about from him? But he was glad she felt safe enough to sleep against him.

He had wanted this as much as she had wanted this, but now he worried even more that she planned to run off on him. As if the sex—like he had worried earlier about her kissing him—was a way to say thank you and good bye. He had to quit thinking in those terms. But he was having a hard time doing so. Especially since with her, she had proved to be so unpredictable.

For now, he just held her close, loving that they'd shared this intimacy, and hoped she would stay with him, and they could work things out with whatever trouble she was in.

He closed his eyes and fell asleep for a couple of hours and woke to her stirring on top of him. That had him hard all over again. The wicked smile she cast him gave him the go ahead to pleasure her all over again before they finally got up and she headed to the bathroom to take a shower. The phone rang again, and he sighed, and grabbed it. Two missed calls from Dan. At least he waited for a while before he called again.

"Hey, Dan, that hound of a reporter, Carl, was asking some questions." Chase told Dan all that had transpired between them.

Dan laughed.

Chase frowned and was going to ask him what was so damned funny, when Dan said, "He asked the same questions of a dozen different people right before Dottie's birthday party. The answer everyone gave was that you were doing some practice police work, seeing how those new handcuffs worked on your wife while she was serving as the arrestee. But once you entered the dress shop, you knew they worked fine and so you were back to your usual loving selves—shopping for your lovely wife and enjoying the day together. I swear everyone has been coming up with stories to explain everything that has happened way before either you or I think of it. Cell phones, text messages, emails, everyone's swapping stories to cover you."

"But he knew about the break-in at Hal's house."

"Right. You're both helping him move, right? She was at the house already packing up some of his household items to help out, and you got this idea about trying out your new handcuffs. She didn't resist you when you left the house, did she?"

"No." Chase couldn't believe it. He loved the people in this town. "I'll let her know. Someone should have told me, though."

"Yeah, sorry. Kind of got distracted at the party. Besides, I didn't think he'd be around to bother you since he hadn't already."

"Did you call about anything special?"

"Dottie said that Shannon told her that she had lost her parents and her twin brother. No names though. And she's been running for four and a half weeks. So that narrows down the timeframe as far as an approximate date that a crime might have been committed. Still no idea where though."

Chase glanced in the direction of the bathroom, the shower still running. "That's a hell of a long time."

"Yeah, I know. The little lady is one survivor. We also know her father served in the military, but that's about it for now."

"All right. We're going to have some supper and watch one of Dottie's movies, I suspect."

"Okay, same goes as before. Learn anything, call me

pronto, and same here."

"Sounds good. Talk to you later."

Chase threw on his briefs and a robe, then headed into the kitchen to see about making supper. He heard Shannon leave the bathroom and then enter the guest bedroom and close the door. He sure hoped she would sleep with him tonight. When the shrimp pasta was ready to serve, she joined him in the kitchen and took in a deep breath of the aroma of the meal.

"Sorry I took so long in the shower. I meant to give you time to take one and then I would have made dinner."

"I think I was a chef in another life," he said. "Do you want to grab a bottle of white wine, and we'll eat in the living room tonight while we're watching a movie?"

"Sure."

Tonight, this was how he wanted it, with her sitting beside him on the couch, the two of them having shrimp pasta and wine, and watching—well, a romance movie. He could deal with it. And if it put her in the mood for more loving, he *really* could deal with it.

After finishing up dinner and their glasses of wine, she snuggled with him like she did before, only this time she stayed awake through the movie, but once it was done, she asked, "Was that Dan who had called?" She carried their plates into the kitchen, and then started the dishwasher while he put the wine bottle away.

"Yeah. I told him about the reporter." Chase explained what the townspeople had made up as their cover story.

She laughed. "That's hilarious. It's a good thing I wasn't in handcuffs any longer when we went to Millicent's to shop."

He pulled her close and looked down at her. "Speaking of which, I need to take you to the store to pick up some more things. Something for you to wear in the snow—snow boots, a hat, a few more clothes."

She almost looked afraid and that had him worried all over again. "No pressure," he said, and leaned down to kiss her wine-flavored lips. "But... you're coming to bed with me."

She chuckled, pulled out of his grasp, slipped her hand around his and headed for his bedroom. "But you know what happened the last time we ended up in your bed."

"Yes, you slept really well."

She smiled at him.

And he smiled right back at her. "You will sleep." But only after they made love again.

He truly wanted this with Shannon, only he was afraid that no matter how much he wanted it, her mind was set on leaving.

***

Late the next morning, Shannon woke and stretched in bed--Chase's bed—not believing that they had been up half the night making love. He was banging around in the kitchen. She realized just how much she had needed the intimacy with a man—not ready to say that Chase would be that man for the long run—not with the way things stood right now.

But he seemed to need the same things as she did, so for now, she was fine with it.

"Hey, are you finally awake?" he asked, smiling at her as she joined him in the kitchen. He was drinking a cup of coffee and started to make her a cup of hot tea.

He sounded friendly and eager to talk with her, not annoyed that she'd slept half the day and missed breakfast with him just because she didn't hold up as well with making love half the night as he did. She really appreciated him for that. She needed that in her life for the moment. No one judging her. Just accepting her the way she was.

"Yeah, I guess I really needed the sleep."

"I'll say. Just glad you were able to. Some guests can't take all the sounds of nature out here. The birds singing, owls hooting at night, the old woodpecker pecking at the old tree near the road, and the wind rushing through the leaves."

"Not me. I much prefer this to the sound of traffic. But that's not what kept me awake last night."

He grinned.

She hated to ask him about getting something to eat. "Did you eat already? I guess it's about time for lunch. Did you want me to fix us something?" She had to do something. She was afraid he'd already given up waiting on her and had already eaten.

"Ham and eggs sound good to me. What about you? I can make them."

She smiled. No man had ever fixed her meals before. And Chase always seemed eager to please. "I may never want to leave."

"You can't. We're married, remember?"

She chuckled. "Right." She set out the plates and silverware.

"I don't have company out here a whole lot, so it's my pleasure."

Before long, she was enjoying her eggs and ham. Despite having eaten well last night, she was hungry and loved Chase's cooking.

When they were done eating, he sat back in his seat and just from his serious expression, she feared he'd begin questioning her again. Maybe he was afraid he'd taken it too far with her last night, and he had to know the truth.

She swore he waited to speak until she finished her meal first in the event he upset her and she couldn't eat any longer. It had to be killing him not to know what was going on, and she appreciated his having had so much patience.

He finally said, "Is there anyone we need to contact to let them know you're safe?"

Here came the questions she knew he was dying to ask. She quickly shook her head. But she suspected he'd gotten an update from Dottie—that her twin brother and parents were deceased.

"Okay, I don't want to push you on this because you're perfectly welcome to stay with us in our town, out here with me at the cabins for as long as you like. So no problem with that at all. I don't want you to feel you have to run again. It's just not safe. We're all like family and protective of our kind here. So if you're in any kind of trouble, we'll back you up with everything we've got. It would help if we knew what kind of trouble you're in and can prepare for it, if anyone comes snooping around, though."

She took a deep breath and let it out. "If anyone comes looking for me—showing off a picture of me and stating I was wanted for something, or I am a person of interest? It's all a lie. Okay? Whatever they tell you--*none* of it's true. And if I go back, I'm dead. Well, I'd be dead before I ever made it back. More expedient that way."

Chase's expression darkened considerably as he sat stiffer in his chair and studied her for a moment. "Okay," he said slowly, his eyes hardening a little. "I'm damn serious about watching out for you. I'm not letting anyone who's under my watch come to harm again."

She wondered if he meant more than losing his wife and baby. She strived to smile, but she was certain the look wasn't in the least bit sincere. Chase might try, but she knew Hennessey was a ruthless killer and he had to silence her before it was too late.

Chase smiled a little back, only his smile was genuine. "You don't believe me. That's all right. I aim to prove it to you."

He couldn't. Not considering what was going on.

A knock sounded on the door and her heart skittered as they both looked that way. "I'll see who it is," Chase said, and hurried to get the door.

Shannon quickly stood. She didn't know what to do, so she waited until he reached the door, and peered through the peephole. "Ah, Hal's here. He's supposed to help me replace the windows on two of the cabins. I nearly forgot about it."

"I wonder why," she said.

He smiled and opened the door. "Come on in, Hal. I'll grab my coat and gloves."

"Morning," Hal said to Shannon who quickly greeted him, then went to take care of the dishes.

Chase said to Shannon, "You've got my phone, right?"

"Yes, thanks," she said.

"Okay, we'll be out there all morning. Weather is supposed to turn really cold for the next couple of days. Talk of snow even. Are you going to be all right?"

"Yeah, sure, go ahead and do what you need to do. I'll be all right here just chilling out. Is there anything special you'd like for lunch?"

He smiled then. "Salmon steaks. And anything else works for me. But remember we're going to the anniversary party tonight.""

"Right."

When the men left, she waited until they disappeared beyond the pine trees, then she hurried to turn on the TV and checked the news to see if there were any reports of a missing woman. She felt panicked, afraid Chase would catch her in the act. This was the first time she'd even thought about checking the news on the TV though. That showed how tired she'd been, and then with so many outings, she'd been tired all over again. She'd wished he'd had a smart phone so she could have accessed the Internet that way.

She flipped from one channel on the TV to the next.

Nothing. Hennessey probably didn't want everyone to go after her. Just himself and a couple of his loyal kin that he could count on. Or it had happened so many weeks ago, it wasn't on the news now.

She found Chase's laptop in his bedroom, and she felt guilty about sneaking a look at it. She was certain he wouldn't mind if she used it. He would definitely smell her scent on his computer. At least she'd been in his room now so he wouldn't wonder about that. While she was at it, she stripped the bed and began to wash the linens. Then, she hoped his laptop wasn't password protected so she could get onto it and do some searches.

She had no idea where Yuma Town was in relation to other locations in Colorado. She needed to know that also when she ran again, where she could go that would be safer than the panicked way she had run off the last time. After researching terrain and the routes she could take, she still considered asking Chase to pay for a bus fare for her. But she was afraid Hennessey would locate her too easily that way, even if Dan could get her false ID. If she ran as a cougar, then what? Unless she could kill Hennessey, where could she go as a cougar?

She was dying to look at her Facebook page and her emails. But she didn't dare. What if someone could tell she had accessed them? Maybe they couldn't, if she didn't respond, but she didn't want to chance it.

She felt bad that Chase wanted to get her more clothes as if she planned to live here permanently. What had happened between them last night was something they both seemed to really need, but she just couldn't stay here forever.

She sighed. Here, the people were sympathetic to her cause. She wasn't likely to find that anywhere else. Certainly not a shifter-run town like this. She turned off his laptop and found some dust cleaner, then began to dust the place.

She needed to wash her sheets and some of her clothes and so it became laundry day. Once she had put the last load in the dryer, she heard the men coming to the door. She headed into the kitchen to begin cooking the meal.

Chase unlocked the door and led the way inside. "I guess I should have said Hal was staying for the meal."

"I figured as much," she said cheerfully. "How'd it go?"

"Another couple of hours on it after we eat and then we'll head on over to the anniversary party."

That night after the anniversary party, Shannon was feeling antsy about the nighttime arrangements. Last night had been impetuous for them both. She didn't regret the intimacy, having needed the release as much as he had, but she knew, with her planning to leave as soon as she could, that they shouldn't do it again. She'd cleaned all the sheets but hadn't made up her own bed yet, so after grabbing her linens from the dryer, she headed for the guest bedroom. She thought it was better just leaving it unsaid.

She felt Chase's eyes on her back and she wondered how Chase would react to her returning to the guest room. Would he try to convince her they should sleep together? Or realize this was for the best? She hoped he'd leave well enough alone because she was afraid if he pressured her at all, she'd cave right in.

***

Shannon had been so quiet at the anniversary dinner, smiling appropriately, nodding, saying a few words to maintain propriety, but Chase knew her heart wasn't in it. He wasn't certain what was going through her mind, but he suspected from when he'd told her he'd wanted to get her some snow boots and other clothes for her for a longer, more permanent stay, she was immediately putting out the stop sign. Even so, he'd called an order in to Millicent when he'd bought Shannon the hot pink sweater, based on the clothing sizes of the purchases he'd already made. Dottie had dropped them off at the house while Shannon had still been asleep this morning. He had put them in the guest room so as not to disturb her while she was still sleeping in his bed.

He hoped she'd be pleased with the slipper boots, snow boots, another bra, another pair of jeans, a pair of turquoise sweats, five T-shirts, three proclaiming *Yuma Loves Pumas! Pumas Love Yuma! Cougar Power!*—because she needed to feel that she belonged here.

When she'd washed the guest bedroom linens, he worried that she intended to leave for good and as a kindness to her host, she had washed them. But then it appeared she was intending to make the bed and sleep in it again. He waited a minute or two, and then figured he'd help her make the bed, and maybe they could talk.

He didn't want to pressure her into staying with him in his bed tonight, though he definitely wanted her in it—with him. Not because of the sex, though he wouldn't discount that. But because he thought the more she got used to being with him, the closer she got to him, the less likely she'd leave.

"I'll help you," he said, before she could object, and he moved to the opposite side of the bed and began to help her make the guest bed.

"Thanks," she said. "Last night was... special. But it's better if I sleep here from now on."

"Did... was I too pushy?" He hated the insecurity in his words but he feared he'd pushed her before she was ready for anything this intimate. Even though she'd acted as though she had wanted him as much as he had felt the same raging need to make love to her.

She shook her head, but she avoided looking at him, and he feared she was tearful again.

He dropped the corner of the sheet he was supposed to tuck underneath the mattress and came to her side, but she quickly held her hand up to keep him from comforting her. "It's… it's nothing. I just need to do this."

He shoved his hands in his pockets. "Are you certain?" His eyes were on hers, watching her emotions, seeing the turmoil. It was killing him not to be able to push through her barrier.

She nodded, her eyes filled with tears.

He let out his breath and returned to the other side of the bed, helped finish making it, then said, "If you need anything, you know where I am. Good night, Shannon."

As much as it killed him to do so, he had to give her the space she needed. Let her come to terms with this on her own. He wasn't letting her go.

He walked out of the bedroom and shut the door, his heart feeling like it had been filled with stones, then ripped out, and thrown into Lake Buchanan where it sank to the bottom.

He hoped she'd change her mind and join him, or maybe even call him and ask him to return to her room, but he knew it wouldn't happen.

He retired to his bed, undressed, and climbed into the clean sheets, disappointed he couldn't breathe in her delightful scent. Was that why she had washed the sheets? To clean away everything that had happened between them last night?

He sighed, wanting to kiss her more, to hold her tight, wished to make love to her again. He shook his head at himself, not believing after vowing he'd never marry again, never find anyone again, he was already thinking along those lines. He would do anything to protect Shannon, he told himself. And she wasn't having any part of it.

Hell, he was really, really interested in her. In more than a protective sort of way. He reached over and grabbed his laptop off his bedside table, opened it up to answer emails and something, maybe his police training, made him check his browser history. He'd smelled her scent on his laptop, but she'd dusted the furniture with a lemon cleaner and moved the laptop to do so. Still, his police instinct and cat wariness kicked in.

In the browser history, he discovered she'd accessed maps, terrain features of Colorado, bus locations, and schedules. He ground his teeth. He'd thought Shannon was feeling safe with him. She was like a deer ready to bolt. He just couldn't let her.

His cell phone rang. Grabbing it off his bedside table, he saw it was Dan. "Yeah, Dan?" He knew his buddy would have news or he wouldn't be calling at this late hour.

"Okay, I have bad news. Are you alone?"

Chase's heartbeat quickened as he set his laptop down on the bedside table. "Yeah, what's going on?"

"I finally got a police bulletin that shows a picture of Shannon that isn't really the best of shots. But between that, her approximate age, and that she has no living relatives, and that her first name is Shannon, I'm betting this is her. In Canyon, Texas, Shannon Rafferty is wanted as a person of interest in an ongoing investigation concerning the murder of her boyfriend, Ted Kelly."

Chase felt numb. She'd said that. That if she was called a person of interest in some investigation to know it was all a lie. "Tell me all about it."

"When her boyfriend didn't show up at work—and get

this, he was a cop—"

Chase couldn't believe it.

"—his family grew concerned. They tried calling both him and Shannon, and there was no response on either of their phones. They discovered a bloody scene where her boyfriend, Ted, was stabbed numerous times in the kitchen of his home and left for dead. They determined he had died approximately forty-eight hours earlier. She and her car were reported missing shortly after that. Her car was found a few days later, purse, ID, credit card, cash, keys, her clothes, and a couple of bags. Everything appeared to have been left intact. They don't have much crime out there or the car would have been stolen along with everything that she had left behind. Instead, the old farmer who reported it was afraid she'd met with foul play and didn't want to leave his fingerprints on anything so he didn't touch anything. The fingerprints that were lifted belonged to Ted Kelly and someone else who wasn't in the database. Had to have been Shannon's since the car's registered in her name."

Chase's head swam with all the possibilities as he tried to see this from Shannon's standpoint. "Was it a home invasion? She witnessed the murder but didn't know who they were, and they came after her? Or maybe it had to do with someone the cop had arrested previously and the man was out for revenge? And she had seen what he'd done to her boyfriend?" Chase asked, grasping at any case that could clear her of having killed her own boyfriend.

"Family and friends are always the first suspects. You know that, Chase."

"Damn it, I know it, but she said if someone came around saying she was a person of interest in a crime that was committed it would be a lie."

"Hell, when did she tell you that?"

"A little while ago. If she witnessed the murder, and I

highly suspect that she had, which was why she ran, she *would* be a person of interest. It might have been a case of self-defense even, but she was afraid it wouldn't look that way because he was a cop and she ran off. That makes her look guilty in the eyes of the law. Was the place a human-run town?"

"Yes. So they're not going to keep it hushed up. They have a dead cop and they need to pin the blame for his murder on someone."

"What have they got on her whereabouts?"

"They thought she was headed for Florida. They'd been tracking her, or they thought they had, but discovered she'd thrown her cell phone in the bed of a pickup truck headed to Florida when he'd stopped for gas at a service station and run in to use the restroom."

"Did she get gas there?"

"Yeah, used her credit card. She had to or she would have had to go inside and pay with cash. That's where they picked up a grainy picture of her by the pumps. No other pictures of her anywhere. Not at her house. Nowhere."

"Except her driver's license," Chase said.

"Didn't look like her at all. She'd had blond hair and it had been cut short."

Chase couldn't imagine her as a blond. Then he frowned. Was she really a blond? No. All of her hair was dark.

"They found her abandoned car in Texas only about two hours from where she lived in Canyon out in some farm land. They said there was no sign of blood or a struggle though, so they assume she was still alive when she left the vehicle. Still, the police think she might have been the victim of a crime because she had left everything behind. Some think she might have witnessed her boyfriend's murder, and the murderer or murderers caught up with her finally. But because they haven't located her body, they're still looking."

"This isn't good," Chase said, rubbing the whiskers on his chin.

"No, it isn't. At least they have no money trail to look for. So that's good."

"Was he a shifter?"

"We don't know and we can't go asking them. Not without alerting them we might know something of her whereabouts."

"If her boyfriend's family are shifters, they could track her trail."

Dan let out his breath. "Yeah. There's the real problem. Her boyfriend's two brothers are police officers also. He's got an uncle on the police force in another town."

"Hell. And how much do you want to bet they are shifters and they're behind trying to have her hung? They know a shifter can't be tried for murder. She can't go to jail."

Dan didn't say anything.

The news really hit Chase hard. "They want to put her down. *God damn it*."

"That's what I figure. They've got to catch up to her before the human police force does. They've got to kill her—in the line of duty. They can say that she killed his brother and ran. She resisted arrest, maybe one of them will cut himself up or something, and then say he had to fatally wound her."

"That's the reason she ran." Chase got off the bed and paced across his bedroom. "Okay, I don't believe she would have killed her boyfriend other than in self-defense."

"We don't know that for sure, Chase. She could be a black widow with dead boyfriends all over the place."

"Dan," Chase said, sounding exasperated with him.

"Okay, I agree, but from the sounds of it, this could be an act of outrage. If she learned he was cheating on her and she killed him for it, she wouldn't have a leg to stand on. Certainly not where his family is concerned if they were very close."

Chase swore under his breath again. "Okay, you're the sheriff. What do you want to do about it?"

"Well, hell, Chase, we've been friends too long for me to say what you can or can't do under the circumstances. You think she's innocent."

"She is until proven guilty, or have we lost that concept somehow?"

Dan didn't say anything for a moment. Then he said, "Okay, listen, believe me, I'm on your side, all right? I'm just trying to play devil's advocate. To protect herself, she might have killed her boyfriend. Hell, she might have killed you up on the mountain for the same reason if you hadn't gotten lucky."

Chase ground his teeth.

"I have to take more of an unbiased view on this."

"So what do you want me to do? Stand down while these men track her down and murder her? Not wanting anyone to learn about it? Oh, sure one of them didn't mean to, but they fought over the gun, and he just happened to shoot her somewhere that she'd bleed out before she could get any medical assistance."

"If I tell you to bring her into town for questioning, would you?"

Chase paced across the floor some more. "I'll talk to her."

"If she admits she killed her boyfriend for a reason other than self-defense? Anger? Something else? What then?"

"I said I'd talk to her."

"Now?"

"Yes. Now. We need to know what to do. Call you back in a little while." Chase ended the call, threw on a pair of boxers, and headed to the guest room. He knew she was innocent of killing her boyfriend in cold blood. He just had to figure out what to do to keep her from being the family's terminal target.

So much for moving a pure cougar out of the territory when Dan had sent him to hunt her down in the first place. This had become a nightmare of epic proportions.

When he reached her door, he knocked. No answer. He worried then that she'd heard him talking to Dan and got the gist of it, and she'd run. Maybe that's why she'd wanted to stay in her own room, so that she could slip out when Chase went to sleep tonight.

She couldn't fight this on her own. He knocked again. She could be sound asleep. But he had to talk to her now and figure out what to do. He shook his head at himself. If anyone had ever said he might one day be aiding and abetting a murderer, he'd have told them he was crazy.

When she still didn't answer the door, he said, "It's just me, Chase." Then he pulled out a tool he could use on the door and unlocked it, assuming the worse. She was gone.

He tried to open the door, but it hit the bedside table. She had moved it to protect herself from him? He felt bad for her all over again.

"Shannon, it's just me," he said, reaching in to turn on the light switch, hoping she was in the room and hadn't slipped out the window, when he saw Shannon in her cougar form crouched and ready to pounce.

***

Shannon had moved the bedside table against the door and fallen asleep, but hurried footfalls headed in the direction of her door had awakened her and she was up on

162

her feet in an instant. Chase wouldn't have bothered her unless something was terribly wrong. She was half asleep and so confused she wasn't sure what to think. Or maybe someone else was here. The sheriff, ready to lock her up and then turn her over to Hennessey.

She'd stripped out of her sweats and shifted and was just waiting across the room, ready to protect herself. The table was still against the door, and she was still concerned Chase might not be alone. That Hennessey would be with him. He'd shoot her if he could get a shot off before she pounced on him, claiming self-defense. Or maybe, he'd wait until he'd had her manacled and driven off with her. And then shoot her and bury her in a shallow grave somewhere in the woods.

Chase was peering in through the narrow makeshift entrance he'd managed to make to see into the room, the table pushed partly away from the door, his eyes wide. "I'll close the door so you can get dressed and move the table. I'll be waiting in the living room. We need to talk." His voice and look told her he meant what he said, that he wanted to reassure her, but that they had to do this.

He closed the door and walked down the hall to the living room. She heard him take a seat on the couch. She shifted, moved the table, shifted again, then headed for the living room—as a cougar.

He cast her an elusive smile. "It works better if you can talk also."

She sat her romp down on the floor and didn't move. If he said anything she didn't like, she was out of here, running again as a cougar.

"Okay, here's the deal." He explained everything that Dan had told him, including what he had thought—that she had protected herself in self-defense. And that her boyfriend and his family were all shifters.

163

He told her he suspected her boyfriend would have been stronger than her. Not some little guy. But then again, in a fit of rage, people were known to do that which no one would ever believe they could do.

***

Hell, if the sheriff and Chase knew as much as they did, there was no sense in Shannon keeping the secret any longer. Chase wouldn't believe her word against another police officer's, but someone had to hear the truth. And yeah, both of the men were six feet-two, and no way could she have killed her boyfriend all on her own. Though she imagined that if someone was angry enough, maybe he'd been doped up or drunk, and the person caught him off-guard, maybe.

But once she told her side of the story, she had to run. And Chase wasn't stopping her this time.

She loped back into the guest bedroom. To Chase's credit, he stayed on the couch, waiting for her. He didn't come after her to ensure she shifted, dressed, and didn't attempt to sneak out through the bedroom window.

Dressed in the gray sweats, one of the Yuma T-shirts, and socks, Shannon rejoined Chase on the couch and pulled the throw over her lap, keeping her distance from him. She was scowling when she asked, "Did Hennessey mention that he and his brother had some kind of business dealings—I assume illegal—and my boyfriend cheated him on it? That Hennessey was furious and they got into a huge fight and he killed his brother? That I was in the house at the time, though he had thought I was sleeping until I heard the fight and it escalated? That after Hennessey stabbed his brother, he came after me? Did he mention that he found the perfect patsy for his crime? Me? And oh, the best part of it? I have to die. I can't have a prison sentence. Cougar shifters in prison would be a disaster. So I didn't have any choice.

Who do you think they'd believe? A police officer who is the brother of a fellow police officer? Or me?"

"Hell. I believe you, Shannon."

But he still didn't offer to pull her close or comfort her, not that she appeared as though she wanted to be touched at the moment. She might look relaxed while she curled up on the couch, but she was coiled to strip, throw open the door, shift, and run.

"Do you mind if I tell Dan the story?"

"Go ahead. It won't make any difference."

"It sure as hell makes a lot of difference." Chase set his phone down before he called the sheriff, and then he did what she hadn't wanted and yet had wanted him to do, feeling like a bundle of contradictions. He pulled Shannon into his arms and held her tight, his one hand keeping her close, his other hand stroking down her back in a tender caress. "I'm staying with you until we resolve it one way or another."

She was stiff in his arms, wanting to relax, but she couldn't. "The only way to do that is to kill him. You know that, don't you? He's killed his brother. I have to take the blame. There's no other way. If I'm dead, his secret will remain. Even if by some miracle he was found guilty of the murder, the same problem exists. He can't live in prison. He'd have to die."

Chase took a deep breath, running his hand over her hair. "We need to clear your name. We'll take care of this one way or another. He's not touching a hair on your head." And then he lifted her chin.

Her darn eyes were filled with tears. Not once had she had any real hope. Not until Chase had hunted her down. And then, she could have killed him!

He leaned down then, and kissed her.

CHAPTER 11

Chase felt bad that he had never considered that Shannon's accuser had killed his brother and Shannon had been the innocent bystander, running for her life. Anyone who had heard the police officer's version would have thought he told the truth, especially since she had run away. He understood why she would have felt that he and Dan might have thought her guilty because they were also law officers.

Now Chase kissed Shannon's lips, his hands cupping her face, his mouth gentle against hers, rubbing, pressing, lightly pulling her lip with his, and kissing again. It wasn't a kiss borne of lust, or the need to quench some sexual craving, though he admitted touching her, being close to her, kissing her, did make him want more. His body couldn't help reacting to hers.

But when he saw the tears in her eyes, the hope there that he would stick by her, help her, and protect her, he had to kiss her, to seal the bargain, to tell her in no uncertain terms that she wasn't doing this alone.

She finally wrapped her arms around his waist, held him close to her, and sobbed.

For a long time, he just rubbed her back, holding her against him, letting her cry her heart out. He realized then she had to have been sick with grief over her boyfriend's death, but she hadn't even had a moment's rest to consider it while too busy keeping herself alive.

He shouldn't have kissed her, but he couldn't help himself. She seemed to need this as much as he needed to comfort her. When she stopped crying, he got her a tissue from the box on the coffee table. She wiped away her tears and collapsed on the couch. He sat next to her and put his arm around her shoulders.

"Tell me about him."

"Hennessey is a bully."

"Right." But Chase didn't mean about him. "Tell me about your boyfriend."

She looked up at Chase then, and he couldn't tell what she was feeling. "I... I was leaving him. I knew something was wrong. I thought he was seeing other women. But after Hennessey and Ted fought, I realized they were dealing in something illegal. Hennessey thought Ted had cheated them out of money. I don't know who 'they' were but I suspect it's his other brother, Roger, and their uncle. They do everything together. Hunt, fish, play poker. They're just really close. Or had been.

"I was leaving early the next morning. Or at least I had intended to. He'd come home only a day after he had left instead of a week later like he'd planned. I didn't even realize he and Hennessey were in the house until I heard their raised voices. Both were angry. Ted said he'd had expenses. I thought from the sound of his voice that he was lying. If I thought so, his brother, who knew him even better than I did, would have known for certain.

"Hennessey told him that this was the last time he'd cheat him out of his money. I heard the struggle, saw Ted sitting on the floor, bleeding with a knife wound to the chest as I ran for the front door. I had already packed a few things, intending to move out of the house the next morning, and the bags were already in the car. Hennessey saw me and came after me with the bloodied knife. I escaped outside and saw a couple walking their yellow Labrador retriever, their three-year-old son on a tricycle behind them. They all smiled and greeted me. Hennessey stayed in the house. He had blood all over him and the knife in his hand, while I was clean. I was afraid he'd kill the young family if I said anything. He would have covered up everything before he called his office. I knew I couldn't call the police. That I was better off running and disappearing for good. So I got in the car and ran."

"What about his car? It had to have been there. The witnesses would have seen it."

"It wasn't in plain view. I think he intended to kill Ted all along. He was trying to learn the truth and once he was certain of it, he killed him. He said he had cheated him yet again, and he intended to put an end to it. I don't know what illegal dealings the two men were involved in. Drugs, I thought, from the sound of it. All I cared about was getting out of there before Hennessey killed me and made up some home invasion story. Or that I had killed him. Hennessey might have planned to just kill me and make it look like someone had murdered both of us at the same time. But I screwed that up when I witnessed the murder and then fled the house. I have no other family. Being a cougar shifter, I didn't have a lot of options." Shannon let out her breath and frowned. "When I realized they probably were locating me through my cell phone, I ditched it, and then later dumped the car and all my belongings, ID, everything, which would make it seem as though I had met with foul play, and then ran as a cougar for weeks after that."

"How long had you been with Ted?" Chase just couldn't get off the subject.

She looked at him, a little incredulous, he thought. And then she smiled marginally. "A month. I hadn't ever had what you would call a stable home environment once my parents died in a bad car accident coming home from a New Year's Eve party."

"I'm sorry, Shannon." He kissed the top of her head. "How did you meet him?"

She curled up against Chase. "I was running as a cougar in the Palo Duro Canyon and he saw me and chased after me."

"Sounds like you have a penchant for that. Not that I'm anything like him," Chase said quickly.

She smiled up at him. "No, you shot me full of tranquilizer first."

"Yeah, and you had to knock me nearly unconscious to make up for it. Sounds like we have a great thing going." He held her close. She was over the boyfriend. He was glad, afraid she was suffering from a kind of shock. He supposed she might still be to an extent after having witnessed some of what had gone on before her boyfriend was murdered, and then being blamed for it, and being hunted down.

For a long time, they just cuddled together.

He needed to call Dan and let him know what was going on, but for now, he just wanted this.

After a good long while, she finally said, "You need to call Dan about this, don't you?"

"I do. I need to tell him that you're innocent, and that his brother is a real danger to you. I need to know what Dan wants to do in this situation, but if it doesn't mesh with what I want to do, we'll go with the plan I come up with."

"And what plan is that?"

"Keeping you safe. Clearing your name. I don't have any qualms about fighting him. But we need to ensure Hennessey doesn't have a chance to kill you first."

"You'll be at risk, too. He could make up a story that you were my lover..."

Chase smiled at that.

"I'm serious. He could twist things around so it looked like Ted found out about us and got angry and..."

"Hennessey couldn't prove any of it. I've been living here for years, working for the sheriff's department on and off. No one's ever seen you before. No one would believe him. I doubt you've been running around all over the place rather than sticking close to home, either."

"True." She sighed.

"I'll call Dan." As soon as he reached the sheriff, he put it on speakerphone.

He wanted her to know just what he said to Dan and what his friend said in return. Chase put his arm around her shoulders, and it seemed so natural for them to be together like this. He'd changed a lot since he'd married his wife and settled down. He could never go back to the way he was before that.

"Hey, Dan, here's the real story." After talking for a good twenty minutes and telling him everything, Chase finally said, "So what do you think?"

"This is one hell of a mess." Dan asked Shannon several more questions.

She answered them based on her recollections.

"We need to discover what dirty dealings the brothers were involved in," Dan finally said. "If we can prove that Hennessey had the motivation to kill his brother, we'll be in good shape. Also, the young couple that witnessed Shannon leaving the house in a panic might help."

"Or not. They might believe she got out of her bloody things and left in a hurry," Chase warned.

"True, unless we can prove that Hennessey had the motive, the timing was right, and he was trying to blame his brother's girlfriend. I'll get right on this. I'll let Rick and Yvonne know what's up also. Will the two of you be all right up there?"

"Yeah. We have a lot of things to discuss." He smiled down at Shannon. She had no reason not to tell him all about herself now. Not about this business, but just about her. And he had every intention of sharing anything with her that she wished to know. He never talked about some of his past so this would be a change for him, but if it helped Shannon to share, he would do it. "Talk later."

"Out here," Dan said.

She was eyeing Chase with a hint of trepidation.

"All right, it's time for the two of us to talk," he said.

She raised a brow.

"I'll start. My favorite pizza topping is pepperoni. In the summer, I love coffee ice dream with hot fudge dripping down the side."

She smiled just a little.

"I love to swim naked in the lake, either as a cougar or a human. Since I'm close to the lake, I can do it in the middle of the night when no one's around."

Her smile broadened.

"But it would be even better if I had someone to swim with," he said, running his hand down her arm. No pressure, just in a gentle, loving way, telling her he really loved being with her, having her here with him like this, beyond the reason why she was here in the first place.

"Why didn't you settle here before? The people are so friendly and they're our shifter kind. The wide-open spaces are perfect for our kind to run as cougars. It just seems idyllic," Shannon said.

"My ancestors were from here. I wanted to go somewhere else where I could do something with my life. Meet new people. I was tired of being called the Buchannan boy. After I served in the military with Dan, Hal, Rick, and Stryker, as soon as we got out, we got interested in law enforcement."

"Not Rick though. He became a financial advisor."

"He and his wife were FBI agents, but got tired of not being able to enjoy shifting and living with our kind."

Shannon frowned at him. "Wait, they weren't just working at the bank? Don't tell me they were secretly investigating me."

"All we care about is keeping you safe. We had to know what we were facing. And yeah, they were, because you weren't forthcoming about any of this."

Fighting being annoyed, she took a deep breath and let it out. "Okay, so where did you meet your wife? In the new area where you'd started working?"

"Yeah. I was a deputy sheriff in Oklahoma. I might have been one of the good guys, seeing that everyone abided by the laws, but I still had a wild side. When I met Jane, she made me see how good married life with a child could be. Honestly, I was happy. When they were gone, I was adrift. Nothing seemed important any longer. When Dan called, knowing what I was going through and said I had to quit my job and move back to my roots, I fought the idea. At first, I felt like I was quitting the people who lived in my jurisdiction. But then I came here for a visit and it really felt like home. A place where I could heal. I thought I could lose myself in the cabin resort and didn't figure I'd have many renters or troubles."

"Was that the case?"

"Sometimes it was booked. I had a case of a teenage stepson abusing one of the walls of the cabins. He had rage issues. Nearly had a swimmer drown—case of getting drunk. And so forth."

"Did you... lose yourself out here?"

"In a way, yes. I had tons of invites to join in the social goings ons. No one would give up on me. The invites kept coming for the four years I lived here."

"You never went to any of them?"

"To my Special Forces buddies' places, sure. No pressure. We grew up together. They understood how difficult it had been for me to lose Jane and the baby."

"What... what happened? If it's not too difficult to talk about."

He had only talked to Dan about what had happened. Never anyone else. "Not much to tell. I was tracking down a domestic violence case that had turned into murder."

"Did you catch the person?"

"Yeah, but at too great a price. I got an urgent call from the sheriff stating that we'd had a home invasion at our place. My wife of two years and daughter of three months had been murdered. The three men had broken into the locked rifle case and my wife walked in on them from the backyard. She headed for the door with the baby in her arms to escape, but they'd already seen her and they killed them. Just like that."

"I'm so sorry, Chase. Did they catch them?"

"Yeah. Every cop in the state was looking for them. It didn't take long. They used one of my guns in a convenience store hold-up, killed the owner, but the police there pinned them down. Two were killed outright, the other died in the hospital several hours later. But they ruined family's lives for what? A few damn dollars?"

"Yeah," she said. "I'm so sorry."

"Jane had a calming effect on me. She made me settle down."

"Then I came along," Shannon said.

Chase smiled at her.

"Then you started working for the sheriff's department part-time."

"Dan knows me and trusts me. So yeah. It worked out well whenever he needed some extra backup."

"Then you had problems with a she-cat. I bet that was an experience you never expected."

"It's one I wouldn't have missed for the world. So tell me about yourself."

"I love bell peppers for a pizza topping. I love ice cream filled with chunks of toffee candy. As to swimming in a lake naked, I've had my wild side, too."

"I think we're going to have to play some watersports at night when everyone's asleep in their tents." He grew serious then, hating to ask the next question, but he had to know how Shannon had felt about Ted. She had to have been in shock to see him killed before her eyes. Was she in denial about his death? So busy running that she hadn't had time to think about it?

"Did you love him?" Chase asked Shannon.

For the longest time, she didn't answer him. He worried he'd touched on a sensitive issue. That maybe she really hadn't had time to grieve and maybe that's why she said no to sleeping with Chase any longer.

She said, "No," so softly he almost didn't hear her. "I was thrilled to find a male cougar shifter who was available and interested in me, sure. But I wouldn't call it a 'candy hearts and roses' kind of courtship. When my parents died, I was fourteen. My twin brother and I had no one to take us in. We were both living in separate foster homes. He was causing lots of trouble, petty theft, nothing major. I'd dropped out of school at sixteen and run away from my foster home, not wanting any more foster parents. It's really tough when you're a shifter, and they don't understand how you need your privacy, or you want to go out at night when everyone's asleep. Not to do anything bad, but because you are dying to let your cougar half go.

"So I was barely making it on my own, waitressing or doing any odd jobs I could to make ends meet. I finally got my GED and have my high school diploma, and my brother kept popping into my life. I never knew if it was to hide out from the law for a while or because he really wanted to see me. I... ended up dating a couple of his friends." She looked up at Chase. "Not at the same time."

He nodded, smiling a little.

She looked back at her lap. "One was killed robbing a convenience store. He wasn't armed, but they thought he was. The idiot had a banana in his pocket. The other was killed in a high-speed car chase. He hadn't even done anything wrong. But he was afraid that the cop would arrest him for someone else's crime and pin it on him. None of them were more than petty criminals. I was twenty-two when my brother ran into some of the criminal element that were really bad news, and he ended up getting himself murdered.

"We were living in Florida at the time, so I left for Texas. I lived in a small out of the way place in the Panhandle and one night was running in the Palo Duro Canyon, frustrated that I was getting nowhere, not meeting anyone that had our shifter roots, and not dating anyone that was strictly human, though I had a lot of offers at the diner where I worked. When the male cougar took chase, I was afraid at first that he was a real cougar and not a shifter.

"I wore myself out, let him catch up to me, and I smelled his cologne. After the chase, we went our separate ways. But he must have been following me or something. I'd never seen him in the diner where I worked before. He was a cop in another town. But he came in to get lunch, knew I was the cougar shifter he'd chased the night before, and struck up a conversation with me. As a cop, he was doing well financially, but now I wonder if it was due to the illegal business he was conducting. He wanted me to move in with him, and I assumed, since he was one of the good guys and a shifter, that was the break I needed."

Chase was glad she hadn't wanted to stay with the cop, though he imagined she was still having a time coming to grips with seeing him murdered in front of her.

She turned her heard toward the window and he heard it, too.

They both got up to look outside. Ice, mixed with snow, was coming down, the ice particles bouncing off the railing around the deck. Shannon smiled broadly and in that moment, she looked like her whole life had changed around. Chase wanted to be there for her and start anew.

Shannon smiled. "It's snowing. Just a light snow, but look." In that moment, she felt like the snowflakes were angels on wings, and she had witnessed a miracle of nature. Feeling more lighthearted than she'd felt for weeks now, she took hold of Chase's hand and squeezed.

Dottie was right. She should have told someone—Chase---what was going on with her. She hadn't been for certain he would have believed her, or that he'd want to still help her, but she finally had to trust in him to do so.

And it felt good to trust in someone again.

"It's late," Chase said, pulling her into his arms, and he kissed her forehead.

He was waiting for her to say where she wanted to go

next in their relationship. She wanted to join him in bed. Yet, she told herself she should stick with her earlier plan and that meant returning to the guest room.

He finally smiled and said, "If you have to think about it that much, you're coming to bed with me."

And that decided it. Well sort of.

"You're not making a mistake with me, are you?" she asked.

He shook his head, his arm around her waist as he walked her back to his bedroom. "I've made a lot of mistakes in my life. You're not one of them."

It was different this time than the last time where he didn't know who she was and now there were no secrets. And he still wanted her.

"I'll understand if you change your mind," Shannon said practically. She was used to relationships ending badly. She didn't want him to think she would make a big scene if he said he was tired of her and that this wasn't working out for him.

"Whatever gave you that idea?" he asked, pulling away the covers so she could climb into bed.

She was surprised he wanted her to just join him in bed and not get naked first and have sex afterward. Maybe he was trying to show that he was okay with slowing things down a bit. She realized just how much she didn't want to do that. She needed the intimacy, the loving, even if it wasn't for the long term.

She shrugged. "Dottie said you dated a couple of women but it didn't work out. That you..."

His brows arched and she was afraid she'd said too much.

"That I what?" He still held the covers up and motioned for her to move over.

She scooted over and he climbed into bed with her and

pulled the covers over them. Then he caressed her arm with his hand and said, "What did she say?"

"That you sort of became a recluse and didn't date again."

"Which is true. But not with you."

"She said that also. That you would never have gone in the dressing room with another woman. That you had a reputation to uphold."

He smiled.

"But, of course, I told her you had removed the handcuffs and had to keep an eye on me."

"I was afraid you'd run off."

"That's what I told her. She said if I was some other woman, you would have had Millicent come inside with me and you would have stayed outside the room."

Again, he smiled.

"Well? Would you have?"

"No other woman has ever knocked me out and escaped from me. That makes you a special case in my book."

She smiled and then she was serious again. "I don't want you to think you're stuck with me. I mean, the other women had places to go once you decided it wasn't going to work out between you. And if we ever resolve this mess with Hennessey and his family—"

"I don't want you to go anywhere, but stay here with me," Chase said, and leaned down and kissed her forehead.

"But if things work out for me that I don't have to worry about the Kellys any longer and you're tired of..."

"I will still want you here. With me. At my cabin. In my bed."

There was no denying she wanted that, too. Not the way her scent was telling him she eagerly wanted his touches. Her heartbeat had already kicked up the pace, and her breathing was becoming ragged, anticipation building.

And then he began to kiss her, not as wildly or as passionately as last night when they felt like they had to kiss or die from the need. He was gentle as if he was afraid she'd change her mind about them. Or that he wanted to show he really cared about her and this wasn't all about having some mind-blowing sex. She had to admit she enjoyed this with him just as much.

The room was cool now, but with his touching her, he was making her hot and they quickly tossed the comforter aside. He slid his hand up her T-shirt and cupped a breast, his mouth kissing hers, his tongue slipping between her lips and tasting her as she sucked on his tongue, which was warm, wet, and wild. She slid her hands beneath his boxer's waistband and cupped his hard ass.

He groaned a little with frustration.

She smiled. But then he pulled off her sweatpants and tossed them to the floor. He moved her thighs apart, and his hand cupped her mound through the silky panties, his heated gaze studying her face, his oh-so-kissable mouth slowly rising at the corners. She felt the dampness of the fabric press in between her feminine folds as he moved his finger so that he could stroke her through the panties.

Every touch was sending her hurtling toward that point of no-return, everything else seemed to be suspended in time. He continued to stroke her core, and she arched up against his fingers, wanting more, wanting the fabric barrier between them gone. Then he slid his fingers down her panties and the contact of his warm flesh against hers sent a jolt straight through her.

He leaned down to claim her mouth again—her hands cupping his face now, angling for a better kiss, deeper, penetrating. How she loved this and wished it would never end. That she had lived here always and could erase her past with one broad-headed eraser. That this could have been her past, her present, and her future.

She reminded herself that she was with him now, enjoying him the best she could, and that only this minute, here and now mattered.

She kissed him for all she was worth, wanting to show him how much she wanted and needed this—him—just like this.

He must have sensed her quiet desperation, as he pulled his lips away from hers for a moment and gazed into her eyes. His were darkened with lust. Hers were blurred with a faint shimmer of tears, but she wouldn't... *couldn't* let him stop what he was doing to her. She tugged him down in a way that said for him to get on with pleasuring her because he was dead meat if he didn't.

He kissed her then, a little unsurely as if he was afraid to upset her, but she was aggressive right back, telling him in no uncertain terms that she wanted this now, and the only way to truly upset her was to give up on her.

Her aggressive kisses, biting softly on his mouth, and sucking at his tongue encouraged him to mirror her assertiveness. And she loved it. Sweet and gentle could be for some other time, or never—because she didn't have forever with him.

Then she was pulling down his boxers, and he was back to stroking her harder, his fingers slipping inside her folds, deeper, and she ground out, "Chase."

Arching into his fingers, she felt the sweet, spicy hit of the climax as it worked its way up her body, and she basked in the warmth and satisfaction of what his touching did to her. His expression subtly changed as he hurried to ditch his boxers, and then her panties—to one of concentration and determination to have her, to claim her.

She thought he would pull off the T-shirt she was

wearing with the bold words stamped across it: *Cougar Power*, featuring a beautiful golden cougar in the middle of it, watching the viewer with her golden eyes, ears perked. But he didn't. He just moved Shannon's legs wider, ran his hand up her shirt to massage a breast, then pressed the head of his cock between her folds and pushed deep.

Chase hoped making love to Shannon would help to convince her to stay with him. He was certain she was teetering on staying or running. When she showed just how much she wanted him now, he wasn't about to stop, though the shimmer of tears in her eyes had given him pause. But the expression on her face was one of either you do this or she would kill him.

Which had made him smile a bit. Her volatility from being one way and then another, her enthusiasm, bordering on wildness, definitely her hotness, made him hard with wanting her.

He thought to remove her T-shirt, but decided against it. He loved the image—her naked and bared to him from the waist down, the cougar imprinted on her shirt challenging him with her eyes as if it was a picture of the cougar splayed out beneath him, and he knew the words imprinted on the shirt were true. This cougar shifter had all the power over him. And he loved it.

Only he wished he knew how to make her stay with him for the long run.

He inhaled in her scent—the wildness, the cougar, and the woman, who had bathed in the rose mint scent, spicy and sweet—that made his cock swell to full attention.

He buried himself to the hilt in her warm, wet sheath and captured her mouth for another long and lingering kiss. Desperately, he wanted her to know how deeply he felt about her, not as a quick sex-fest and he was done with her, but like he wanted to make a lasting impression. Like he wanted to show her how much he cared.

And then he was pulling out and working into her again, as she kissed him just as passionately, her fingernails lightly scratching his back like a big cat's claws in play, gently, not drawing blood. Her golden eyes were open, watching him, her fingers trailing down to his buttocks and squeezing. And then she wrapped her legs around his hips, and he dove even deeper, loving this, loving her.

He wanted to tell her how much he wanted her to stay, but he was afraid it would push her away—as if this was the only bit of pleasure she'd allow herself, and that she couldn't commit to anything further. Nothing permanent.

He realized how much he was at odds with the notion and slipped his tongue between her lips. Her hands moved up to his waist, clutching as she rolled her hips a little, making him groan into her mouth. Wild cat was all he could think of as he spilled his seed deep inside her, continued to thrust, to finish what he had begun, when she arched her back and closed her eyes and cried out.

"Ah," he growled, sinking against her briefly before he rolled onto his back, pulling her with him. He wanted to keep her pinned down beneath him, unable to squirm her way out from under him, and out of his grasp. He was reminded of the day when he'd had to handcuff her, and she'd rocked against him, trying to unseat him, how much her actions had stirred his blood even back then.

But he wanted the shared feelings of mutual respect, that she wanted to be with him and not that he was forcing it on her. Though he would do anything he could to convince her how staying with him was the only option left to her. Not only the best option, but that she truly wanted to be with him.

He let out a frustrated sigh, vowing to enjoy each and every moment with her for as long as they had. But he wanted her to know that he wasn't about to think in terms of her leaving, but in terms of her staying. "Next time, I want to see you in that little pink nightie you bought at Millicent's shop that had all the women who saw it already speculating about us."

Shannon smiled.

CHAPTER 12

For two and a half weeks, Chase and Shannon gone to all kinds of social gatherings to family's homes for dinners, movies, tea parties, just anything anyone could think of to keep them busy and for Shannon to practically meet everyone who lived there.

So when Chase told her they were staying home for the day so he could get some work done on the cabins, Shannon was secretly thrilled. She knew that all the invitations were a way for the other shifters to reach out to her and let her know they cared about her and wanted to form friendships. And she truly loved them for it. She had to admit, it was the reason she had put off leaving for so long. Although, that was only part of it. Most of it had all to do with Chase. Despite her saying no to him getting her anything else, he had gone out of his way to buy more clothes for her so she felt like she wouldn't have to wash clothes constantly, and she had some choice in what she wore. And because he kept taking her out to see people.

She knew when she left he would not be happy, just like her leaving him behind would make her despair for him.

She was straightening up the kitchen after they'd had pizza last night and had gotten a little frisky while watching one of Dottie's romance movies, Chase telling her the hero was so lame and Shannon challenging him to prove to her what the hero should really be like.

That had led to wild sex on the couch, forget the movie. Then he'd turned it off, and tossed her over his shoulder, carried her to bed and he showed her again what a romantic hero was all about, which had her laughing and loving him all the more. But they'd left a mess of everything that she was now cleaning up.

This morning was the first time since Chase had come into her life that he was up later than she was.

She guessed her waking him to make love to her a couple of more times during the night had worn the poor guy out. She smiled at the notion when he joined her in the kitchen all dressed—jeans, a shirt, and boots. She greeted him with a plate of hot French toast and a kiss. She sure could get used to this.

"You said you were going to paint this morning. Can I help?" she asked, wanting to do something more than be a fixture around the place.

They took their seats at the table. Chase poured maple syrup on his French toast.

"Sure. Do you really want to?"

"I'd like to feel like I'm being useful around here. I've painted some... well, it's been a long time ago. Maybe when I was five and I used my hands and not a brush."

He chuckled. "I can't say enough how much I enjoy your company. You don't have to do anything, but wake me up at night to keep me on my toes."

She smiled. "I've... I've enjoyed being here with you, too. I still want to help."

"Sounds good to me. I checked last night on the supplies and we have just enough to paint the living room. Are you ready?"

"Sure am."

She was wearing the gray sweats, figuring they were

perfect for painting since she didn't care for the color anyway, in case she dripped a little paint on them.

They headed to the cabin furthest from Chase's, and once inside, they first moved the furniture out of the way, then taped, and laid down plastic to protect the wood floors. That took about an hour, but with the two of them working well as a team, that had probably saved them a lot of time. Chase began rolling paint on the walls while she was doing the detail work, the corners and edgings. He had brought over some wild music to play while they were working, and she had to pause to observe him dancing to the beat.

She chuckled and he smiled. "Painting has never been this much fun before, I have to admit," he said, turning back to face the wall and rolled another layer of paint over it.

"You make it fun," she said. She filled up her tray with more paint and was just crouching down to paint along the baseboard when a mouse scurried across the plastic and she fell back, annoyed with herself for her reaction to seeing a mouse. She was a cat, for heaven's sake! A big cat.

But she tipped the tray of paint she was holding and spilled some of it on her sweatshirt and pants. Trying to avoid getting it all over herself, she tried to stand and stepped back and realized too late that the object behind her that she had bumped into was the can of paint.

Normally she could react quickly, but with the tray of paint in her hand, the paintbrush in the other, and being off balance, she knew there was only one way this was going. Her falling, knocking over the can of eggshell white paint, making a mess, and creating a total disaster.

Between the beat of the music and Chase working on the wall behind her with his back to her, he didn't see the catastrophe going down. Not that he could have done anything to prevent it, rescue her, or save the paint.

All she could think of as the paint poured out of the can and she was sitting in a puddle of it, soaking it up with her sweats, he would never want her helping him to paint again.

As quickly as she could, she jerked the overturned can of paint right side up, but the damage was already done. She was just glad they'd covered most of the floor with plastic and all of the paint was either on her or on the plastic. She looked over to see if Chase had even noticed.

He was still shaking his booty to the music and rolling the paint on the wall.

She smiled, shook her head, and sighed. "I hate to tell you this, Chase, but I think we might need another can of paint."

"There should be plenty enough in that can to cover the walls," he said, glancing at her. For a second, he just took in the sight of her sitting there, covered in white paint, a mess of it on the plastic, and of course, there wasn't any sign of the mouse so she couldn't even point to him as the culprit.

Not that she'd really want to, either. A big cat shouldn't get spooked by a little mouse.

Then Chase burst out laughing. That made her smile. She was glad he wasn't mad at her.

He joined her and peered into the can of paint. "You're right. We're going to need some more paint."

"I've got to get cleaned up. I'm soaked through to my panties and bra."

He was still chuckling. "Sorry, I can't help it. You are so cute. Okay, can you manage to get back to the cabin and get washed up on your own? I'll clean this up and run into town for some more paint. If you still want to help me finish the job, you can join me then."

"You still want me to?" she asked skeptically.

He laughed. "Yeah, I do. I hate doing the detail work and you've made a great start on it. Maybe I should get two cans of paint, just to be sure we have enough."

"You have mice," she said, as he helped her to stand.

He started chuckling again. "You saw a mouse."

She rolled her eyes and headed out the door. She stalked back to his cabin, and when she got there, she stripped off all her clothes, and wiped up most of the excess paint that had seeped through to her skin with the unpainted part of her sweatshirt, then dumped it with the rest of her clothes on the grass. She'd have to wash them out as soon as she took a shower. She didn't envy Chase having to clean up her mess at the other cabin.

But she was glad that he was so good-natured about it.

When she reached the bathroom, she saw she even had splatters of paint on her face and in her hair. She groaned, started the shower, climbed in, and began to soap up.

"I'll be right back," Chase hollered to her. "If you need anything..."

"No. Thanks. I've got to wash my clothes out next, and we can finish painting when you get back."

"Okay, take me no more than half an hour or so."

"See you shortly," she called out, and then she relaxed and enjoyed the shower. She didn't look forward to cleaning her sweats. What a mess.

When she was finished with her shower, she threw on her jeans and the gray sweater, grabbed a trash bag, and headed outside. After dumping her clothes into the bag, she took them inside and began cleaning them out in the kitchen sink. This was a hundred times worse than cleaning paintbrushes. The paint just kept pouring out of her clothes no matter how much she ran the water over them and kept squeezing out the paint. If she'd had a lot more clothes to wear, she would have just figured they were now her paint clothes. But she wore them to snuggle up with Chase on the couch while they watched movies, warmer than her pink nightie that was more suitable for cuddling with him in bed later.

That had her thinking about how long she was staying and how she was fighting with herself over leaving, and letting Chase and the others help her. Every day she'd tell herself she'd stay just a little longer.

But she felt strangely at home here—with Chase. Every day she'd look at the calendar, feeling a little panicked, telling herself she couldn't keep putting off leaving here forever. That she should have already left well before hunting season had arrived—and it had already begun.

Thanksgiving was nearly here. And when she knew she shouldn't, she'd promised to go to the Muellers' for Thanksgiving with Chase in just a few days. He'd told her how he hadn't celebrated it in years and how much it would mean to him if she'd go with him. He'd already done so much for her, and she had to admit the lure of turkey and the works and spending the time with him and his friends appealed more than her wanting to leave.

But after that, she needed to go. She was certain her good fortune wouldn't last forever.

Over the spray of the faucet water, she thought she heard a vehicle pull up outside.

She couldn't believe it had taken her that long to shower and wash her clothes—that she was still washing. She listened to the sound of the vehicle's engine. It wasn't Chase's hatchback. Her heartbeat quickened, and she quickly turned off the kitchen faucet.

The engine ran rougher, sounded noisier, more... ominous. Maybe someone wanted to rent a cabin. Or maybe someone had come by to see Chase. But she didn't believe so. Everyone knew her situation. She was certain they would have called ahead and let him know, and he would have warned her if they were coming. Maybe it was that pesky reporter again, and he knew she was alone.

She dried off her hands and ran to the bedroom to get the phone. She pulled it off the bedside table and called Chase. "Chase—"

"Yeah, did you need something while I'm in town?" he asked, sounding cheerful when her blood was running cold. "I'm just about through with getting the paint mixed. I'll be there in about ten minutes."

"Someone just parked outside your cabin."

Three doors opened, but they didn't slam shut. Whoever it was she thought was attempting to be quiet. With her enhanced cat hearing, she heard everything.

"At least three people." Her voice was soft, but trembled. She hated feeling like she was the hunted, the prey again, when for the past two and half weeks she'd felt almost normal, living like anyone else in the town, happy with Chase and with those who had welcomed her so warmly. She glanced at the rifle cabinet and noted it was locked.

"I'm in my car and headed back. Is the front door locked?" he asked, his voice hard, police-like.

"Yes."

She eyed the door, listening to their movement, heard someone's boots walking across the deck toward the living room window. She was thankful the curtains had remained shut—her wish, feeling safer like that, hating that she still hadn't felt entirely safe here. Chase had been sweet enough to accommodate her in anything she had wanted.

At least the men couldn't see her through any of the windows.

"I'm on my way back, Shannon. Do you know how to

shoot a rifle?" Chase asked, giving her a chance to see what was going on before he intruded on her thoughts.

"Yes, but I already checked, and the gun cabinet's locked. There are at least three people out there and no one has spoken a word." Which made her believe they were men, that they were after her, and they were motioning with hand signals. She hoped she was just being paranoid.

Someone knocked on the door, and she jumped a little, her heart beating hard, her eyes fastened on the solid oak, but she was listening for where the others were. Hennessey wouldn't bother knocking, would he?

The one at the door could very well be a distraction while the others tried to find a way in. Instantly, she thought of Hal's house and how she had managed to find an unlocked window. She'd known, from her brother and his friends' scrapes with the law, that often people left a window unlocked, second-story windows usually, figuring no one would climb up to reach them.

Now, she worried that Chase might have an unlocked window somewhere in the house. She thought she heard someone try to lift the living room window. Nothing happened. It was locked. But the fact someone would try the window, meant these people were trouble.

"They're trying to get in through an unlocked window," she said to Chase, her voice unsteady.

"I'll be there, Shannon. I'm only minutes away. The lock combination to the rifle cabinet is—"

"Shannon," Hennessey called out, making Chase stop talking to her on the phone. Chase had heard.

"We know you're in there and that the boyfriend has left you all alone. Open the door and make it easy on yourself. All we want is to know where Ted hid the money," Hennessey yelled. "Your boyfriends always end up dead, don't they? Let this one live. Come on out. We just want that money. I'll only give you one chance to cooperate. Wait—you don't think I killed Ted in cold blood, do you?"

Of course he had. What did he think? She was an idiot?

She swallowed hard. They'd been watching the cabin. For how long? They couldn't have been watching it all that long or they could have grabbed her when she went out to get her clothes that were covered in paint.

But she knew Hennessey lied about Ted. She hadn't thought anything of the money that Ted had stolen. He said he'd paid expenses with it. She'd figured he'd spent it. But his brothers must have thought otherwise. How much had he stolen? Why would they think Ted would have confided in her?

And then she remembered the last things that were said right before she escaped. Hennessey had asked where he had the money. Ted had seen her and said her name, as if he had forgotten she was in the house, or that she might be hurt next. Had Hennessey thought Ted was saying Shannon knew where the money was?

Even if she did know and could tell Hennessey, he would still want her dead. She had witnessed him murdering his brother.

"What you saw was a case of self-defense. Ted came after me with one of your butcher knives. I only just managed to wrestle it away from him. I didn't want to hurt him. I had to know where the money was."

"It's them," she said to Chase in a hushed voice. "Hennessey and two others. I... I love you, Chase. Always remember that." She didn't believe Hennessey had accidentally killed his brother. Maybe they had fought over the knife, but he still wanted Shannon dead.

"Shannon, the combination on the gun cabinet is..."

She didn't hear the rest of Chase's words as she shoved the phone in her jeans pocket. She was already running for his bedroom. If she could strip off her clothes, make it to his bedroom window, and open it in time, she could shift, leap out into the woods, and run.

Even if she'd managed to get into the rifle cabinet in time, she couldn't kill all three men, and she'd be a sitting duck. But someone was likely to hear her shoving the window up at the back of the house, and then he would run around the back while alerting the others. Or someone might already be at the window. She hoped they were watching *her* bedroom window instead.

She had her sweater off and tossed it in the hall. She had to pause to kick off her socks, and when she reached Chase's bedroom, she pulled off her jeans and panties. Even as a cougar, she would be able to fight at least one of them before they shot her dead. A crash sounded as something struck the glass in the living room window, making her heart skip a few beats. Someone banged hard against the front door. It was solid oak and wouldn't budge.

More tinkling of breaking glass in the living room sounded as someone must have been trying to make it safe enough to climb through the window.

Heart hammering against her ribs, she locked Chase's bedroom door, and ran to his window, still unclasping her bra, then tossed it aside. Then she peered out through the curtains. No sign of anyone.

Footfalls ran down the hall, two pairs. One of the men threw open the door to her guest bedroom and it banged against the wall just as she unlocked the sash to Chase's window and shoved the window up. Thank God it wasn't stuck like the one at Ted's house. She felt a case of déjà vu all over again.

She shifted just as the bathroom door was thrown open and then the hall closet door was opened.

Tears collected in her eyes and she thought of leaving

Chase behind, as she leapt through the window. Angry at herself for being upset now, she fought to keep a clear head. Adrenaline poured into her veins, boosting her ability to fight or flee. Not having a choice, she had to escape these men for now because she couldn't make a stand alone. But realization dawned: she had to quit being the prey and become the hunter.

She, who had never committed a crime in her life— until she came here—had every intention of killing at least one of the three men if she could. *If* she could manage to get the advantage before they got her first.

***

Fearing for Shannon's life and his own heart doing double time, Chase sped back to his cabin, only minutes away from his resort, still listening on the phone when he heard the glass breaking at his place. Shannon had quit talking to him, and he knew she had to be trying to save herself. He quickly ended the call and got hold of Dan, who would have Dottie call every cougar shifter who was a capable hunter in the area to join him at his place. Well, not exactly join him, but follow him. Because if Shannon managed to escape, she'd be gone, running as a cougar. And the men after her? They would have no choice but to shift to catch up to her if they intended to take her down.

With their longer legs and more powerful muscles, they would be able to catch up to her even if she had a head start.

He couldn't lose her and his stomach twisted into knots as he felt he was reliving his wife and baby's deadly ordeal—home invasion, three ruthless men, no one to protect his family in time.

"Three men," Chase said, "and she said the one man was Hennessey."

"I've got Dottie calling everyone. Everyone will be on

their way in a heartbeat. They're grabbing rifles and whatever other gear we need. Medical supplies, the works. I'm on my way. My deputy's headed back from his vacation, saying there's way too much excitement around here to bother soaking up the sun in Costa Rica any longer."

He'll be too late, Chase thought morosely. This was going to end now.

"I'm at my place now, black Humvee out front, living room window shattered, no smell of any of the three men in the vicinity. They have to be cloaking their scent with hunter's spay." Which made sense or they would have alerted Shannon they were here.

Chase unlocked the front door and raced through the cabin. All the doors were open except his bedroom door. "They couldn't break through my solid oak bedroom door. She's got to have gone out the window from there."

He raced back through the cabin. He could have just stripped and shifted and run, but he had to discover if she'd managed to get away and if the men were in pursuit as cougars or humans. He had to let Dan know what they were up against so he could tell the rest of the hunters. Though he suspected Hennessey and the others were still chasing her or they would have returned to their vehicle and left already.

When he came around the outside of the house, he saw his bedroom window was open. He ran up to it and peered inside, ensuring she wasn't lying in there wounded or dead. Shannon's clothes were tossed every which way. "She's running as a cougar," he said to Dan.

Not that he'd had any doubts. Unless she'd had a gun and knew how to use it, she'd be better off with her cougar's teeth and claws.

Then he ran a short distance into the woods and found where the men had ditched their rifles and clothes.

"They've shifted, Dan. They're going to kill her as cougars."

"The hell they are," Dan growled. "Be there in three minutes."

"Okay, I'm stripping and shifting." Not only would Hennessey and his men be after her, but so would every human hunter if they spotted her, looking to make their kill for the season. "Ready," he said, now naked. "See you soon."

Chase dropped his phone onto his clothes, shifted, feeling like one growly mountain lion ready to kill a bunch of males. He smelled her panicked scent and prayed she could hold out until he reached her.

He was feeling the same gnawing panic when he'd been too late to save his wife and baby. He couldn't be too late *this time*.

***

Shannon headed to her old stomping grounds—at least it felt that way to her—the cave near the waterfall. She needed the height, the advantage of knowing the area, what was below her, and that they couldn't get to her from up above without her seeing them first. She didn't have much hope of killing all three of the men. Maybe not even one of them, unless she got damned lucky. But she had to give Chase a chance to reach her. She knew he'd let the others know and everyone who could, would be on their way to help her out.

She just had to manage by herself until then.

She had never wanted something so badly—a home with Chase, with these people who had made her feel so welcome, a chance to set down roots and never have to run again. And now it was all about to be taken away from her.

She'd reached the cave, but she stayed near the ledge where she laid down. A few golden grasses had managed to sprout up there and with her golden coloring, she was well hidden as long as she kept her head low. They wouldn't have to see her though. Just smell her scent and follow it.

The cats could move so quietly and with the waterfall muffling any sound of their movement, she didn't think she would hear them before it was too late. Just suddenly, three cats would leap into her space, and she'd have to decide which one to fight before the others lunged for her.

She envisioned that Chase had reached the cabin already and that he was in hot pursuit of the men. He might even reach one before they managed to find their way to her. Then she'd have only two to deal with.

On the other hand, she could see Chase getting himself killed over her. If he tackled one of the men, the others would return to help him out. They wouldn't come after her then. Not until they finished him off. He would be the greater threat to one male.

She couldn't allow it. He had to wait for the others to join him as backup. She'd never felt she was cursed, but what if she was? With three dead boyfriends to her name?

She stood up and snarled and growled and screamed in the way only a cougar could to tell Hennessey she was ready for him. She couldn't allow the three of them to gang up on Chase and kill him.

***

As soon as Chase heard Shannon's cougar calls, he felt ripples of chills run through his blood. She was alerting her pursuers where she was.

Why?

They would already know the way she had gone. She had to know that he would go after the men and be on his way so she didn't need to alert him. She needed to be quiet and keep low.

She was silent for a moment, and then she began snarling again. It wasn't a *"fight for a life"* sound, but an angry *"come and get it"* sound. As if she was tired of running, and she was ready to make a stand.

But she couldn't. Not against even one hefty male cougar.

Chase leapt over fallen trees and moss-covered rocks, dove through the underbrush, no longer tracking her, but following the sound of her growly calls, which he thought were bouncing off the cave where she'd been before she saved the boy at the waterfall. He rushed to join her so they could make a stand together. He thought that at least one of the men would have reached her by now. But she wasn't fighting for her life yet. Had her actions startled them? Made them regroup a bit? Trying to figure out what her ploy was?

If she was one thing—she was unpredictable.

And he loved that about her. Hell, he loved her for all her vulnerability, her sassiness, her caring, everything that made her the she-cat that she was.

Somehow, he would save her.

What he didn't expect was to see a male cougar he didn't recognize standing still up ahead. He was slightly overweight, which would make him harder to take down, but Chase could maneuver quicker. The cougar had a few gray hairs, so he was older, too. He probably wasn't Hennessey then, but maybe his uncle.

He was just standing there, his ears twitching as he listened to Shannon's calls, not moving an inch, wary, uncertain. Chase didn't see any sign of the other two men in their cat forms, and lunged, jumping a good twenty feet to make the connection just as he heard Shannon's snarls change to fighting posture. One of the men had reached her.

His chilled blood turned to ice in his veins as he bit into the cougar's shoulder. He hoped to hell Shannon could hold out until he reached her. The cougar had seen Chase in his peripheral vision just before Chase had pounced, and attempted to swing around to face him head on. Which was why Chase had only bitten him in the shoulder and not the back of the neck where he could have made a quick and sudden killing blow.

He'd gotten in a few good scratches, trying to avoid tackling the bastard head on. With his weight, the other cat might be able to pin Chase down. But then the sound of men running through the brush stole his attention. Chase's first thought was that the men were some of their kind, and would be armed with rifles and take out the cat he was fighting. It was already cougar hunting season though and Chase couldn't be certain.

A shot suddenly rang out. The round nicked Chase's ear and hurt like a son-of-a-bitch. Granted, he and the other cat clawed and snarled, and attacked, both trying to angle in the right position to get a killing hold on his opponent. So he understood it was hard to get a bead on the right cougar.

Another shot slammed into a nearby tree, missing him and the other cat. The one he fought snarled and leapt away into the woods to safety.

Chase didn't wait to ensure the men were off to hunt the other cat down, but ran to save Shannon. Another round smacked into a tree near his rump. Damn! They weren't some of his kind. They had to be cougar hunters. Not cougar shifters!

He was liable to lead them straight to Shannon, but he couldn't help it. She was fighting for her life up in the rocks. He couldn't deviate from taking the most direct path to her. The only good thing was he didn't hear a second cougar fighting her. Just the one, which could mean he was waiting in the wings.

As soon as Chase saw the rocks up ahead, he suddenly

felt an eerie bit of déjà vu. Except this time he wasn't climbing the rocks as a human, Shannon was fighting a cougar, and hunters were hot on his tail. As soon as he began his ascent, he would be exposed to the woods until he could get far enough back on the ledge and out of the hunters' sights. The good thing was that they would have to catch up to him, and he was running far too fast for them. Still, their boots tromped through the brush some distance back, and he wanted to turn his anger on them. But his focus had to remain straight ahead.

Once Dan arrived with reinforcements, *he* could stop the men from hunting the cougars even if they had the license to do so. He'd come up with a damn good reason why they suddenly couldn't hunt in the area. Dan just had to get there in time.

What if a bunch of shifters in their cougar forms arrived to help Chase and Shannon? The hunters would be assured that there were plenty enough of them to kill. And then? All it would take would be for one cougar to die and turn into a human in front of the hunters.

Chase finally reached the rocks. He leapt onto one ledge, and then the next, getting closer to the growls and snarls of the two cats, Shannon's and another's. Before he could reach the cave ledge, he growled to let her know he was coming to her rescue and to warn the cougar fighting her that he had more of an opponent to battle, hoping Chase would garner all his attention. To Chase's horror, Shannon, bloodied and injured, jumped off the cave ledge above him.

No ledge jutted out below her in that direction to afford her a safe way down. Only a seventy-five foot drop to the waterfall pool below existed. She plummeted to the water, her legs stiff, as if she was about to land on the ground. She plunged into the deep, cold water nearly giving him heart failure.

Desperately, he wanted to see her swim to the surface, but the cat she'd been fighting jumped onto the ledge where Chase stood. The cougar appeared to be about his age, as well muscled, but bleeding on his shoulder and leg. His mouth sported blood. Sickened to think the blood was Shannon's, Chase tore into him. Chase had to end this quickly before the hunters saw two cougars fighting and shot them both. He had to get to Shannon. What if she had drowned? Or had injured herself badly? He couldn't think of that now, not with the cat in front of him trying to rip out his throat.

A gunshot sounded and the round pinged off a rock to Chase's right. *Hell.* Chase leapt onto the rock above him where he could fight the other cat nearer the cave and the hunters couldn't see them.

For a moment, Chase didn't think the cat was going to follow him. Had he decided to leave before he got shot, or had to face a male cat instead of a weaker female? *Bastard.*

Without warning, the cat jumped onto the ledge. Before the cougar could get the first bite in, Chase pounced and took the advantage.

***

Forever Shannon swam toward the surface of the waterfall's pool of water this time. She had been wrong about how deep it was. Thank God. The water was much deeper than ten feet, and she hadn't killed herself as she feared she might. She couldn't have fought Roger any further. When she heard Chase's growl, she did the only thing she could do—she jumped—a last desperate chance to save herself.

Men were coming, their boots running through the brush as they searched for the cat that had jumped from such a height and landed in the pool. Was it Dan or his

201

men? She couldn't take the risk that it was if it was not. She had to do what her kind should never do. Not wet and in this cold weather. Not when the last the men had to have seen of her, she had been a golden cougar. If they found her, which was inevitable, and they were hunters, they wouldn't hesitate to shoot and kill her. Their boots crunched through the fallen leaves, and if they were hunters, they'd be excited with the chase and the promise of a kill. Even if she was half dead already. Some mighty hunters that would make of them.

She was spent, wounded, bleeding, and struggling to paddle to the rocky beach. She intended to hide under the shelter of the rocks where she had taken the boy who had fallen in the pool so long ago to save his life.

She dragged herself out of the water and limped to the rocky overhang. She shifted out of sight, right before the first of the men scrambled down the rocks to reach her. Her leg and side burned as if they were on fire.

She was bleeding and freezing all at once, shivering, and not believing she could hurt any worse than she did this minute. The water-pummeled rocks serving as her bed were smooth at least, but cold and hard beneath her naked body as she collapsed on top of them and shivered uncontrollably.

Way up above in the rocks, Chase and Roger's angry growls persisted, and she prayed Chase came out the victor. If she could have, she would have helped him. But she couldn't have done a thing and it was better for Chase for her to get out of his way.

She heard the first of the men land on the rocks nearby. She glanced at him briefly. His bearded jaw was slack, his rifle in his hands, blue eyes wide, and he was wearing camouflaged hunter's gear. He was a hunter, not a shifter. He had fully intended to shoot and kill a wounded cougar.

For a second, he stared at her naked, bruised, and bloodied *human* body as if his mind was still trying to recall what he had last seen—a wounded, bloodied, golden cougar.

"Holy shit," the hunter finally said.

That's just the way she was feeling right before her world vanished in a sea of black.

CHAPTER 13

The hunters shouted to each other down below, warning each other about the badly wounded woman. Chase knew then that Shannon had made it out of the pool, but she wasn't out of danger. She must have shifted before the men saw her do it. It was the only thing she could have done under the circumstances. She would be naked, freezing, and badly injured.

"She's alive. I'll give her my coat. Someone else have something to bind her wounds?"

"Yeah, wait. I'll give you my flannel shirt."

Chase was glad the men were taking care of her.

The cougar that Chase was fighting heard the conversation, too, and paused to listen to hear what else was being said. Chase lunged at him in what he hoped was the last time he'd have to in an attempt to kill the cougar. Both of them were wearing out. He wondered briefly what had happened to the other men who had been with this one.

For now, he concentrated on killing *this* cougar. Chase attacked and bit into his neck, sinking his teeth deep. The cougar struggled to get free, but Chase held on, determined to make this the final killing blow.

The cougar finally collapsed on the rocky ledge, his heartbeat slowing, and then it was gone. Chase released him.

Desperate to get to Shannon, Chase couldn't go to her as a cougar. And he sure as hell couldn't reach her as a naked man. Loose rocks below him fell as someone climbed up the face of the rock headed in his direction. Hell, the hunters couldn't be foolhardy enough to climb up there and try to shoot him. If Chase had been a real cougar, he could kill the hunter before he had a chance to ready his rifle. He glanced down at the dead man. This looked really bad though. A bloodied, naked, dead man lying at Chase's cougar paws. *Really* bad.

Chase didn't have any choice, either. He shifted. He was nearly as bloody as the dead man, shivering, and pissed off that he couldn't go to Shannon.

The climber's head crested the rock ledge, and Chase saw that it was Dan. Relief washed over him in waves.

"Hell, Chase, what did you go and shift for? It's too damn cold for that." Dan continued to climb up the rock face.

"What about Shannon?" He couldn't talk as a cougar and he had to know about Shannon.

"Where in the hell is she?" Dan asked.

"The same place she was when she protected the boy—down on the rocky beach next to the waterfall pool." Hell, he'd thought Dan was already on it.

Breathing hard, Dan reached the ledge. "Hell, I didn't think I'd ever have to come this way again. Not as a human. Shift. I'll watch your back with the hunters."

"What about the other men that were after Shannon?"

"We've got men and cougars after them. We'll catch them before long."

"They're wearing hunter's spray."

"Hell, I know, but they're tracking other signs they've been running through the brush. We need one of them alive so he can take the word back to their police station to let them know that *this* was the man who killed his brother."

"Hennessey? This is the one?"

"Yeah. Now shift before you catch pneumonia."

"Shannon…"

"I'm on it." Dan had already yanked his phone out of his pouch and had punched in a number, waiting for a response. "Rick, you know where Shannon saved the boy at the falls? She's at the same beach, same area she was in when she protected him."

"She's badly wounded and in her human form," Chase said.

"Did you hear that? Get the word out to everyone, whoever can reach her quickest needs to get there ASAP."

"Hunters are with her," Chase warned.

"No cougars. Hunters are on the scene," Dan added.

Despite having a million more questions to ask, like how the hell they were getting Hennessey down from here, Chase was too cold to do anything else but shift.

Then he paced as a cougar, tail whipping back and forth in agitation.

"Yeah, she's where she rescued the boy," Dan said to Rick. "Naked. I've got Hennessey and he's dead. Chase is beat up a bit, but he's going to live. I want the others caught and taken alive if possible. We've got to get Hennessey down from here. All right. Out here." Dan glanced at Chase. "We'll get her and take care of her. We'll ensure she never has to run again. If you want her and she wants you, the whole town is ready to celebrate."

Hell yeah, he wanted her. And if he had any say in it at all, she was staying with him for the long run.

Dan's phone rang and he frowned. "Okay. Good show. Bring up the gear and we can get down from here." He ended the call. "Some of our men have reached her. One of the hunters had already wrapped her in his parka. She'll live. They're carrying her back to the lake where the closest vehicle is. They've told the men to clear out of the area as this is a police matter."

Chase wondered how the hunters would take that. Cougar nearly kills woman and suddenly the police don't want anyone involved in hunting down the cat?

"A couple of our guys are going to give them a ride to their vehicle and they can drive about ten miles from here and hunt to their heart's content. Our men will let us know when the hunters are far enough away so that you can join Shannon."

All of this was taking too long. Someone else began climbing up to the cave and Chase was ready to shift and take Dan's parka. No, two more people. Dan peered over the edge. "Hey, Hal, Jacob, glad you made it okay." Then Dan got a call. "Yeah? Okay, I'll tell him." Dan said to Chase, "The hunters are out of here."

Chase didn't pause to consider the news. He leapt to the ledge below this one, and kept going until he reached the slope. From there he tore off, leaping and running for the cover of the woods. Once he reached the relative safety of the forest, he raced through the underbrush, his heart thumping hard, his pace frantic.

He wanted to be with her for the ride to the clinic. Not once had Dan said how bad off she was. She needed Chase at her side. To know how much he cared about her. Moving too fast, he wasn't his usual wary self and watching his surroundings while running as a cougar. A branch broke beneath someone's footfall. Chase dove beyond a tree. The rifle blast sounded and the round hit him in the flank. Sharp pain stabbed him. He stumbled. Snarled. Damn it to hell.

He got back to his feet and kept on running. He prayed the hunter couldn't reach him in time before Chase made it to his place. His side burned and ached. He was in the most god-awful pain, but he had to reach the cabin before the hunter could get him in his sights for a second time. Chase stumbled again, cursing himself. He just had to reach the safety of his place. Another hundred or so yards. Just a little farther.

Blood coated his flank, the pain excruciating, and he felt lightheaded. The woodpile came into view and it would provide a little shelter for a minute while he caught his breath and made his next move. The hunter crunched through the woods, running after him.

Just a little farther. Another shot pinged off a tree. Damn it.

Chase skidded through the fallen leaves and dashed around the wood pile. Panting he stared at the back of his cabin. He had to get into his house, shift, and apply pressure to his bloody wound. And he had get word of his injury to Dan. Eyeing the bedroom window, he judged if he could make it. But the hunter might see him leap inside and could even shoot him as Chase made the jump. If Chase managed to get inside, the hunter would come in after him, feeling it was his duty to finish off the wounded wild cat.

Running around the house to the front door would expose Chase briefly, too. But he believed he could get inside before the man saw him enter the cabin. Chase had to risk it.

He crouched at an angle, then sprang forty-five feet, a record for himself, and landed at the corner of his cabin. Close to being out of sight, but not all the way. The man fired another shot, but Chase tore around to the front as a round struck one of the ends of the logs of his house, splintering it with a crack. Chase was ready to arrest the hunter for trespassing, shooting at his house, endangering him... and whatever else he could charge him with.

Briefly, Chase thought of jumping through the broken window in his living room, but as much as he was hurting, he was afraid he might skim a jagged piece of glass and injure himself further. He stumbled to the front door, saw that it was wide open and remembered he'd left it that way when he was in such a rush and had searched for Shannon and the men after her. Without any time to waste, he shifted, sank to his knees as a jolt of pain ran all the way from the bullet wound in his side to this brain. He fought the dizziness washing over him, not wanting the hunter to see him naked and bleeding like this. He managed to push the door shut.

Despite the broken window, the curtains still hid the living room from the hunter's view.

Trying to block the pain, Chase forced himself to his feet and locked the door. Then he stumbled like a drunk into the kitchen to get a towel. Pressing a towel featuring a bottle of wine against his wound, he fought the blackness that continued to battle for control. *Phone.* He had to call Dan. No one would know of his condition if he didn't reach Dan. He tried to remember where he'd last used the phone. Where...

Crap! He'd dropped his police-issued phone outside with his clothes when he'd shifted and taken off after Shannon. He'd never be able to reach it.

Shannon had been on his other cell phone though. Where had she left it? In the bedroom? Where she'd shifted? The phone had to be in there. Holding the towel tight against the wound, attempting to stop the blood flow, he made his way down the hall to the bedroom, trying to remain conscious, keeping his body against the wall, which was helping him to stay on his feet.

Every step, as quickly as he tried to make them, brought another wave of dizziness and nausea and pain, slowing him down. When he reached the bedroom, he recalled too late that she'd locked the door. He needed a nail, thought of the spare hardware he kept in a kitchen drawer, but didn't think he could make it. He glanced at one of the pictures hanging on the wall. He made it to the closest one and yanked it off and dropped it on the floor, the glass breaking in the frame. He grabbed the nail that had held the picture up, yanked a couple of times, glad for once for hollow board walls, and pulled it loose. Returning to the door, he felt his strength ebbing. He poked around at the doorknob hole until he felt the lock click open, heard the pop, and quickly twisted the knob. Throwing the door open, he stared at Shannon's clothes, but no sign of the phone. Thinking the pocket of her jeans was bulging a bit, he stumbled across the floor as fast as he could and leaned over to dig out the phone, if that's what it was.

His vision turned dark and he fell to the floor. In pain and barely able to keep his wits about him, he managed to pull the phone out of her pocket, hit Dan's number, and said, "I've been shot. Home."

Then without his damned permission, he fought surrendering to the darkness and lost.

***

Dan shouted into the phone, "Chase! Damn it, Chase, talk to me!"

"What's going on," Hal asked as they managed to carry Hennessey's body down the cliffs and to the base.

"Chase was shot. He's home. You guys get this piece of shit to the morgue. I've got to get to Chase."

Dan ran through the woods as fast as he could. After as many harrowing missions as he and Chase had been on while abroad in the army and at home, and with his woman—because Dan couldn't see Shannon as anything but—going into surgery soon, they couldn't afford to lose

Chase now.

"Chase, answer me, buddy!" Dan's heart couldn't have beat any faster as he raced through the forest to reach his friend's place.

It seemed to take forever to make it to the woodpile at the back of Chase's cabin. Chase's bedroom window was still open. Dan headed around the cottage to the front door, when a man wearing hunter's camo gear came around the side of the house, rifle at his shoulder.

"Sheriff Dan Steinacher," Dan said, pulling out his badge and his gun. "Drop the rifle."

"Hell, sheriff. I tracked a cougar here. I shot it and..."

"Drop the weapon, now," Dan growled. He needed to get to Chase and he sure as hell didn't need the delay.

"I'm in my rights..."

"You fired a weapon this close to a house. You're under arrest. Down on the ground."

"The cougar nearly killed a woman."

"*On... the... ground*. Now!"

"Hell, sheriff." The man set his rifle down, then laid face down on the ground. "You're making a big mistake. I need to finish the cat off. It's wounded and more dangerous than before."

Dan could have killed the man. Yes, he was just shooting cougars, but firing a weapon this close to a residence could have killed someone, and Chase could be dying or dead. In his desire to kill the cat, the man had broken a number of laws, including trespassing, the least of them.

"You're making..."

Dan handcuffed the man, then called Dottie. "Let one of my deputies, any of them who might be close enough to Chase's cabin, know that I need a man picked up for shooting Chase there. And I need an ambulance!"

"What? I shot a cougar," the hunter protested.

"Yeah, well, you fired so close to the house one of the rounds penetrated it and struck my deputy."

That made the hunter's eyes round a bit.

"He's inside bleeding to death." Dan left the man on the ground and raced around to the front door and yelled, "Chase!"

The door was locked. Dan backtracked to the front window and carefully climbed through the broken glass.

Chase didn't answer him and Dan feared the worst. He followed the trail of blood through the house and down the hall and found him passed out on his bedroom floor, a bloodied towel lying on his wound.

"Get an ambulance up to Chase's place, STAT," Dan said into his phone, and pressed the towel against Chase's wound. He reached over to grab a blanket off the bed and cover him. Chase's body was ice cold.

***

Three days after Shannon's run through the woods and her subsequent fight with Hennessey's triplet brother, Roger, she blinked at the doctor, recognizing her voice from the first time she'd been admitted to the clinic. Shannon felt much better and was ready to leave, hating confinement of any kind.

"How are you doing this morning?" Dr. Kate Parker asked.

"I'm ready to leave. Where's Chase? Is he all right?" Shannon was worried that the couple of times she'd awakened, she'd seen Dottie and Dan, Hal had even dropped by, but no sign of Chase. And she thought she'd asked, but in her drug-induced state, she couldn't remember what they'd said. Or if they'd said anything. She noticed a ton of flowers on a table by the window, smelling fragrant and heavenly and couldn't believe the outpouring of love for her.

The doctor smiled. "He's beyond the curtain, sleeping still."

Not realizing he'd been injured that badly, Shannon began to sit up, but the doc made her lie down. "Rest a while longer. You should be well enough to leave by tomorrow morning."

"Chase, what happened to him?"

"He was chewed up a bit, but it was the bullet in his flank and the blood loss that resulted that was his downfall. He'll be fine. He should be able to leave tomorrow also. He's asked for you whenever he's been awake."

"Can I see him?"

The doctor pulled the curtain aside. He looked pale, his chin covered in a light stubble, his eyes closed in sleep. She wanted to leave the bed and kiss him—for everything he'd done for her, for everything he was.

"Did... did they catch Hennessey?"

"Chase killed him."

Feeling relief, Shannon studied Chase, listening to his light breathing and sleepy heartbeat. Then she realized he was wearing a penguin gown like she had worn the first time around. She smiled, then realized she was wearing one, too. They were a matched pair.

"You should be able to eat a regular meal today. You let me know how you feel. Once you're able to make it to the bathroom on your own, we'll see about releasing you tomorrow."

"What about the other men? Hennessey's triplet brother? I injured him, but probably not badly enough, and I'm sure if he got away, he would have healed by now."

"They didn't catch either of the other men, I'm afraid. They were wearing hunter's spray. The sheriff and his men had hoped to grab their vehicle, but when the sheriff returned to learn what had happened to Chase, he discovered the men's vehicle was gone."

Shannon let out her breath. "As long as Hennessey is dead."

"He is. I'll let you get some rest. I'll check back in on you a little later."

"Thanks, Doc."

"Kate. Everyone calls me that."

"Thanks, Kate."

Kate studied her for a moment, then said, "You're the best thing that ever happened to Chase since he returned home four years ago. You're good for him."

Shannon shook her head. "I nearly got him killed. Wait, who shot him? I thought Hennessey's men were all in their cougar forms."

"A hunter. He was sure confused though. He's had his hunting license revoked, rifle confiscated, going to court in a week or so over trespassing on private property and shooting Chase, a deputy sheriff on top of everything. Of course, he shot the cougar, but Chase managed to shift inside the house. A round had struck the corner of the log cabin, so the word was that a stray bullet went through the window and struck Chase while he was changing a light bulb. It was the only way to explain how Chase was shot in his side while he stood that high in front of the bedroom window."

After all her hero had risked while fighting the cougars aiming to kill her, that's how he would be remembered?

Kate smiled at her. "We all know the truth. That was the best that the sheriff could come up with on really short notice. The hunter's got a lawyer, so they had to make it work. The bullet definitely came from the man's rifle, so no problem there. If you need anything, just call the nurse." Kate walked out of the room and closed the door.

Shannon climbed out of bed, glad to be feeling so much better and walked to the bathroom, intending to prove to the doctor she was ready to leave sooner than later. Then she remembered that Hennessey and his kin had broken the window to Chase's living room. Would she even feel safe there again? Not alone. Not with Roger and his uncle still on the loose. And even then, not for some time.

When she came out of the bathroom, Chase was watching her. "Hey," he said, smiling a little.

She smiled back at him. "Thank you for saving my life." She went over to the bed and took his hand, and leaned over and kissed him.

He pulled her down for a bear hug.

"Ooh, you're pretending to be all weak and bedridden when you're awfully strong."

"Yeah, it's due to the workout I get with changing light bulbs."

She laughed. "I love you."

"I sure hope so because you and I are getting married."

She smiled, raising her brows. "Did... I just hear a proposal in there?"

"After all I've been through, you don't think I can get down on one knee and propose, do you? I will, if I have to, but..."

"No. But I was thinking more like over a pizza and wine, and maybe some kind of a fun movie to watch."

"No violence though?" he asked, looking like that's what he would prefer.

"Romance. Dottie sent over several cute movies. Remember?"

He groaned. Then he pulled his covers back and she eyed his naked legs as his hospital gown barely covered his tantalizing hardware—that was already tenting his gown.

She smiled. "You look like you're ready to leave the

bed."

"I've fallen madly in love with a she-cat. Haven't I told you? I'd have you join me, but I think the best alternative is to get out of here."

"The doctor said we couldn't leave until tomorrow."

Chase pulled her on top of him in the bed and began to kiss her, really, really kiss her, like he had thought he'd lost her. She kissed him back, hoping she wasn't injuring him further.

He groaned as she tried to take some of her weight off him. "I'm hurting you," she said, wanting to get off him at once.

"Only one part of me and it has nothing to do with my wound, so stay right there. I love you, Shannon Rafferty."

She kissed him again, slowly, thoroughly, until she heard the door open, and she realized her gown was open at the back. Instead of getting off Chase, she yanked the covers over them and turned, figuring it would be the nurse.

Dan smiled. "Ah, I guess the two of you are feeling better?"

Both she and Chase groaned.

"I came by to tell you that some of our men replaced your window and cleaned up the mess. The cabin is ready for you to return to, but since we haven't apprehended Hennessey's brother and uncle, I'm concerned that it won't be safe for Shannon there yet. They might have given up after Hennessey died, figuring he'd be the patsy for the crime, since he had actually committed the murder. Hopefully, they'll believe hanging around here is bound to get them into more trouble than it's worth. But we don't know that for sure."

"Hell," Chase said.

"The two of you are welcome to stay with me," Dan said. "I've got two spare bedrooms. Hal said he'd bunk in one of the rooms as extra backup."

"We can't do that forever," Chase said.

"Rick and Yvonne are pinning the crime on Hennessey as we speak to clear Shannon's name. They've got a couple of FBI agent buddies of theirs investigating their police departments for the narcotics trafficking, believing that these men were involved in shaking down drug dealers and then selling off their stash, taking their cash, and making them disappear."

"Murder," Shannon said under her breath. Why hadn't she realized they could have been involved in murder, beyond Hennessey murdering his own brother, Ted?

"Yeah, these guys are bad news. They can't return to their police departments now. *They're* on the run this time. But it doesn't mean they won't want revenge."

"Now that they're wanted by the FBI, what if the agents kill them? The same problem exists as they had with me, not being able to allow me to live, no incarceration for our kind."

"The two agents are shifters. That's why Rick and his wife sent them the 'intel' and they've been tasked to take care of it. I've already identified the cougar you were fighting with and the man that Chase killed as Hennessey Kelly, but family or close friends usually are called in to make a positive--"

"Wait. The man I was fighting with by the cave was Roger Kelly. His triplet brother. Ted was the one I had been dating, and he was the one Hennessey murdered. But I didn't fight with Hennessey."

"Are you certain?" Dan asked, his eyes wide with surprise.

"Yes, yes, the three men are identical triplets, but even so, Hennessey is a little stockier than Roger, and his hair was a little darker because Roger was out in the sun more often. But otherwise, all three men were hard to tell apart. Unless you were a shifter and knew the brothers by scent, or knew them in person. Their voices sound the same, too. It was hard to distinguish them when I heard them on the phone."

"Hell. All right." Dan let out his breath and ran his hands through his hair. "Okay, I need you to come to the morgue and look at the man just to make sure. Are you well enough to do that?"

"Not without some clothes."

"I'll get you something to wear over your gown and wheel you down there."

"Are you kidding? Chase and I are ready to leave. We just need some clothes."

"Before you leave this time, you're getting the doctor's permission," Dan said. "I'll get a wheelchair."

"I'm going, too," Chase said.

Dan shook his head. "I'll speak with the doctor, but if she says you're not going anywhere, you're not leaving the bed." He stalked out of the room.

Shannon kissed Chase on the lips, but before he could respond, she got off him, grabbed a sheet off the bed, wrapped it around her, and said, "Where's the morgue? Are you coming?"

CHAPTER 14

Once they had the doc's permission to leave the clinic, Chase and Shannon had agreed to stay at Dan's place, have pizzas and beer and watch movies, though Dan hadn't said what kind. But Chase felt like he was having a poker game night with his buddies with Hal and Dan there, and even Stryker showed up unexpectedly to join them.

Though for now, everyone was observing Shannon make a snow angel on Dan's front yard. After the fear of nearly losing her, Chase watched her in wonder, how she could be so happy as if nothing bad had ever happened to her.

"Ah, come on, you guys. Make some, too," she said.

Chase just chuckled.

"If you won't, I will," Hal goaded him.

Chase shook his head at him, talk about being dared to do something that he really didn't want to do. Dan's place was in a residential area, and Chase really didn't want anyone to see him making angels in the snow, especially with his Special Forces buddies waiting to see if he'd do it.

But he did anyway to Shannon's delight, and darned if Hal didn't take a picture of them. "For posterity's sake," Hal teased.

Chase was still smiling at having witnessed Shannon's

exuberance when she saw the snow everywhere that had fallen overnight.

As they shook off the snow and headed into Dan's house, Stryker said to Chase, "You didn't think I would be left out in the cold this time, did you? After I missed the first of the action and got in on this last deal, I'm sticking close to the two of you. We never have this much excitement around here."

Still, Chase wished he could have been alone with Shannon, watching a movie, having some downtime together. And not spending the time with his friends, too. Though he had to admit he did feel Shannon was safer this way and that meant everything in the world to him.

"I doubt anyone would be foolhardy enough to come here while all of us are watching Shannon," Dan said, carrying a bunch of bottles of beer into the living room and setting them down on the coffee table. "If we could hunt them down, it would be a better scenario. By the way, we already fixed your broken window and finished painting the cabin you had been working on. Who spilled the paint?"

Shannon looked at Chase. She thought he'd cleaned it up.

"I wanted to get into town and get more paint. I just rolled up the wet plastic and set it by the door," Chase told her.

The guys were all smiling at them.

"So who spilled the paint?" Dan asked again.

"I did," Shannon and Chase both said at the same time.

The guys laughed.

"Well, we cleaned up the place also," Dan said.

Then Shannon wondered about her sweats still covered in paint and sitting wet for three days in the kitchen sink. They had to know she was the one to have spilled the paint. But if her clothes hadn't soured, they would still be a mess.

She hated to bring up the issue of her paint-soaked clothes, but she also hated the idea that they'd be sitting there for any more time and the paint would have to be scrubbed off the sink also.

"I had some clothes I was soaking in the kitchen sink," she said.

"Taken care of," Dan said, winking at her.

So he had known. "Did they get washed out okay?"

"Chase said to get you a new pair."

She couldn't help it—she thought the world of the guys.

"I did. I know you really don't care for gray, so I had Millicent get you a couple of other colors to wear to lounge in," Chase said.

"But I could have used those to paint in."

Everyone chuckled.

She realized her sopping wet paint-covered sweats must have been the topic of conversation among the men while she and Chase were recuperating at the clinic. She was glad they had something to laugh about after all that had happened. It made her feel a little better, too.

Hal had already started a fast action thriller, but Chase knew they weren't really watching the action. He hoped that Shannon would get her mind off everything that had happened, but he and the other guys needed to figure out a permanent solution to this problem for her.

The doorbell rang and Dan got up to answer it. Shannon's expression instantly turned to worry. Chase and his friends all pulled guns.

"Pizza delivery," Dan reassured everyone.

Everyone holstered their guns, then grabbed slices of pizza and took their seats to watch the movie and eat.

"You didn't get a license number on the vehicle they

had at your place by chance, did you Chase?" Dan asked.

"Yeah, right. A little too busy at the time or I would have disabled the damn vehicle, too," Chase said, wishing he could have and killed all three of the bastards at the same time and then this wouldn't be an issue.

Shannon snuggled closer to Chase as if she wanted to let him know she understood he was trying to reach her and save her life and hadn't had time for anything else. He squeezed her tighter against him in a hug. "You saved my life," she said, as if the others needed to be reminded of that. "That's all that matters. But Hennessey is a hard man and will seek revenge if he could kill his own brother for cheating him out of some money. His pursuit of me has cost him his other brother's life and by tangling with you all, he's wanted by the FBI and is now on the run.

"He has to be pissed beyond measure. For now, I'm afraid he'll bide his time. He knows people in his line of work—the kind that are into shady dealings. I assume he'll be able to keep out of the reach of the police and FBI. He can gain a new identity. Become a ghost. And he won't have to run as a cougar like I had to, either."

Everyone was quiet while staring at the TV screen as if watching the movie, but Chase knew better. They were taking in her words, knowing she knew Hennessey better than any of them there did.

Then Shannon suddenly said, "What can I bring to the Thanksgiving dinner?"

With losing three days at the clinic, he hadn't realized Thanksgiving was tomorrow already.

"Chocolate cake," both Dan and Chase said.

Hal and Stryker smiled. "We heard you baked a mean chocolate cake for Rick and Yvonne's dinner," Stryker said.

"I'm ready for it," Hal said.

"If she starts baking it here, we won't want her to take

it over there," Chase said, smiling.

They finally got into the action of the rest of the movie and finished off the pizzas. When the movie ended, Chase wasn't sure what to say. He knew the guys would want to discuss Hennessey further, but were reluctant to in front of Shannon. She kissed Chase's cheek, then stretched like a sexy she-cat, and got off the couch.

Chase joined her.

"I'm going to take a shower before you all use up the hot water," she said.

They all smiled at her.

Chase walked her back to the bedroom and kissed her. "I'll come to bed in a little while."

"Sure. Just don't stay up too late."

"No. I'll be in bed with you before you know it," he promised, wanting to join her before she fell asleep. He released her. She headed into the bedroom to get her things, and then he rejoined the men in the living room, waiting for Shannon to go to the bathroom before they began to talk.

***

When Shannon walked inside the bedroom, she was rewarded with the fragrance of roses and other sweet flowers that people had so graciously sent her, and she began reading the cards. Despite the fact that Chase had been injured so badly that he had been hospitalized along with her, he had ordered three dozen red roses for her. She vowed the first chance she got, she'd make him a special chocolate cake just for him. She saw a couple of bags and inside were several days' worth of clothing. Everyone had thought of everything for them.

Shannon knew he and the other guys intended to talk about Hennessey and what they were going to do about him. She didn't know why they didn't want to discuss the situation in front of her, maybe because she was a civilian, but she didn't care. She just hoped their plan was a good one because she didn't have a clue as to what she would do if she had to face Hennessey down alone.

She'd attempt to kill him, of course, with teeth and claws, or if she could get hold of a gun, she'd use that on him, but she really was hoping it wouldn't come to that because if she thought Roger was hard to fight—and she would never have lasted fighting him if she hadn't made an escape—Hennessey was bigger, stronger, and lots more scary.

She peeked out the curtains to see the fresh fallen snow again. They'd get it in the Texas Panhandle, but she loved to see it here and everything looked so crisp and clean and... Christmassy. And when she thought of that, she realized she and Chase would be spending their first Christmas together.

If she wasn't still so worried about Hennessey, she would have been cheered by the notion. No sense in worrying about what she could do nothing about, she told herself, and headed for the bathroom.

Everyone talked about the weather and what they were doing for Christmas while Shannon took her shower. Chase hadn't even discussed Christmas with her. Or what they would do. For the first time in years, he wanted a Christmas tree, lights, decorations, and wassail cooking on the stove, pies, and a turkey.

All the guys were looking at him while he was lost in a Christmas wonderland and he lost the smile. "What?"

Hal grinned and shook his head. "I would love to know what you were thinking about."

Dan and Stryker were smiling just as broadly. Getting in some hot loving with the she-cat, he figured they were thinking.

"Christmas with Shannon," Chase said, and everyone quickly sobered. Chase had avoided Christmas celebrations for the four years he'd lived there. The same as far as Thanksgiving went. They knew how hard it had been for him to lose his wife and child and how Christmas had never seemed the same after that. "I hadn't even thought about it until she brought up Thanksgiving dinner." He suddenly felt uncomfortable with the silence.

Dan nodded. "She's good for you, Chase. I'm so glad for the two of you."

Hal snorted. "It could have been me."

"Hell," Stryker said to Dan, "the one time you forced me to take a vacation and I missed everything—the excitement, the glory, but most of all, the hot she-cat."

Hearing them, Shannon walked out of the bathroom, smiling at them, her wet hair in a towel, while she wore a fresh pair of sweats---only these were turquoise and he was glad he'd gotten them for her as much as she loved them. "Night, guys."

"Join you in bed soon," Chase said.

Her cheeks colored, she nodded, and the guys all said good night. She slipped into the room down the hall, situated between the one Hal was staying in and Dan's. Stryker planned to sleep on the couch tonight.

Chase took in a deep breath and then let it out. "Okay, we need to decide how we're going to do this."

"Track him down?" Dan asked.

Hal took another swig of beer. "Or lay in wait?"

"If Shannon's right, I'd have to agree he'll have the resources to bide his time. On the other hand, when he came after her initially, he had tracked her to my place, but he didn't realize just how dedicated our people are in protecting our own. He didn't count on there being so many of us and that at a moment's notice, we would band together. If we go after him, I'm sure he'll lead us on a merry chase. But I suspect that he doesn't want to hang around here forever, risking that some of us will spot him or his uncle. He has to know we expect him to return out of vengeance, for no other reason, and we'll be waiting for him," Chase said.

"So we lay in wait," Dan said. "Or maybe you think he's not going to come."

"He wants the money that Ted absconded with and if it's sizeable enough, that'll keep him coming after her if nothing else. He might leave the area for a while and return when we least expect it," Chase said.

Dan frowned. "Christmas Day. He might decide to attack the two of you when you are up at your cabin for the holidays. Everyone else would be busy with their own Christmas Day activities. That would be far enough in the future that we might figure he's given up on Shannon."

"What if he sends someone else to do his dirty work?" Stryker asked.

"That's always a possibility. But if he wants the money, I doubt he'll want anyone else to know about it. What I don't understand is how come Roger, his triplet brother, seemed eager to kill her," Chase said.

Dan cleared his throat. "She was injured. What if they wanted to injure her badly enough that she couldn't run? Then they would have forced her to tell them where the money was and after that killed her."

Hating the scenario, Chase nodded. "What are we going to do in the meantime? We can't spend a month here camped out at your place."

"Sure you can," Dan said.

Hal said, "I'm good for it."

Stryker said, "I'll be headed to my place after tonight. But you know I'm only a call away."

"Okay, then we'll plan for some kind of an ambush for Christmas," Dan said. "And we'll keep watching for any signs of them in the meantime. If they come back, we'll be on it."

Chase bid everyone good night, though everyone else remained in the living room while Hal put on another movie, and turned it up nice and loud.

Chase smiled. They had his back. At least so he could have some quality time with Shannon in relative privacy.

Chase closed the door to the bedroom and noticed the damp towel hanging over a chair back and her turquoise sweats spread out on the seat of the chair.

Her shoulders were bare and her eyes were watching him in the semi-dark, a greenish gold glow to them. Cat's eyes. He began stripping out of his clothes. Not saying a word. He could have lost her this last time and as long as she was feeling up to it, he wanted to make love to her, to share the connection he'd felt ever since he'd tackled her as a cat near the river and then again when he'd pinned her to the kitchen floor at Hal's place.

As soon as he was stark naked and seeing the way she was watching him with a speculative gleam in her eye, his dick stood at attention. Which made her smile.

But then she frowned a little as he pulled the covers aside and climbed into bed with her. "We're not going to make love, are we? Just cuddle?" she asked.

She reached over and ran the palm of her hand over his nipple and the warm, soft sensation against his sensitive nipple made it harden in appreciation. She licked the hollow of his neck, her dark hair tickling his chest.

"They turned up the TV so that we could be as noisy as we want," Chase said, lifting her face so he could kiss her mouth.

"They'll hear anyway."

"If you want, I'll ask them to go outside and make snow

angels or a snowman until we're done, but I'm making love to you, no matter what. Unless you don't want me to."

Shannon shared the most wickedly devilish expression with him. "Would you? Make them go outside? Would they do it?"

He chuckled and kissed her instead, ignoring the shouts and battle cries going on between armored men and the blue-painted Picts in the movie on TV—instead, concentrating on Shannon, every soft curve, her dark hair, her sweet and already musky scent, the sound of her heart ratcheting up a few notches.

He still hadn't gotten over the fear of having nearly lost her. Even though it had been three days ago, he'd been out of it for most of that time. So it seemed to him like it had only been yesterday.

He kissed her mouth again, cupping a breast as her hands held onto his shoulders, and she kissed him back. With Shannon, starting slow didn't seem to work as he planned.

Whether it was because she was afraid the movie would grow quiet and the men would hear them or some other reason, Shannon's sweet kisses turned passionate in a heartbeat and before he knew what to expect, she climbed onto his lap, facing him, spreading herself to him.

Once again, she was showing that side of her that was so wildly unpredictable, and he loved her for it.

His back was pressed against the soft padded headboard, her legs bent at the knees and spread outward, her dark curly short hairs already wet for him.

He took handfuls of her long, silky hair and luxuriated in the feel of it as he breathed in her scent, tasted the spices on her tongue, heard the rapid beat of her heart—felt her alive and wanting and real. She was like a dream that he had captured from the moment he'd shot her with the tranquilizer dart and taken her in. As much as she had meant to run away, he had held her heart hostage, whether she was ready to freely admit it or not, just as much as she had held his hostage.

Even now, he remembered the way he'd been shivering in the cold, naked, his head pounding from the slight concussion she'd given him, but instead of running off and abandoning him to his fate, she'd stayed with him, protecting him like she'd protected the boy, no matter what the risk had been to her own safety.

He kissed her hard on the mouth with the kind of passion that said he had claimed her body and soul, before he began to stroke her into climax.

She reached between them and began to stroke his cock and that had him groaning against her mouth as she stopped only long enough to run her thumb over the head with an erotic sweep. Then he continued the assault on her senses—inserting two fingers into her tight sheath, running his thumb over her swollen nub.

She stopped stroking him and arched backward, her hands planted on the bed, a sheen of light perspiration on her silky skin, her breathing ragged. He continued to stroke her, his free hand sliding down her calf, watching her lose herself in the way he was bringing her pleasure. He felt the tension, saw the way her body responded, smelled the excitement, both his own and hers. And smiled as she cried out. He would have covered her mouth with his and muffled her cry of pleasure, but he wasn't able to the way she had been leaning away from him, caught up in the moment.

He leaned her back then, moving his legs out from under her, until her head was to the foot of the bed. He pushed into her, driving his cock between her folds slowly at first, placing kisses on her breasts, licking her nipples, nibbling her earlobe with his teeth and connecting with her in the most intimate way.

Her knees were bent on either side of him as he drove into her, wanting her to be his forever. He licked her nipple and sucked, then pumped hard into her, hot and eager. Her hands slid down his skin, her touch making his blood sizzle. She was exquisite, his, just as much as he was hers and he loved making love to her.

When she'd told him she loved him over the phone, her parting words spoken when she thought she was going to die at Hennessey's hands, or teeth, Chase hadn't had the chance to tell her how much he loved her in return. It had nearly killed him to think he might lose her and he had never even had the opportunity to tell her that he loved her. He vowed to do so every day of their lives with a word or action to let her know just how precious she was to him.

Her eyes were half-lidded, her fingers sweeping over his buttocks, her sweet body pushing against his.

He felt the end coming and claimed her mouth, thrusting his tongue between her lips, and spilled his seed deep inside her.

"Shannon," he managed to get out as he sank down on top of her. "I can never lose you." The fear was still there that Hennessey would come for her.

She wrapped her arms around Chase's body, her legs around his hips as if to say she was claiming him for her own.

"I was so scared…," he said, never having admitted such a thing to anyone.

"I was, too. But I knew you were coming for me. I was just afraid…"

"You called out in a cougar's way, offering yourself as bait. Why?" He kissed her cheek and combed his fingers through her hair.

"I realized once you fought one of them, the others

would go to his aid. You couldn't fight all three at once. Then they'd come after me. I had to taunt one of them to come after me. Had you been fighting Hennessey? What happened?" She slid her hands down his sides, her touch warm and soft.

"I assumed he was the uncle with a few gray hairs. Hunters shot at us. At me. He ran off."

"So Roger came after me and you were fighting their uncle. Where was Hennessey all that time?"

"Maybe backtracking to move the vehicle and pick the others up, along with you, at a different location. I was so injured, I wasn't thinking much about anything else when I returned to the cabin after being shot, but to protect myself and get help. I vaguely remembered noticing only my vehicle was there and the Humvee was gone."

"He probably figured they were soon going to be outnumbered and outmaneuvered. Then when their uncle took off, he probably headed back with Hennessey. I wonder if they knew Roger was dead."

"Probably assumed it because of the hunters and the shifters who were coming to your rescue. They might have had a rendezvous point and if he didn't meet them by a specified time, they would assume the worst," Chase said.

"They were wearing hunter's spray," she said.

"Which was to be expected. They didn't want you to smell them prematurely."

She took a deep breath and exhaled it. "We're upside down on the bed."

He smiled at her and kissed her cheek, then he moved off her so they could climb under the covers with their heads on the pillows again. Or at least his was. She snuggled up against him, her cheek resting against his chest, her warm breath fanning his skin. "They won't wait for Christmas, will they?"

"If there's a lot of money involved, they believe you know where it is, they're afraid someone else might get hold of it, and they are worried they're going to get caught, no."

Which was why he feared Hennessey would come after Shannon again—and soon.

CHAPTER 15

Early the next morning, Stryker had left to oversee a three-car pileup because of the snow and icy conditions on the road. Dan was at the hospital interrogating a case of a kid breaking another kid's nose. Hal was still sacked out, but he was there to watch Shannon and Chase's backs if they needed him to.

"I haven't shared Thanksgiving in a while with anybody," Shannon said to Chase as she baked the chocolate cake while he was making up a bowl of fruit salad. "My twin brother got into trouble a lot. He was... he was in jail at Thanksgiving, and then he was murdered before he made it to Christmas."

Chase stopped what he was doing and crossed the floor to take her in his arms. Once they had learned who she was, Dan had discovered everything about her, including all about her brother and the two guys she'd dated before she got involved with the cop, who had also died. But he'd learned that she had never had as much as a traffic violation. And changing boyfriends, from those who broke the law, to one who was supposed to uphold the law, hadn't made any difference.

Someday, Chase figured she'd talk to him about it, but none of that mattered. He'd also been thinking a lot about that birth control implant she was wearing and how much he'd love to see her carrying their children and how much he'd love to adore them as much as he adored her.

"When did you want to get married?" he asked, kissing her forehead, holding her tight, his hand stroking down her back. She was wearing that hot pink sweater again, and he was glad she loved it so much because he sure did.

"Shouldn't we wait a respectable period, like a year?"

"Hell, no."

She chuckled.

"We've known each other long enough. And if you didn't know, I hadn't ever planned to let you go."

She looked up at him and smiled. "You said I could leave anytime I wanted."

"I lied."

She laughed. "I was planning to, you know. I kept telling myself I'd wait just a couple of more days and then I needed to leave before Hennessey caught up to me."

"I know."

She raised a brow.

"I caught you looking at the calendar a couple of times. Didn't you notice that I'd stick closer to you, not leave you alone as much right after that?"

She smiled and curled her arms about his neck. "I thought you were just lonely."

"I was. But I also alternated between thinking you were having a hard time leaving because you'd miss me too much, and worrying you'd stayed too long because Hennessey was sure to find you."

"I was."

"So, when are we getting married?"

"Three months from now?"

"How about next week?"

She laughed. "I thought you were asking *me* when I

want to get married."

He smiled. "If your choice of date was close to when I want to get married, I would have just said I'd go along with it."

"You want to marry before Christmas? How can we get the paperwork done that early?"

"Dan will take care of it. So that's a yes?" He looked so happy she was about to say yes, when she remembered her cake.

"Oh!" she said, and pulled away from him to check the oven. "It doesn't pay to distract me while I'm baking." She pulled it out of the oven.

"If it's ruined, I'll eat it," he said, taking deep breaths and enjoying the chocolate aroma.

"Then I'd have to make another and it wouldn't be done in time. No, it's just perfect."

Hal poked his head into the kitchen. "Tell me we're having that for a late breakfast."

She laughed. "It's for Thanksgiving dinner. When are we headed over there?"

"Early," Chase said. "Weather reports show another winter storm headed our way. We might as well get over there and just enjoy ourselves, visit and play games, until we eat."

"Where's everyone else?" Hal asked.

"Dan's at the clinic questioning a couple of boys about a fight that left one of them with a broken nose. And Stryker's working a traffic accident. We'll have to take it slow to reach Rick's place out in the country," Chase said.

"What about Dottie and the kids?" Shannon asked.

"Dan will head over there and pick them up right after he finishes with the kids at the hospital. Is your cake done?"

"Sure. It'll cool down on the way over there and I can add the frosting then. We might as well go now. Are we all going in one car or two?"

"My truck," Hal said. "It's got four-wheel drive, snow tires, heavier than Chase's hatchback."

"I'll just grab my coat, hat, and gloves," she said.

Hal said, "Me, too. Wait, what can I bring?"

"Dan said to bring a couple of bottles of wine. He's got them in the cabinet there. Dottie's bringing something she baked. A vegetable casserole, I think. Stryker said he picked up a pecan pie yesterday and he'll drop by his place to get it," Chase said.

Before long, they were out the door with the cake, bowl of fruit, and two bottles of wine.

The roads were messy, though Shannon felt safe in Hal's truck. Several cars had slid off the road into piles of snow, but thankfully the occupants of the vehicles must have been rescued because the cars were empty.

When Hal drove out into the country, they came upon another stuck car. A man and woman were trying to clear the snow out of their path. Hal stopped and two ten year-old girls got into the truck with Shannon to stay warm while the mother drove the car back and forth as Chase, Hal, and the husband tried to push the car back onto the road. They managed to get onto the road and the kids rejoined their parents and were on their way. Only a mile down the road in the blinding snow, the car was in the ditch again.

"Where were they going?" Hal asked.

"To their grandmother's house," Shannon said.

"Which is where?" Hal asked.

"I have no idea."

Hal sighed and pulled next to their car again. Only this time they all crammed into the double cab of Hal's truck along with a damp German shepherd, too. Shannon had never known cat shifters who owned a dog before.

Everyone but Hal—well, and maybe Chase, but he was

only smiling and not saying a word—wanted the dog inside the cab with them.

Hal complained nearly the whole time about how dogs and cold weather were meant for each other. That the dog would love to see the sights and not be jam-packed into the back seat with the family. He'd feel squished. That he was way too big to be a lapdog. That he would feel way too confined.

The two girls giggled. "He's sleeping on all of our laps," the one girl said.

Shannon smiled.

The trip was way out of their way and took them up a country road that made Shannon worry that even they wouldn't make it. The family's low-slung car would never have made it. When they reached the house, the lights were on inside and a cheery fire was blazing in the fireplace. A gray-haired grandma came out to greet them in a sweater and dress and snow boots. She looked a little surprised to see Hal and Chase and Shannon.

"Oh my goodness, you're that wild she-cat the sheriff and his men were trying to catch," she said, then smiled. "Come in. Come in. Have Thanksgiving dinner with us."

Chase and Hal smiled at Shannon as she felt her cheeks heat.

Two more German shepherds rushed out to greet the family and the family's dog, and then checked Shannon and the others over.

"We've got to be at Rick and Yvonne Mueller's place, Ma'am," Chase said. "We were glad to be of some assistance."

"Will you need a ride home tonight?" Hal asked.

"No, they're staying a few days to help me put up my decorations for Christmas."

They all made their well-wishes and Shannon, Chase,

and Hal drove back the way they came. Chase texted Rick to let him know they would be late because they'd gotten held up on the drive over.

Rick responded by saying Dan had texted him that he couldn't make it to Dottie's place to get her and the kids in time. Could Hal?

"Okay, another run. At least Dottie doesn't have any dogs," Hal said.

"I saw you pet that dog," Shannon said.

He smiled. "I would have loved him, if he'd been riding in the back."

"It's not safe for them," she said.

"My whole truck smells like wet dog now!"

"And chocolate," Chase said, wrapping his arm around Shannon.

It took nearly an hour to reach Dottie's place. A light was on in the living room, and they saw Dottie wave out the window at them, then leave to get the kids.

Hal parked and everyone got out. "It's like moving day taking Dottie and the kids anywhere. Remember that when you have kids. You don't just go. You have to get car seats and toys, and special food to keep them happy, and diapers and…"

Shannon started laughing. "No dogs and no kids, eh, Hal?"

He smiled back at her. "Now if…"

Chase punched him.

Hal and Shannon laughed.

Hal opened the front door and walked inside but a shot rang out and Hal hit the floor. Chase had been to the right of him, Shannon behind. She let out a startled shriek, and ran the other way.

Praying Hal and Chase would be all right, she dashed outside into the snow. It had to be Hennessey and he'd taken Dottie and her toddlers hostage. Shannon knew the only thing she could do was run and hope that Hennessey would come after her. She began stripping, which wasn't easy as many clothes as she had on. She ran into the blinding snowstorm and into the woods. She hoped Chase was safe, but she knew he'd go after the shooter and have to rescue Dottie and her little ones. He'd already lost his wife and baby. He couldn't see it happen again. She worried that Hal had been hit, though she'd also assumed he might have hit the floor as a soldier would do when under fire.

Naked, she shifted, willing the warmth of her cougar coat to cover her skin, and ran blindly away from the house, the snow stinging her eyes.

And then she saw him. Hennessey, the bastard. He was outside wearing his cougar form and coming after her. She hesitated. She could either run away from the house, and she knew she couldn't outrun him, or head back to the house and hope Chase or Hal had taken down the shooter. She darted back toward the house at a full run, leaping through the screen of cold, white flakes. She was certain Hennessey was chasing her, but she couldn't hear his silent approach while the cold wind whipped the snow about.

Gunshots went off inside the house. Four.

And then a massive tan body slammed into her from behind and she rolled onto her back, unable to do anything else. Snarling and growling, she bit at the bastard as Hennessey tried to grab her throat. She kicked at his belly, claws extended, trying to keep him away from her throat.

The wind swept the white flakes around her as she was half buried in the soft snow, kicking and biting at the devil himself. He knew he had to kill her quickly if Chase or Hal were still alive. But then he wouldn't learn where the money was, if he still believed she knew where it was.

She bit him in the leg and he snarled and hissed but

before he could pay her back, another cat slammed into him and sent him into the bank of snow.

She jumped to her feet, panting from exertion, the snow clinging to her fur. *Chase*. He tore into the cat and she was torn between staying with him this time and going to see to the others. Hal had dropped like a rock when the first shot was fired, and she feared he might have been hit and was seriously injured or dead. And she worried about Dottie and the kids... But she couldn't leave Chase.

Her heart pounded furiously, the adrenaline still rushing through her blood.

Had Dan really texted Rick and told him to ask Hal to pick up Dottie, or was he in the house hurt or dead?

She feared the latter. Hennessey had to have used Dan's phone to text Rick so that they would come here.

Chase was just as viciously trying to kill Hennessey, and she couldn't wait for Chase to be victorious any longer on his own. She had to see to those in the house. She whipped around in the deep snow, crouched, and sprang at least fifteen feet to where the two cats were fighting, raked her claws down Hennessey's back, and took his rabid attention off of Chase for an instant.

He snarled and snapped at her, but Chase closed his jaws around Hennessey's neck and clamped down hard. They waited until they no longer heard his heart beat and his breath no longer blew out puffs of frosty air. Then she dashed back toward the house and inside. Hennessey's uncle was dead on the floor, shot twice. Hal was unconscious, his head bleeding profusely.

Chase joined her inside and shifted, then began getting dressed. "I'll get your clothes," he said, then he ran back outside, gathered up her things, and trudged back through the snow at a run.

When he reached the house, he dropped her clothes

on the floor for her, and shut the door. "Dottie and the kids are tied up in the bedroom at the back of the house. You can free them. I've got to take care of Hal."

She had already shifted and was throwing on her clothes. "Hal," she said, tears in her eyes. She had caused this. By coming here, she could have caused so many deaths.

"Head wound, bleeds a lot. Bullet grazed him and he'll have a hell of a headache when he comes to." Chase stalked toward the bathroom.

Shannon got on the phone to Rick, telling him Hennessey and his uncle were dead as she raced down the hall to the bedroom where the door was closed. She threw it open.

Dottie was tied to a chair, her eyes red with crying. Dan was tied up on the floor, struggling to get free, a raised welt on his forehead, red and already bruising. Both Dottie and Dan had been gagged. The babies were on the bed, a quilt covering them, but her heart nearly stopped when she worried they were dead. She quickly checked them out and found they were just asleep.

"Everyone's all right," Shannon said, reassuring them. Then she put the phone on speaker as she untied Dottie's wrists and said, "Hennessey and his uncle were here lying in wait to ambush us at Dottie's house. Hal's been wounded, but Chase said it's not serious." She sure hoped he was right. "Dan looks like he has been struck in the head, but he seems like he's going to be all right."

"I was worried when I couldn't get hold of Dottie or Chase to learn why none of you had showed up here. I tried Dan's number and I couldn't reach him, either. I'm actually on my way there now. Stryker had gotten hung up on another car pileup. I'll let him know what's happened there. And we'll get a clean-up crew out right away."

"Thanks," Shannon said, as Dottie untied Dan. The toddlers were still sound asleep on the bed. "See you soon."

"Ten minutes tops."

In about twenty minutes, owing to the weather, Stryker and Rick arrived along with another couple of men that she didn't know in three different vehicles. Hal was lying on the sofa with his head bandaged. Dottie was packing up the kids and Dan, though he was normally in charge of an operation, wanted to get her and the kids out of there because of the dead men, and Hal being injured. Everyone assured him they'd take care of everything. Dottie, Dan, and Chase had wanted Shannon to go with them. But she wasn't leaving Hal or Chase behind.

Shannon worried about Dan having been knocked out also. But he assured everyone he was fine.

Once the clean-up crew arrived to take the two men to the morgue, Chase drove Hal's truck while he stretched out in the back. And Shannon sat up front.

"Doc's going to be angry you didn't go in to have your head looked after," Chase said.

"It's Thanksgiving. She doesn't need to have to come in for stuff like this. She already had to set that kid's broken nose."

"Stryker looked upset that you didn't ride with him," Chase said.

"Hell, I have to watch the way you're driving my truck in this weather."

Chase chuckled.

Hal was lying down in the backseat and couldn't see anything. "Besides, where you and Shannon go, that's where all the action is. Already Stryker's complaining that he missed out again."

"At least no one's going to say you got shot changing a light bulb," Chase said.

Shannon smiled.

"No, they're going to say I didn't duck fast enough though."

"Good thing or the guy would have shot Shannon." Chase looked over at her.

She took a deep breath. "All of this was my fault."

"No, it was Hennessey's fault," Hal said harshly. "The bastard was a cop, too." Then he said, "Hell, as soon as I arrive at the feast, I'm going to be smelling like a dog."

Shannon and Chase chuckled.

Once they arrived at Rick and Yvonne's house for the Thanksgiving feast, the whole place smelling of turkey and pumpkin and pecan pies, and chocolate cake, Shannon felt relief and ready to share this truly special holiday with Chase and friends.

She kissed Chase, wanting more, but not here in front of everyone else, and though he appeared to want to hold onto her longer, she smiled and said, "I've got to frost the cake."

His arms still wrapped around her, he said, "I can't wait for dessert."

The glint of the devil in his eyes and the way his mouth curved so wickedly, she was sure he wasn't talking about the cake. He released her then, and while she mixed up the frosting, Chase opened a bottle of wine, and Yvonne set the dishes of food on the dining room table.

But just as Shannon finished frosting the cake, Chase was standing beside her, catching her at doing what she'd always done as a little girl helping her mother to frost a cake—sliding her finger around the inside of the bowl to catch the remaining ribbons of chocolate, then licking it off.

The next thing she knew, he was licking her fingers, her mouth, kissing her as if no one else in the house existed.

Yvonne finally finished pouring the wine and asked,

"What exactly happened? We need the full details of what went down."

Shannon gave Chase one more chocolaty sweet kiss, then they washed up to join the others, though she was thinking about just how much fun sharing chocolate with Chase could be—when they were alone.

Dan was sitting on the couch with Hal, neither of them looking really great. Dottie was taking care of feeding her toddlers. Stryker acted like he didn't know quite what to do, his hands shoved in his pockets as he watched everyone else work. Rick began to carve the turkey.

Then they all sat together at the dining room table.

"I finished talking to the two kids who had gotten into a fight, then spoke with their parents. After that, I called Dottie and told her I was on my way to her place and that we should be able to make it in time to Rick and Yvonne's place. I'd told her that Shannon was with Chase and Hal and they had been delayed getting there, too," Dan said and passed the bowl of potatoes. "And I said that Stryker was still dealing with the traffic accident, but that he'd join us as soon as he could."

"So they were monitoring your conversation using a scanner," Shannon said.

"Yeah, they had to have. I was on the phone to Stryker about the car accidents when I entered Dottie's house. When I stepped into the place, I didn't even have time to call out that I was there or get a chance to smell Hennessey or his uncle's scent. Though I realize now they were wearing that damned hunter's spray again. The ape hit me in the head with something and I went down. I don't remember anything after that until I woke up in Dottie's bedroom and we were both tied up and gagged. I was trying to get myself free when I heard Shannon on the phone coming for us. I guess the bastard used my phone to text Rick," Dan said.

"Which was my fault," Dottie said, passing the gravy to Dan. "They forced me to verify that Shannon and Chase were going to Rick and Yvonne's for Thanksgiving. I said that I didn't know where they were going, but the older man said I didn't have to confirm it was so, but that he'd kill either one of my kids or the sheriff and see if that might help me to remember. He said they weren't going to hurt any of us—"

Dan snorted.

"I agree. He said they just wanted the money Shannon had stolen from them," Dottie said. "I didn't believe them about the money or that they didn't want to hurt anyone. I told them that they nearly killed Shannon the last time, and Hennessey said she wasn't supposed to be hurt, but she fought Roger and didn't just go along with them. That they just had to convince her they meant business."

"Ha!" Shannon said. "Well, maybe that's why Roger didn't kill me. He could have. Maybe he figured he'd injure me enough, and then they'd force me to tell them what they wanted to know. But he would have killed me afterward."

"Just my thought," Dottie said. "I wanted to be the one to make the call to Rick so I could say something that would alert everyone that something was wrong, but the older man just texted Rick, pretending to be Dan and must have said he couldn't reach my house in time to pick us up. They knew about the traffic accidents and that Dan had been at the clinic. I suspected Hal might be driving because he has a heavier truck, but I didn't say anything. I hoped if they asked if Chase would come and get me, Rick might figure that something was up."

Rick shook his head as he served more wine to everyone. "I didn't give it a thought. My only concern was that everyone was late getting in. I had never considered

Hennessey and his uncle might be there. We thought it was a case of you getting stuck somewhere in this snow."

"How did they know to go to your place? Even if they were monitoring Dan's calls, how did they know who you were exactly? And where you live?" Chase asked.

"You know that reporter? Carl Nelson? He learned of the accidents and was still wanting more information about those cougar sightings," Dottie said.

Dan grunted. "Hell, he was pestering me at the clinic right before I left to see you. I heard him tell his boss that he was checking out an accident that Stryker was working and that he'd gotten nothing from me about the cougars as he hurried out of the clinic."

"Hennessey said something about usually hating reporters, but they got lucky with that one in town. Since the reporter isn't a shifter, he wouldn't have been suspicious of them asking him about me. So that's how Hennessey and his uncle learned just where I lived," Dottie said. "They must have talked to him, and left town right afterwards before Dan departed the clinic. Only a few minutes after they arrived, Dan parked out front."

"We were just lucky Carl hadn't come around to your house about that time or what a mess that would have been," Dan said.

"Agreed," Chase said. "I don't think any of us want him to join our exclusive cougar club."

Shannon explained how she'd run out of the house, stripped, and shifted so she could draw one of the men away and give Chase a chance to get the advantage inside.

Chase took a deep breath and looked at Hal, who was forking out a potato onto his plate. "When Hal fell beside me, I was certain he was dead and that Shannon and I were next. I saw her dash back outside and I dove for the couch. I had my gun out and came around the corner of the couch to shoot the shooter, but he had dashed toward the hall, and I knew he intended to grab a hostage to use as a shield. I fired a couple of shots and took him down. Then I heard Hennessey and Shannon fighting in the snow and I quickly stripped and shifted and took off after them. I'd briefly thought of trying to shoot him, but I believed I'd have a better chance killing him in my cat coat than if I took a chance shooting at the two cats fighting."

Everyone was eating in earnest when Hal cleared his throat and said to Shannon, "So... where is the money?"

"Like *I* should know."

"Did he have a safety deposit box?" Rick asked.

"I wouldn't know. He paid the bills. I still had my own personal checking account, but once I stopped working, I didn't have any more money coming in that I could call my own."

"Did he spend a lot of extra money on stuff?" Chase asked. "Maybe he spent it all."

"He said he had expenditures, but Hennessey didn't believe him. He was certain he'd lied about it."

"Did he garden?" Yvonne asked.

"Garden?" Shannon asked.

"Like he might have dug a hole and hid it."

She shook her head, trying to remember if he'd been doing anything different lately.

"Grand Cayman accounts?" Stryker asked.

"Not that I would know about."

"He hunted and fished with his brothers and uncle, right?" Dan asked.

"Yeah."

"Did he have a freezer?" Chase asked.

She stared at Chase. "Sure, but I never went into it."

"Why not?"

She shrugged. "He said he had organized it his way and

if I went in there and began digging around, I'd end up pulling out the wrong meats to eat first."

Rick was on his phone immediately. "Hey, Jenks, we think we have a lead on where the stolen money is."

"I can't believe I had been so naïve," Shannon said as they left the table and helped to clean up.

Everyone there gave thanks for the people in their town, for the feast they shared, and for Shannon coming into their lives. She snorted at that. But everyone smiled at her, and Chase took her in his arms and kissed her, telling her just how much he had to be thankful for.

"When's the wedding?" Dottie asked, all smiles.

"Next week," Chase said.

Shannon had opened her mouth to say a couple of weeks, but when he looked at her, she sighed and said, "A week. And then he's taking me to an island for a honeymoon."

He looked down at her and smiled. "I did promise that, didn't I? But we have to be home for Christmas."

"I'm all for that." But she wasn't sure what she was going to get him to show him just how much she loved him.

"We got some bottles of champagne, and they're chilled, just in case," Yvonne said and Rick helped her to get them.

The glasses of champagne were passed around.

"To a long life and happy marriage," Dan said, raising his glass for a toast.

"Here, here!"

Toasts continued until everyone had their say. And then later, they enjoyed some of Shannon's chocolate cake and Stryker's pecan pie. As they were cleaning up again, Rick got a call and smiled.

They all waited in anticipation. "Thanks. I'll let everyone know." He ended the call and said, "A million and a half dollars."

"In the freezer in the basement? How could he have even had that much money in there?" Shannon asked, incredulous.

"He had a whole slew of Grover Cleveland thousand dollar bills in a secret compartment in the basement floor *underneath* the freezer. He was taking a lot of sudden trips out of town. Probably depositing the illegal gains at different locations, then transferring them to an offshore account. Only this time he didn't have time to before his brother confronted him."

"So they hadn't needed to go after me in the first place. Except that I had witnessed Hennessey killing Ted," Shannon said.

"And they needed a scapegoat." Chase wrapped his arm around her shoulders.

Dottie glanced at her toddlers sound asleep on the couch cuddled up against Hal, who looked like he was having a difficult time staying awake. "Looks like it's time to call it a night."

Stryker offered to take Hal home with him, and he'd watch over him for the night. Dan was taking Dottie and her kids home.

And Shannon was going home with Chase, only this time it was going to be her home, too.

She still was afraid she'd have the nightmares, but she hoped they'd soon go away. This was the first real home she'd had since her parents died, but more than anything, Chase was who made it home for her and she was happy to set down roots.

First, they had to drop by Dan's house and exchange Hal's truck for Chase's hatchback. She hoped they would make it to the cabin all right in the snowstorm.

"I have to admit for the first time in four years, I'll be

sitting in the cabin with a fire going and the snow coming down outside with a wild cat in my arms. You can't know how good that makes me feel," Chase said.

"I haven't had a real home since my parents died," Shannon said. "You can't know what it's like to be going to a home of my own with a cat who's one of the good guys and as close to being the perfect hero as a woman can get."

"Close?" he asked, smiling.

She smiled. "Yeah. You shot me the first time we met, remember?"

And it was the best mistake he'd ever made.

###

ACKNOWLEDGEMENTS

Thanks to my beta readers—Donna Fournier, Bonnie Gill, Dottie Jones, and Loretta Melvin, for helping make the story the best it can be!

ABOUT THE AUTHOR

Bestselling and award-winning author **Terry Spear** has written over fifty paranormal romance novels and five medieval Highland historical romances. Her first werewolf romance, *Heart of the Wolf,* was named a 2008 *Publishers Weekly*'s Best Book of the Year, and her subsequent titles have garnered high praise and hit the *USA Today* bestseller list. A retired officer of the U.S. Army Reserves, Terry lives in Crawford, Texas, where she is working on her next werewolf romance, continuing her new series about shapeshifting jaguars, and having fun with her young adult novels. For more information, please visit www.terryspear.com, or follow her on Twitter, @TerrySpear. She is also on Facebook at http://www.facebook.com/terry.spear. And on Wordpress at:
Terry Spear's Shifters
http://terryspear.wordpress.com/

Call of the Cougar coming Fall, 2014

CPSIA information can be obtained at www.ICGtesting.com
Printed in the USA
LVOW08s1449100914

403438LV00001B/108/P